THE LIVING PROOF GETS THE BLUES
Neighborlee Book 13

Michelle L. Levigne

www.YeOldeDragonBooks.com

Ye Olde Dragon Books
P.O. Box 30802
Middleburg Hts., OH 44130

www.YeOldeDragonBooks.com

2OldeDragons@gmail.com

Copyright © 2022 by Michelle L. Levigne

ISBN 13: 978-1-952345-31-9

Published in the United States of America
Publication Date: May 1, 2022

Cover Art © Copyright Ye Olde Dragon Books 2022

Welcome to Neighborlee, Ohio.

Where? Somewhere on the North Coast of Ohio, south of Cleveland, right off I-71, north of Medina, in the heart of Cuyahoga County.

What is it? That's a little harder to explain.

Neighborlee is a place you need to experience.

The most important thing you need to understand: Neighborlee is *magic*. Some people say the town is alive. It exists to protect the weird and wonderful (and sometimes a little bit scary) from the cold, practical, material world.

More important, Neighborlee protects the outside world from the weird and wonderful that come to visit … and sometimes come to stay.

First stop: Divine's Emporium, a four-story Victorian house sitting on a hill overlooking the Metroparks. Whatever you really need, you can find at Divine's. Even if you don't know what you're looking for when you walk in the door. The shop is often bigger inside than it is outside. Angela is the proprietor. Please stay on the first floor. You don't want to find out what is hidden and locked safely away upstairs. Like Aslan, Angela is good, but that doesn't mean she's safe. And neither are the secrets and wonders and doorways to other worlds that she protects … and keeps securely locked.

Come in and explore. Meet the people who help Angela guard Neighborlee. Share their adventures of magic and wonder, danger and sacrifice. You never know who or what you'll run into as you walk the streets and listen to the stories of their lives.

Chapter One

Happily ever after?

If only.

You'd think after all these years, the guardians would know that peace was a temporary thing, if not an utter illusion. But we could always hope.

Honestly, that summer when Angela and Ethan were reunited, we were just plain worn out.

A lot more things happened in that moment when the Hunt and the Hounds of Hamin were fighting the traitor, Wolcott, and the shield around Neighborlee rippled, going unsteady for a few seconds. While that "burp" of energy acted like a flare or a beacon, drawing a few more members of the Hunt to Neighborlee, it also acted like a signal for enemies, helping them pinpoint us and Angela and Divine's Emporium. Kind of like clanging that metal triangle outside the bunkhouse kitchen on a ranch, and shouting, "Come and get it!"

A whole lot of really vicious, sneaky, cold-hearted schemes and schemers combined, culminating in an attack late in the summer. This latest attack in the centuries-long battle tried to use Pastor Rocky as a weapon.

Note to evil masterminds and wannabe dictators over the various realms and dimensions of reality and universes: Never, ever go up against a man of God who knows how to pray.

Really stupid choice.

The whole scheme actually started in the late winter, while we were dealing with the whole doppelganger problem. So we were a little distracted and missed some warning signs. Pastor Rocky was feeling the first tendrils of the enemy trying to wrap around him and manipulate him. He had no idea what exactly was happening and why, but he knew something was wrong. And he reacted in the smartest way possible.

First, he prayed.

Then he got our church involved.

Wednesday night at prayer meeting, in mid-January, he stood up and announced he had a confession to make. He started out giving a little background, and it didn't surprise anyone who was there.

We all knew he had been a rock'n'roller back in his youth. We knew he had run away from Neighborlee Children's Home two months before his eighteenth birthday to take advantage of an offer from a talent scout.

The administrator of NCH back then was a Mrs. Baumgartner, who was the polar opposite of Mrs. Silvestri. That is to say, she was a Grandstone supporter. When Stephen and Rosco Grandstone were harassing residents of the orphanage, her tactic was to lecture the victim to stop being so sensitive, or selfish, or ridiculous, or dramatic, and learn to get along. Girls who were being sexually harassed were told to stop being such prudes and remember their proper place in society.

Yeah, she was a real gem. *Not.*

What Pastor Rocky didn't say in the prayer meeting, but the guardians knew, was that the Grandstone brothers were focusing on Lost Kids, recruiting them into servitude. They were after Pastor Rocky's gift.

None of us knew he was the kind of Lost Kid to have an extra-special gift, until he met with us to discuss his past.

His gift let him influence people with his singing voice, guided by the lyrics he sang. The Grandstones, or at least their overlords, the Rivals, figured out Pastor Rocky's talent and wanted to recruit him. Probably to brainwash people.

Back then, when his name was August Miller, Pastor Rocky was just figuring out that odd things happened when he sang. Gut instinct told him that when Grandstones were being friendly and Mrs. Baumgartner was pleased with him, that was a bad sign. Especially when friends of his who worked in the administration building at NCH found mail addressed to him that ended up in the wastebasket or was put aside to pass on to the Grandstones. Mail from talent scouts and music industry people who were responding to his audition tapes and wanted to sign him. He knew better than to confront Mrs. Baumgartner about the opportunities she was trying to steal from him. He also knew better than to keep saying no when Albert Grandstone, Stephen and Rosco's father, told Pastor Rocky the Grandstones were sending him to a special music camp, and he would accept the destiny they had mapped out for him.

At church that night, Pastor Rocky told us the day after graduating from Neighborlee High, he packed his clothes and cleaned out his savings account, and ran away in the middle of the night, to meet up with the talent scout.

He told the guardians his savings included a big gift check Albert Grandstone had deposited there, to celebrate the "glorious future" awaiting him in service to the Grandstones. Pastor Rocky was ordered to be ready for a car that was coming for him, and go quietly and meekly to the music camp. But he was never told where the music camp was. Mrs. Baumgartner's lecture about how he should be grateful just sealed the deal. Anything the Grandstones thought was a good idea, and Mrs. Baumgartner approved -- a smart boy ran the other way.

As soon as he turned eighteen, he spent what remained of that bonus money to buy a new name, on the shady side of legal: Drake Abbott. He didn't become Peter Simons, the name we knew, until he got his soul back and went to seminary.

He told our church that the talent scout helped him arrange to ship his clothes and musical instruments to a boarding house in Detroit. Then he got on a bus in the middle of the night and followed his gear to Detroit and the talent scout.

And never looked back, never even thought about Neighborlee, until things just got too weird and he hit rock bottom.

He told the guardians that from the day he left Neighborlee, he never sang another note. He was strictly an instrumental man. The ability he had discovered to influence people with his singing voice scared him. Bad.

He told us at church the minimum details about how he bounced from one talent scout and shyster manager and con man to another. Then at the age of twenty-three, as Drake Abbot, he met up with Frankie Leonides, a drummer, who needed a guitar man for a bluesy band he was putting together. They called themselves Magna Magma.

Why this big confession to the church congregation? After nearly fifty years of being ostracized by his former bandmates, they had contacted Pastor Rocky. The first concern was *how* they had found him, since he had changed his name. The second was *why* they contacted him, to give the fans what they wanted and do a ten-concert reunion tour. They wanted Pastor Rocky to come back. All was forgiven.

Forgiven for what?

The band breakup was his fault. He was getting scared by odd things happening to the band, odd things the fans were getting into, odd things and scary things some of the members of the band advocated. Spiritually strange things. Rumors of Lavaheads -- that was what the extremist fans were called -- participating in strange rituals that went beyond drugs and hints of orgies. He got "scared straight" before that phrase became popular, and when he left to follow God, the band disintegrated.

Pastor Rocky wasn't afraid of his past catching up with him and his sins being revealed. He had always been honest with us about it, without bombing us with shameful details. He feared Lavaheads invading Neighborlee, maybe attacking Neighborlee Gospel Church to punish him for refusing to return to relive the "glory days" as the fan sites called it.

Yes, sites. Plural. Five sites, none of them able to get along. No wonder Pastor Rocky stayed away from social media. I checked out some of those sites, and those people were more than freaky.

He asked our entire church to pray. Protection for our church. Protection for our town. Protection for the members of Magna Magma, and the Lavaheads, so the evil influences that had frightened him back then wouldn't arise and awaken and destroy more lives.

When he met with the guardians, he asked for help from London and Sherwood, our resident Artificial Intelligences, to track the activities of the band, and look for warning signs of trouble, so we could pray harder, and maybe pass along warning to authorities who could do something and intervene.

Pastor Rocky knew about a lot of things that made our town so unique, and they didn't freak him out for more than a few seconds. We had to tell him, since Maurice and Holly wanted to get married in our church. He noticed pointed ears almost as easily as the guardians did. We had even more fun with his reaction when we introduced him to London and Sherwood. Especially when she asked if he thought they had souls, if they could die, and if they did, would they be sent to Heaven or to Hell. It was his opinion that if they were worried about having souls, that was a good sign they had souls. If they had been observing the recorded church services posted on YouTube and the church's website, they knew the proper way to get their tickets stamped for Heaven. London and Sherwood contacted him about once a month for deeply spiritual and philosophical discussions, and all three of them enjoyed the challenge and mental and spiritual stretching that came from it.

So our church was praying hard, and the guardians were on the lookout, and our friendly AI's were scouring the Internet for warning signs.

One good result came from that searching. Pastor Rocky reunited with one member of the band. His spiritual reformation and awakening had triggered one in BoJo Taggert, who played keyboard and saxophone. After Magna Magma had their big split, he took back his real name, Marty Haggerty, joined a monastery, took a vow of silence, and went into seclusion for approximately ten years. At that time, he emerged to publish a book of worship songs written for the saxophone and set up a ministry to reach troubled youth through music programs.

Unlike Pastor Rocky, Father Marty was open about his "wicked past," and referred to Magna Magma regularly to warn kids away from the path he had taken. So, the Lavaheads didn't like him. One site posted threats to his life if he didn't support the reunion tour. Father Marty's superiors thought it might be wise to send him on a long vacation. When London found him, Pastor Rocky made contact and offered him sanctuary.

Those heavy-duty prayers for the safety of our town got a reaction from the enemy. Or at least one of our enemies. We didn't realize the connection between things we were doing, and our church was doing, and what the different factions of the enemy were doing, until much later. The dust was still churning from the trouble we had with the doppelgangers and then some black-clad nasties who tried to interfere with the long-awaited reunion between Angela and Ethan.

The next salvo in the effort to penetrate Neighborlee's shields began quietly. "Welcome to Neighborlee" signs started popping up at every single street that crossed the border into town. Even where the border crossed through residential sections. Sure, there were complaints from people who came home from work and found the signs in their tree lawns, without any warnings from the city that signs were going up. They went up too fast to be believed, as in holes dug, cement poured, big wooden signs put into place, all between people leaving for work and coming home. Suddenly, the signs were just there.

Those who complained discovered nobody knew who had ordered those signs, who had approved them, or who had paid for them. We didn't hear about the mystery for several more weeks because the signs were on the *other* towns' side of the dividing line. The people complaining weren't Neighborlee residents. They called their own town officials.

It was like the people who were putting up the signs couldn't cross over into Neighborlee.

Sound familiar?

When the other towns' officials investigated and got no answers, they called Mayor Wellington to accuse him of some dicey activities. He didn't wait for a city council meeting. He called in Chief Tanner, and John Stanzer. They got to work asking questions and studying incident reports, to see who might have a grudge against Neighborlee and didn't care about the expense and hard work of pulling a pretty odd trick like that. The Chief and Stanzer spent about an hour looking over what was known about the situation so far, and they agreed that some details were too similar to other incidents that were pretty much kept quiet, so the general population didn't know what was going on.

The Chief basically didn't want another blow-up like with the sleepwalkers, which was still having some reverberations. Most of that came from the people who had awakened outside in all sorts of weather, not sure how they got there, and were being treated by the specialists provided by Hoax, Inc. The media had let go of the story because Hoax was so good at deflecting interest and attention, so people didn't realize that something was far weirder than anyone realized.

The Chief handed the police department side of the investigation over to good old Gordon Priebe, who was getting far too much experience with Neighborlee's weirdness, and had him work with Stanzer. They came to the guardians.

The weirdest detail in the mystery of the welcome signs? The people on the Neighborlee side of those signs never noticed them until the ward representatives got nudged into action by the mayor and started walking their wards and asking questions. Gordon drove around to determine exactly which streets had those signs, and how long they had been there.

Sherwood made a map, noting each sign's location. The little red dots on a street map of Neighborlee, small enough to fit on a sheet of copier paper, pretty much created a solid line circling our town. Kurt and Ford headed out to investigate those signs. They soon determined the signs needed to be removed. ASAP. Each one gave off an itchy-tickly hum of suspiciously, faintly familiar energy. Enemy energy.

The only opposition they might run into would come from the owners of the property where the signs now sat, because removing them would create holes in their tree lawns.

Kurt called me after he and Ford checked out the third sign, to contact Angela and Ethan, who had just gone to their garden, accessed through the wall of the second-floor landing. They couldn't be reached without someone going through the dimensional gate. Maurice couldn't, because he and Holly were in the Fae Realms, so she could meet his relatives. Kurt and Ford were busy with the signs, so Jane and I were the best bet for going through that gate without trouble.

We needed to bring Angela and Ethan back, because while Kurt and Ford were examining the third sign, the energy they sensed surrounding it suddenly flared to life. They hid behind a convenient hedge, and less than a minute later, a vintage black Ford sedan drove past, with four black-suited, black-hatted young men, their faces half-concealed with dark glasses. Kurt swore they could have been the Blues Brothers or Men in Black wannabes who had crashed the New Year's Eve party, right as he was about to propose to Jane.

The shield seemed to keep the doppelgangers, Kerri, and her black-suited minions out of Neighborlee, so why not this new batch of black-suited creeps?

London and Sherwood were pretty strained already, as hard as it might be to believe, with their unlimited access to the Worldwide Web and all the resources, and their ability to tap security cameras and sensors practically anywhere. Finding power to add to the shield around Neighborlee was their main focus, and they had been pretty busy dealing with constant fluctuations in the shield at multiple locations. They added watching for the black-or-blues, as we came to call them, shortened to BoBs, to their regular routine.

And after just a few days, discovered something really disturbing.

And encouraging at the same time.

The downward fluctuations -- weak points -- occurred any place one of those welcome signs appeared. They were small, almost not worth noticing. Except that our sloppy enemies messed up there by having so *many* weak points, a pattern became visible.

The downward spike doubled in size any time the monitoring program caught one of the BoBs crossing over into Neighborlee, and crossing out again.

On a positive note, there were regular upward spikes in strength in the shield, sometimes strong enough to close the weak spots completely. Three times, upward spikes hit when a black car with four BoBs approached, and they weren't able to cross over. The cars swerved, diverted by something the drivers couldn't see.

Those spikes of energy lasted long enough to be traced back through the ground. In time, Sherwood determined they were coming from -- get this -- Neighborlee Gospel Church. The spikes happened during prayer meetings, or when the prayer warrior teams got together to pray over Pastor Rocky's concerns, and the defenses of our town.

Pretty cool, huh?

And yeah, a little embarrassing. Kind of like an action movie hero finding out he had the weapon to defeat the evil mastermind all along, but he had neglected to practice using it, and had even let it get damaged.

Ford and Kurt and a handful of guys from our Star Trek club went around and took care of the unwelcome "Welcome" signs, putting in the physical labor to remove them. Pastor Rocky got the prayer warrior leaders together and asked them to rework the schedule. There were fewer people praying at any one time, but we had nearly constant prayer shifts, to deal with the Magna Magma threat and the defenses of our town.

By the time the quartet of kids belonging to the Hunt showed up, and a really nasty millionaire named Wolcott followed them to town, all but five "Welcome" signs had been taken down. Some people didn't let the removal teams come onto their property to pull up the signs. They were among the loudest of the complainers. General consensus said they wanted the signs to remain so they could use them in a lawsuits, as soon as they could figure out who to sue.

So, we had times during the day and night when we didn't have a prayer shield, and we had five spots that needed constant monitoring for BoB entrances and exits. If London and Sherwood could have followed the BoBs all through town, we could have figured out what they were up to, but there were too many holes, too many streets where residents and businesses didn't have security cameras or those video doorbell contraptions or other devices for spying on their neighbors.

All we could do was be vigilant.

And wasn't that what the guardians had been doing all along?

The big power burst or burp or whatever it was when the Hunt came up against Wolcott set off a reaction. Angela and I both heard and felt a deep ringing through the foundations of the town. We found out later there was a momentary weakness in the shield. Enough to let Angela's enemies, led by a really cold, creepy old woman named Von Helado and her black-suited minions, to get a good idea where she was.

Why were all our enemies dressing their minions in black suits?

We found out soon that the "burp" brought some other changes to Neighborlee. It was like sending up a signal flare in some ways.

The most important and positive change was Pendry. She felt the power surge and followed it, but not to the end of the trail. Pendry was a runaway, fifteen years old, a member of the Hunt, and she had been chased by some pretty grim and scary characters that she just didn't want to talk about. She didn't know who to trust, so she settled down to camp in the Metroparks until she could scout and find out who had set off the energy beacon and whose side they were on.

The Hounds of Hamin weren't putting up with it. One of them grabbed Dawn and hauled her down to the swimming hole in the Metroparks, and another Hound grabbed hold of Pendry and dragged her to meet Dawn. With an introduction like that, Pendry couldn't deny that Dawn and the other members of the Hunt were legitimate, and they were good guys, but that didn't mean she would open up any time soon. It was enough to have her in Stanzer's building, settling in and slowly defrosting. We got to work on legal arrangements. Pendry needed legal protection and supervision, so some other creepy traitor like Wolcott wouldn't falsify documentation saying she was a long-lost granddaughter, to put her into his clutches.

The other reaction to that "burp" came from Earnest B. Tass. He called himself the Right Reverend Apostle Earnest B. Tass, but since his ministerial license came from a mail order catalog and he proudly proclaimed he had never polluted his soul by attending seminary, most people referred to him as Tass, if they didn't refer to him as "that wacko." Most people refused to put him in the same class with Pastor Rocky and the other legitimate ministers in town. Tass had a little storefront chapel, as he called it, in a four-unit strip shopping center on an intersection everyone referred to as "four corners," where Neighborlee, Darbyville, Titustown, and Centerville Heights met. The shopping strip was on the Centerville corner, kitty-corner from Neighborlee. Tass had been there, trying to build up his congregation and going door-to-door, ignoring the Do Not Knock legislation and the stickers passed out by NOPEC, for about six or seven months before the burp. He had a regular routine, annoying residents in all four towns equally. After the "burp," he spent three days a week in Neighborlee.

Of course, we didn't make the connection until much later, after the big explosion at the Sunday school picnic in the Metroparks. Then London and Sherwood did a lot of backtracking of his patterns, and harvested all the security camera memory throughout town.

All the guardians noticed him, stomping up and down the sidewalks in Angela's neighborhood, whenever we went to Divine's for meetings.

We paid more attention after Ethan and Angela were reunited. Ethan noticed Tass several times standing on the sidewalk across the street, his hands clasped behind his back, scowling at the building. By that time, we were all used to him being around, dragging his stormcloud behind him. Those of us who attended Neighborlee Gospel Church asked that Divine's Emporium be added to the prayer teams' lists, to protect the shop and Angela from the sour old pharisee. But that was all we did, that was all the time and worry we spared to Tass.

Until Ethan awoke in the middle of the night and followed a trumpet call through the gates on the wall of the second-floor landing, to his and Angela's private garden. His suit of armor was there, waiting. It turned into mist that enveloped him, and then soaked into his skin. He didn't mention it to anyone until two days later, when Tass stood across the street. Ethan's sword solidified, in his hand, ready for service.

That was kind of a hint that maybe Tass was going to be trouble.

Ya think?

About three weeks before the Sunday school picnic, several boys reported to Angela that Tass had asked them to take pictures inside Divine's Emporium. He would pay them to go into every room in the shop and take pictures of the contents. One of the boys asked what he wanted the pictures for, and Tass told him, with a straight face, that he was on a mission from God to rid our town of "evil influences." If the boys took "evil goods" from the shop when he asked, they would be paid even more. When one boy said that sounded like stealing, Tass told him it wasn't stealing if it was a mission from God.

The boys were smart enough to know there wasn't enough money in the world to convince them to steal from Angela. Taking something without paying for it was stealing, no matter how much the slick-suited, big-voiced, crazy-eyed man twisted words around. The boys went straight to Angela and told her. She called Gordon, who confronted Tass.

I was so proud of Gordon. Tass got all self-righteous and snarly. He spit when he got really wound up, and declared that his mission from God overruled everything that mere mortals might say. Gordon snapped out one of my favorite lines from *Ladyhawke*. "Sir, I talk to God all the time, and He's never mentioned you."

Tass threatened the destruction of his soul. Gordon just smiled at him and told him his soul had already been given to Jesus, and Tass had no say in what happened to it. Then he took the body camera recording and gave it to Chief Tanner, putting the whole encounter on record.

From that day, Tass went on the offensive -- as if he wasn't offensive already? -- against Divine's Emporium and the Neighborlee Police.

Meanwhile, Stephen Grandstone had started harassing Pastor Rocky.

He knew he had been Drake Abbot, in Magna Magma. How? How

did the Grandstones find out anything? Shady sources, at the very least.

Get this: Grandstone wanted an inside exclusive to the reunion of the band. He wanted a reunion concert in Cleveland. Playhouse Square. One of the venues at Cleveland State. The I-X Center. All Pastor Rocky had to do was name a place and date, and he would arrange it.

He got kind of nasty-snippy when Pastor Rocky told him he wasn't in the reunion tour. He accused Pastor Rocky of lying, and then trying to game him and force him into negotiations.

All this was done over the phone. Grandstones had never stepped foot into our church, even when they tried to prove they were the legitimate owners of the building. We suspected any Grandstone who stepped foot onto church property would burst into flames.

The phone calls were a regular occurrence, according to Vivian Holt, our church secretary. At least once a day, six days a week, Stephen Grandstone called and Vivian had to pass him to Pastor Rocky. On Sundays, he called and left a message on the church answering machine, because no one was in the office.

Then after two months, the phone calls and demands to meet the band and sponsor a concert stopped abruptly.

It was the day after the third reunion concert. I knew the schedule because Pastor Rocky tried to stay on top of things, to have us praying for his former friends. He had a bad feeling about the whole situation, how the whole concert came together, the nastiness of the Lavaheads, and especially how the organizers for the tour had found him. How difficult was it to get through three false identities to track someone down?

Sherwood contacted me at work. It was a Tuesday, paper delivery day, and I had just gotten to my desk. My computer screen lit up with his face on it. Pretty neat trick, since I hadn't turned on my computer yet. The little light in the camera lit up and he looked around the office before speaking. Which was a relief, because I was bent down to pick up a pack of flag stickers I had knocked onto the floor and didn't see him watching me for a few seconds.

"Lanie, Pastor Rocky is going to need you," Sherwood said. "Right away. I have bad news to give him."

"What kind of bad news?" Honestly, my first thought was that Stephen Grandstone was on his way to the church with a car loaded with Magna Magma memorabilia and a couple machine guns.

"According to the news, Pastor Rocky should be dead."

Chapter Two

"What?" Somehow, I managed not to shriek that word.

"Just go. I'll tell you in the car. Father Marty is reading the news on his computer right now, and we want Pastor Rocky to know before he tells him."

"Okay, I'm going." I turned my wheelchair away from my desk, and nearly forgot to grab my backpack, which I had slung onto my desk to unload it. Kind of needed my backpack, because it had my keys.

Daniel was just getting out of his truck when I reached the parking lot. Oh, great, we were supposed to have an editorial department meeting. How did I manage to forget that little detail? Maybe because I was trying to forget anything having to do with Daniel, thanks to the weird looks he had been giving me ever since we celebrated Angela and Ethan's wedding, and she threw her bridal bouquet right into my face.

"Hey, no running out on me," Daniel called, laughing, as I sped down the ramp in my wheelchair.

This was one of those days when I was even more furious with all the damage done during the whole doppelganger situation this past winter and spring. My healing had been set back by years. I should have been leaving the office on my own two legs, and maybe even run to my Jeep and jump in. No delays to get out of my chair and fold it up and sling it into the back seat.

"Pastor Rocky needs me," I said, and nearly ran him over, when he stepped into my path.

At the last moment, Daniel pivoted aside and grabbed the handles of my chair and turned me toward his truck. He nearly tipped me out of my chair, but I caught on to what he was doing, and levered myself up onto my feet in time to avoid doing a face-plant against his passenger door. I was in and pulling the door closed by the time he had my chair in the back of his truck and was getting into the driver's seat.

Then I turned on my phone and told Sherwood to fill us in.

"Read this," he said, and kindly took over my phone so it switched over to a music website devoted to rock'n'roll bands.

It featured Magna Magma's reunion tour. Sherwood only let me read a few paragraphs before he took over again, blowing up several pictures.

"That's Pastor Rocky. But it's not." I squinted at the images. "And there's Father Marty. But --" I swallowed, fighting a queasy sensation. "But that's not them. They're … younger."

We got to a stop sign and Daniel leaned over to look. I showed him the phone. All I had to do was hold it, while Sherwood scrolled through the images. Pastor Rocky and Marty scowled at the camera, looking like they did in the pictures from the band's glory days. Except …

Except they were wearing current clothes. None of the grunge rock outfits. Black t-shirts and jeans and cowboy boots and black leather jackets. Their hair was short -- well, Father Marty had hair, period. The man I had been running into when he practiced with Pastor Rocky's retro band wore the typical Friar Tuck haircut, glossy dome with a straggly fringe. In all the pictures I had seen from Pastor Rocky's boxes of memorabilia, they had had long hair, past their shirt pockets -- if they wore shirts at all.

"This is a story that was slated to release next week," Sherwood said, when Daniel sat up and continued driving to the church.

"How did you get hold of it ahead of time?" Daniel asked.

"I didn't. It was released in reaction to an accident last night. Read."

My phone showed a series of newspaper articles and police reports and online news bytes. Sherwood didn't give me time to read much more than the headlines and a few of the first lines. I didn't want to read more than that, because the headlines and lead lines told me the whole story.

Magna Magma's tour bus had collided head-on with a semi hauling a fuel tanker. There were no survivors.

Okay, we were going to comfort Pastor Rocky on the tragic deaths of his former friends. So why were we trying to get there before Father Marty?

My phone display stopped on the final article, and I realized I was wrong. There was a whole lot more to last night's accident.

The last article was a list of the dead. With a few sentences talking about what they had been doing before they reunited for the concert tour.

Pastor Rocky and Father Marty were listed near the top.

The article gave their current names, the names they had been using when they were with the band, and where they ministered now.

I read the information to Daniel, and my voice broke a little when I got to "Neighborlee Gospel Church, Neighborlee, Ohio."

"But they're not dead," he said. "So who died in the crash?"

I flipped through my phone, moving backward through the screens of information Sherwood had put there, then increased the view to navigate through the article. I was reading when Daniel pulled into the church parking lot, and while he unloaded my chair and brought it around to the door.

"It doesn't say anything about getting lookalikes or body doubles or whatever to fill in for them," I said, when I couldn't delay any longer, and slid out of the truck to settle in my chair.

"Sherwood?" Daniel said.

"You want it sent to Pastor Rocky's computer?" he asked through my phone.

"Please."

When we came in the back door by the church office, Vivian was hurrying down the hall away from us, trying to keep up with Gabe McIntosh, our head custodian. All the lights were off in the office, but not in the hallway. Okay, so now we knew how Sherwood was keeping Father Marty from reaching Pastor Rocky before we did.

"They're kind of scary, you know?" Daniel murmured, as we slowed and watched Vivian and Gabe vanish down the hallway, probably heading for the utility room at the other end of the church. I knew all the back rooms and hallways and storage rooms, from part-time custodian jobs in high school.

"Yeah, but it's good to have them on our side," I said, and turned my phone to look at the blank screen and make a face, betting myself that Sherwood was listening and watching.

I was right. A cartoon of Groucho Marx flashed on my screen, waggling his huge eyebrows and his big cigar, and saying, "With friends like these, who needs enemas?"

Daniel laughed, then he sighed and straightened his shoulders and looked around. "So, what do we do? Just go in and hope he isn't busy?"

"Doing what? No computer, no phone." I checked my watch. "He's probably still in the sanctuary with the prayer vigil team. The current shift isn't done for another fifteen, twenty minutes."

Pastor Rocky has always believed in putting his knees where his mouth is, so to speak. Prayer vigil teams signed on for one hour at a time, but he made a habit of putting in two shifts in a row. I've always had a hard time praying, mostly because my prayers seem to be more "gimme" and "can I?" than an actual conversation with God. Which, when I really take time to think about it, is kind of lame. Considering the miracle of my whole life, the crazy saves we pulled off, the battles with otherness we have won, my multiple brushes with death, and the fact I'm at least partially on my feet, when I should have spent a greatly shortened life paralyzed and probably on a respirator, you'd think I'd be a lot closer to God, right?

Thank God we had Pastor Rocky to give us the best example possible.

So we headed down the hall to the back doors of the sanctuary, and slipped in to try to find Pastor Rocky, so we could snag him as soon as the chime sounded to end this prayer vigil shift. The door creaked, sounding like a haunted house soundtrack. I was glad I was sitting down. It put me lower, about three-quarters hidden by the last pew in the row. Poor Daniel didn't have that protection.

Only one head raised up, and the tall, thickening body it belonged to got up almost before I saw Pastor Rocky's face. He had a long walk from the front pew, and he tipped his head slightly to the right and stared at us as he came down the right-hand aisle to the back of the sanctuary to meet us. He licked his lips, and for a moment looked like he might say something. Then he shrugged, gestured for us to follow him, and led us out of the sanctuary.

"Now I know what you go through," he said, once the doors had closed and we were heading down the hall again to the church office.

"Who?" Daniel said.

"Lanie. With her dreams." He rested a hand on my shoulder and walked with me as I wheeled down the hall. Not an easy thing to do, but it helped that he had long arms, otherwise there was a risk of my running over his foot once or twice.

"What did you dream, exactly?"

"That door creaking, and you two coming in and looking like you were about to tell me the Grandstones finally found legitimate reasons for throwing us out of the church." He managed a coughing kind of laugh. "But it was all tied up with that Magna Magma concert he wants."

Daniel choked. That got a frown from Pastor Rocky.

The moment we walked into the front of the church office, the lights came back on. Pastor Rocky looked up at the ceiling, where one of the fluorescent tubes flickered, and his lips moved, silently counting. He shuddered when the flickers stopped, then offered us a crooked grin.

"In my dream, the light flickered like that ten times. This was only six times, so I guess we're still safe from the Grandstones." He took a deep breath and let go of my shoulder, to move ahead of us down the hallway with staff offices on either side, to where his office sat on the end.

"Sherwood, are you all set?" I asked, once we were all inside and Daniel was reaching to close the door.

In answer, Pastor Rocky's desktop computer monitor flicked into life.

"They found something?" Pastor Rocky walked over to his desk to turn the monitor around more so we all could see what was on it.

"We've seen it. You might want to read it for yourself," Daniel said. "We'll wait until you're ready to talk. Sherwood asked us to come here. He thought you might want to have company when you --" He gestured at the monitor.

"O -- o -- kay." He sat down and turned his monitor around. "Let's see what you've got, Sherwood."

Daniel and I settled at the table on the other end of the office, where Pastor Rocky counseled people or had business meetings. We both took the time to text the newspaper to let them know where we were and we wouldn't be back for a while. Vivian came in while Pastor Rocky was still reading. His face just had a slightly puzzled frown, instead of shock or confusion or grief, so he was still reading the online magazine article.

"Father Marty has been trying to reach you," she said, when he looked up from the monitor. "He's left a few messages, but with the power outage …" She shrugged. "His last message said he was on his way over."

"Send him in as soon as he gets here, would you? Thanks, Viv." His smile looked weary as he turned back to the monitor.

"Is he going to be all right?" she whispered, as she backed toward the door.

"He's getting some bad news," Daniel said, just as quietly.

A choked sound and Pastor Rocky bowing his head to rest it in his hands told us the moment he read the headline of the first accident article.

"I've been thinking about the younger version in the pictures," Daniel whispered.

I was glad he spoke, because my eyes were aching a little, trying to watch Pastor Rocky but giving him some privacy.

"Doppelgangers strike again?" I said, and glanced at him.

He nodded. "How much good can we do him? Other than knowing how he has to feel, since we had our own lookalike problems."

"Yeah, but ours didn't … well, yeah, one of my doppelgangers went to dust when it hit the sunlight, and yours kind of burned up against the shield. Maybe. But neither of ours left behind a body to be declared dead at the scene. What is going on?"

"Peter?" Father Marty tapped on the door frame as he peered around it. His gaze landed on us, then shifted to the other end of the office. Pastor Rocky had his head in his hands again. I was pretty sure he was praying. And knowing him, grieving for the friends he had known so long ago, and had lost when he chose God over Magna Magma.

"Did they have anybody left behind?" Pastor Rocky said, raising his head. "How do we reach out to their families, whoever is grieving right now, when we wouldn't have anything to do with the reunion? What good can we do?" He took a shuddering, deep breath. "We failed them, trying to keep our hands clean."

"London and I are searching to see what family they had," Sherwood announced.

"Thank you. That's a start." A choked little chuckle escaped him when Father Marty turned around, looking for the source of the voice. "Bo, meet Sherwood. He's the Neighborlee equivalent of Maxx Headroom, without the stutter."

"Excuse me?" Father Marty shook his head and blinked rapidly.

"I guess I went too slow, breaking you in to the wonderful weirdness of Neighborlee." He sighed and looked over at Daniel and me. "Thank you for being here for me, but I think we need some privacy to grieve."

"Sure." Daniel stood up and I gave my chair a good shove forward with brain power. Father Marty didn't notice. He was giving the office some searching looks, probably looking for the speakers and maybe video cameras that fed into Sherwood.

"Are you thinking what I'm thinking?" Daniel said, once we were back out in his truck, and he had my chair in the back.

"Time for a run to Sweeties' candy warehouse? Time for a death by chocolate feast? How about a *Buffy* marathon?"

He snorted and just grinned at me for a few moments. Then the smile faded, and he sighed and closed his eyes. "If those were doppelgangers, like the ones we fought ... what do they have to do with the reunion tour for Magna Magma? Is Pastor Rocky a target? Why is he involved?"

"Big Ugly doesn't slap at anybody unless they're a threat," I said, more thinking aloud than offering something he didn't already know. "What did Pastor do to get attention and make himself a target?"

Ford came up with the possible answer. We weren't able to get the guardians together and meet with Angela at Divine's Emporium until that evening. I had to get to work, and Daniel had some meetings for the company. I wrote up a report and London took care of getting it out to the guardians, along with our questions and theories, and linked everyone to all the articles on the Magna Magma concerts and the crash. Everyone had the same information, and we all had most of the day to think about the questions. Ford didn't even wait until everyone was gathered in the backyard behind Divine's.

"The prayer vigil," Ford said. "It interfered with those crazy welcome signs, finagling the whole requirement that the enemy has to be welcomed, invited inside. The cyber kids even told us that the shield got stronger during the times that matched up with the prayer vigils at church. People were praying to protect our town. Big Ugly or whoever arranged for those signs has put a target on Rocky, because he's getting in their way."

"But why go to all the trouble of killing the entire band? And halfway across the country?" Arthur Sheridan said. "Don't they know Pastor Rocky is right here, within reach?"

"Yeah, that's a complication, but it goes back to the whole prayers thing. Maybe he's invisible to the enemy. They know enough about him to link him with the band. Remember, that article gives his name and location. Whoever caused the accident thought he was on that bus." He shrugged. "Yeah, I know there are logic holes, but that's the only thing that even makes halfway sense."

We all agreed. Mostly that there were logic holes big enough to drive the *Enterprise* through. But if those were doppelgangers and not some impersonators hired by the rest of Magna Magma to make the fans happy, then Pastor Rocky's contribution to protecting our town had to be the driving factor for the attack.

London and Sherwood found a few relatives of each of the members of Magna Magma, but couldn't verify if they had any recent contact with them. They found some ex-wives and estranged children, but again, very little evidence that there had been contact in the last ten years. Which was kind of sad. Wasn't there anyone who mourned them, other than Pastor Rocky and Father Marty? Well, yeah, the fans. The people who had bought tickets for concerts that would never take place. The rabid Lavaheads who were screaming about conspiracies and gathering their resources to sue the city and county and state where the accident had taken place, scrambling to find someone to blame.

After five days, rumors started floating to the top of all the Internet chatter. Bodies had vanished from the morgue. Then the rumors said some of the bodies hadn't been dead, but the police had lied to protect the survivors. Then other rumors said the survivors had been spirited away to protective custody, that they had seen something dangerous. Now the search was on to identify who had survived, who had attacked the band's bus, and who was the enemy.

Sunday afternoon, self-anointed Rev. Earnest B. Tass attacked our Sunday school picnic.

We were at the swimming hole area of the Metroparks, rather than on the church property, combining our church Olympics competition with a rib cook-off and baptism service. Later, after studying security videos from businesses around town, we realized that not only were the BoBs that got into town stopped at the edge of church property, but so was Tass.

He couldn't step foot onto Neighborlee Gospel Church property, any more than he was able to get past the gate of Divine's Emporium. Talk about holy ground being a real, defensive phenomenon.

Pastor Rocky stepped onto the sand of the little beach between the snack shack and the swimming hole, and held out a hand to Tami Lee Trumble, who was about to be baptized. He had on boat shoes, and walked right into the water, wearing baggy swimming shorts and a muscle shirt. Tami's parents were standing to the right, holding a beach towel and waiting for her to come up out of the water, and the deacons were standing to the left, with my Pop holding a towel for Pastor Rocky. I had a front row seat, with my wheelchair right on the edge of the grass, because sand wasn't too friendly to my wheels.

Tass bombed through the crowd. We found out later he pushed a couple people aside hard enough they fell into other people, kind of like a chain reaction of dominos.

"For shame!" he roared, his voice rising to a shriek while adding six syllables to "shame." "For shame! Who are the misguided parents of this innocent child who is about to be lowered into the waters of false repentance, to be condemned to spiritual death? How dare you abuse your child so?"

He was about to splash into the water, and I wouldn't have been surprised if he blamed Pastor Rocky because he didn't walk on the water. The deacons leaped forward like this was a move they had practiced for years, with my Pop and Chief Tanner leading the way. They became a wall dividing Pastor Rocky and Tami from Tass. Then they surrounded him. Those were brave men, because there was just something sweaty, slimy-looking, and plague-carrying about the man in his designer suit that made Herb Tarlek of *WKRP* look like a fashion plate. It had to be a designer suit because I couldn't imagine any clothing manufacturer risking its reputation on producing more than one of those things, in neon orange and brown plaid, glossy like he was covered in oil. Who would wear a three-piece suit like that in the 90-plus-degree August weather?

Somehow, those twelve men hustled Tass off the beach, past the snack shack, and across the parking lot, short-circuiting his shrieks into stammers. The crowd parted like the Red Sea, but I bet the Red Sea didn't snicker and whisper as it parted before Moses. I was willing to believe God temporarily granted all of them superhero powers, like telekinesis, or maybe just a force field that protected them from physical contact. Or maybe it was the badge Chief Tanner flashed in the wacko's face, close enough it could have gone down his throat if he had kept his mouth open long enough.

"This looks like a job for guardians," Ford said, leaning over my shoulder. He followed the deacons before the crowd surged back to their positions. I looked at Mum, who was standing next to me, looking especially demure that day with navy blue hair and a long, silvery-white shirt over denim capris. She rolled her eyes and nodded, and I turned my wheelchair to follow Ford.

"Well, let's get on with the Lord's business," Pastor Rocky said as I gave my chair a mental push, to let me catch up with the deacons. They were heading for the grassy amphitheater on the other side of the parking lot. "If Dave and Mercy are willing to trust me?" he added, with a nod to Tami Lee's parents.

That got some people chuckling. I felt the tension ratcheting down behind me. Then a shiver of apprehension got me pushing with my arms, to save my telekinetic strength for any emergency handling of the nutcase. I caught a flicker of movement from the corner of my eye and turned my head enough to see Angela and Ethan following me. He had his phone out, and I didn't doubt he was calling more guardians.

The amphitheater was a little stage of sandstone slabs at the bottom of a half-moon curve of slope, with a three-sided shelter across the back creating a backstage area for outdoor performances. The depression in the ground was surrounded by a thick wall of hedges, and provided surprising sound muffling, so concerts and plays taking place on the stage didn't create much disturbance for people using the swimming hole or the picnic pavilions scattered around the curve in the Metroparks road. The situation couldn't have been better for getting Tass away from the congregation, without having to drag him all the way to the police station.

"Repression!" Tass bellowed as I came through the gap in the hedge at the top of the slope. "Silencing the voice of holiness!" It took him long enough to recover from being surrounded and hustled away. I had to wonder if he was shocked because he wasn't used to people responding so quickly and efficiently. And without violence.

"Holiness isn't rude," Pop said, leaning forward so he was nearly nose-to-nose with him.

When Pop was serving as a deacon, he dressed a little more formally than usual. That meant wearing a brown sport coat over his tie-dyed T-shirt, with his long gray ponytail tucked into the collar of his jacket. But he was wearing his ugly orange and brown Bermuda shorts under the sport coat, showing off his extremely hairy legs. I was close enough to see the moment Tass got an eyeful of the T-shirt and the ponytail that had worked loose. His eyes bugged and he went bleach white for two seconds before an angry red flush washed over his face.

"Hippie! Spawn of Satan! Heretic!" Then he reached into that huge coat of his and pulled out a bottle with a sports pull-top, yanked it open, and squirted Pop in the face.

Whatever he expected to happen, it didn't. He stopped, eyes bugging out, and stared at Pop and couldn't seem to figure out what to say for a few seconds. Only a few seconds.

"I'm adding assault to disturbing the peace," Chief Tanner said, and took his life into his hands by grabbing Tass and shoving him down onto a bench to one side of the stage's shelter. "Start making some sense before I call for the nice young men with nets and tranquilizer guns," he added, a growl rumbling at the back of his voice as he leaned down, getting nose-to-nose with the wacko.

"He didn't -- he should have -- someone defiled my holy water!" Tass wailed.

Pop burst out laughing. He tugged off his sport coat and tugged up the hem of his shirt and wiped his face.

"Good one, Charlie," Ford said from behind me. I was making my way down the slope, letting gravity pull me down to the bottom, with my hands acting like caliper brakes on the wheels. He grabbed the handles of my chair and guided me down to the pavement in front of the stage.

Tass started to stand, gasping and pushing at the bench with his hands. I was ticked at him, despite Pop laughing. I telekinetically grabbed his hands and yanked them up over his head. Pop turned around and looked at me, nodded, and winked. I took that to mean he knew what I had done, and he approved.

"You want to start over?" he asked. As if I could read his mind, I knew what Pop was doing. Give the intruder a chance to hang himself with his own words.

"I demand --"

"You have disrupted a worship service, and you have just assaulted the head deacon," Chief Tanner said. "We can also get you on trespassing, since we paid to reserve the swimming area for our church's use today, and the bulletin board clearly states the beach isn't open to the public. While we welcome visitors, that welcome is for worship and fellowship, which does not include slander and public displays and false accusations and assault. You want to choose your next words carefully, mister."

Tass whimpered and looked up at his arms, which I still had pulled straight up in the air.

Pop turned around and made the cut signal, finger across his throat. I let go and Tass sagged down on the bench.

"Demon possession," he croaked.

"How could a demon get hold of you, surrounded by church folk?" Pop said calmly, with just a hint of amusement in his voice. "Aren't you supposed to be a preacher? Or are you a fallen sinner who surrendered to the devil's power?"

That got Tass. He went white again. Pop had him there. He couldn't claim demons were at work without admitting that he wasn't holy and inviolate and not there on a mission from God. That was a phrase he loved to use. He justified everything he did whenever people complained, by loudly proclaiming he was on a mission from God.

By this time, we all had a good idea of Earnest B. Tass's method and his message and tactics. Athena had put together a nice fat electronic dossier on him, with blog postings and YouTube tirades about this fat, self-satisfied, self-righteous creepazoid who was traveling the country on a mission from God -- his own words -- cleansing the churches in America. In one he had even said he would do all it took, even if that meant burning the building down around the false ministers who lined their own pockets at the cost of the innocent lambs of God.

The really mystifying part was that Tass had been in Arkansas just five days before he suddenly appeared in Neighborlee. His press releases declared he was working his way across the country, so why skip all those states and jump to Ohio in his campaign?

Pastor Rocky joined us then, coming through the gap in the hedge at the bottom of the slope, squelching slightly in his wet boat shoes. He had a VeggieTales beach towel wrapped around his hips.

"Uh huh. Uggy Bear is handling announcements and the singing, but I need all of you out there to take care of communion in about twenty minutes," he said, as he climbed the four steps from the pavement to the stage.

Uggy Bear was the nickname for our youth minister.

"Blasphemy," Tass whimpered. "You have no right to serve communion --"

"Don't get me started, boy," Pastor Rocky said, his voice going colder and quieter than I had ever heard it. "I tried to be polite and respectful when you contacted me. Don't make me regret not calling my friends in the Cleveland Browns and asking them to make you their new tackling dummy." He stopped about five feet away from Tass and jammed his fists into his hips. "I told you I'd be willing to meet and talk about your accusations, but you had to be civil and not involve my church family in your sideshow. You like using props? You like making everything a Hollywood spectacle? You keep demanding a welcome in writing and in front of witnesses, but I'm not going to play your game. If you come in peace, then you're welcome here, but you aren't here for God's peace, are you?"

I didn't hear what he said next, because his words about welcome set up a ringing feeling in my head, and a dropping sensation in my stomach.

This was late summer, and just six short months ago, we had been dealing with enemy forces that would have Earnest B. Tass shrieking for holy water and an exorcism. They had tried to trick us into welcoming them into Neighborlee. In essence, giving them permission to cross the border and walk through the energy shield defending our town.

I looked at Ford, and from the wide-eyed look he was giving me, he had caught exactly the same thing I did. Pastor Rocky had narrowly avoided officially welcoming this self-righteous, vindictive creepazoid that gave me warm and fuzzy feelings for Torquemada.

"This where the party is?" Kurt said from the top of the amphitheater slope.

I looked up and saw him and Jane standing there with Angela and Ethan. They hadn't come to the picnic because they had plans to spend the day in Sandusky. Jane was attending our church and she had managed to convince Kurt to give church and Pastor Rocky a try, when all my invitations over the years had failed. That was a sign of true love.

Pop exchanged one of those looks with Chief Tanner that made me suspect even more strongly than ever that the Chief knew a whole lot more about the guardians and what we were doing to protect our town than he had ever let on. Tass tried to get up from the bench, but I held him down. I suspected from the way his eyes widened at the sight of Angela and

Ethan approaching the stage now with Jane and Kurt, he knew who they were, and he probably feared a comeuppance for his efforts to get boys to steal from Divine's Emporium.

The deacons left to take care of the communion service, leaving Pastor Rocky, Ford, Kurt, Jane, Angela, Ethan and me to deal with Tass.

"Pastor, we need to have a long talk with you about not being so hospitable. Specifically, the teaching in the Bible about not welcoming foul spirits and enemy forces into your home," Ford said.

"Foul --" Tass again tried to rise off the bench.

This time, I didn't hold him down. I kind of hoped he'd fight so hard to get up he'd trip over those too-shiny expensive shoes and fall flat on his face. Instead, his eyes bugged and his mouth worked with no sound coming out. Then he grabbed at his throat. I looked at Jane and Kurt. Which one of them was doing the Darth Vader silencing routine on him? Both of them had very convincing poker faces.

"What does Torquemada here want with you?" I asked.

Pastor Rocky and Ford were on the stage with Tass, while Angela, Ethan, Jane and Kurt were on the pavement in front of the stage with me. If looks could kill, the one Tass aimed at me, for equating him with the leader of the Spanish Inquisition, would have turned me to cinders in about five seconds.

"Magna Magma," he gasped, when there was an almost audible ping sound, and quite obviously the restraint on his voice was released.

Later, Jane admitted she had formed a tiny bubble of Ghost field around the lower part of his head, so he could breathe but couldn't make himself heard. Now, that was fine-tuned control.

Pastor Rocky shook his head. "I haven't had any contact with them in years."

"Liar," Tass growled. "You were on that satanic reunion tour with them. Until you made a deal with the devil and walked away from that accident that should have wiped your poison off the face of the world!"

"Should have?" Kurt said. "And how do you know what that accident *should* have done? Like maybe you caused the accident?"

Chapter Three

Tass gaped at him, and for a few seconds I seriously considered the idea that the accusation, which I knew Kurt had made just to be sarcastic, might have some truth behind it.

Creepy, anyone?

"I haven't even left the county in probably five months. How could I be on a tour?" Pastor Rocky said, looking more amused than upset at being called a liar.

That got Tass. He stopped with his mouth open, about to respond. He got that little boy lost expression that a lot of self-righteous jerks get when they realize they've made a mistake, and they think the world is about to implode, and it's just totally unfair that they have to confess to that mistake. Then the moment passed and his enormous lower lip pouted out until it was twice its normal size.

"You played three concerts. All of you, making deals with the devil to ..." Then he blinked and leaned forward, and I had the strongest impression he was getting his first good look at Pastor Rocky since the whole circus started. "Evil, black magic of the worst kind. You prove how false the power is by returning to your true face between ..." Then he sighed and slumped and deflated a little. "Incredibly skilled makeup artists. I'm willing to admit that, rather than black magic."

"What is he talking about?" Jane asked.

"All of them, strutting around the stage, shredding the air with their demonic music, wearing their faces from forty years ago, seducing foolish, scantily clad women, endangering the souls of children with your demonic lyrics," he finished on a hiss that had me looking for a big snake providing sound effects. It amazed me how much hissing he could get into a sentence with so few sibilants.

"In case you haven't read the fan sites, I'm the reason Magna Magma broke up. I left and went to seminary. None of them wanted anything to do with me. I haven't talked with any of them --" He hesitated, and I suspected he was thinking of Father Marty, which kind of made his statement a lie. "I was surprised when they invited me on the reunion tour, but they cut me off when I refused to go. Just like always."

"You were on that tour," the fat idiot insisted. "You snuck away from your church and you played that devil music and then you came back and you endangered --"

"Jane?" Pastor Rocky gestured at Tass.

She grinned, and the invisible Ghost field gag slapped across his mouth again.

"I have a communion service to perform, and a sermon to preach, and I'm going to need some quiet and some heavy-duty praying before I go back. Could you … entertain our guest somewhere else?"

"We could take him to Divine's," Ford said, with a rather nasty gleam in his eyes.

"You sure he wouldn't burst into flame the second he steps over the threshold?" Kurt muttered.

Tass writhed and fought to get his mouth open, until he was red-faced and sweating. Jane flicked her fingers at him and the gag popped off with an almost audible pop.

"No! You can't! Don't take me into the hell-hole of that witch!" Tass shrieked, and pointed a trembling hand at Angela.

I laughed. The accusation was so ridiculous, and so melodramatic. Angela shook her head, wearing her usual superior smirk. Ethan and Kurt, however, had thundercloud expressions. Both of them were ready to pound Tass for his words.

Jane called up the Ghost field completely, making him vanish as well as silencing him.

We didn't take Tass to Divine's, for the simple fact that we were far too sensitive lately about welcoming people or things or whatever Tass was into our homes. What Pastor Rocky said about Tass wanting a formal welcome set off loud alarms in my head, and Ford had caught it too. We didn't want to take Tass into Divine's, because while he would have been contained and controlled, that would have been, in essence, welcoming him. He would probably claim that the evil he imagined filling Divine's had kept him from entering, but we knew better. Tass hadn't been *able* to step onto our church property, just like the BoBs.

We took him into the quarries. Jane and Kurt flew us there in the Ghost field. Tass probably had seizures, between being paralyzed and silenced and then flying about one hundred feet up in the air, going fast enough that the ground underneath us blurred. When Jane released him, on the plateau where we usually went for private conversations, he fell to his hands and knees and gasped and shivered for maybe ten, fifteen minutes. Then he shifted onto his sizeable bottom and looked up at us all in terror. I was surprised that he didn't come out with shrieking accusations of demonic powers, or something like that. He whimpered quite a bit, and shook, and sweated. The guy didn't have a very healthy diet, judging by the stink of chemicals and the greasy tone of the sweat pouring out of him. Fortunately, none of us had to touch him.

"All right," Ford said, when the whimpering died away and Jane signaled she had taken the gag off Tass's mouth. "Why are you so interested in Pastor Rocky's old band?"

"He's lying to you," Tass said in a strangled voice.

"Prove it," Kurt shot back.

Well, the slimy, fat weasel did have proof, on the smartphone in his coat pocket. He had all those articles Sherwood and London had gathered up for us, talking about Magna Magma's reunion tour, complete with pictures of the lookalikes of Pastor Rocky and Father Marty. Ford flipped through the files for less than a minute and told us what he found. Tass seemed disappointed that we knew about those articles.

"Here's proof that ain't him," Ford said. "No matter what those pictures look like, that man isn't our Pastor Rocky. See these dates?" He pointed at a line in the article. "He was right here in town, leading our retro band and playing for the mayor's birthday party. I've got a couple hundred pictures, and just as many witnesses."

Tass didn't call Ford a liar, and his bottom lip quivered like he might burst into sobs in another moment. He just shook his head.

"And this one." Ford tapped another date on the screen. "Pre-marriage counseling session with my granddaughter. That was a long one, because all the families were involved, so don't tell me Rocky snuck out. What we got here is --" He stopped, his eyes going wide for a few seconds. Then Ford swallowed hard. "We got some imposters. Lookalikes. Rocky and his friend, Marty, refused to get involved in that mess again, so they got lookalikes, and those poor guys died with the rest of the band."

"But he told me ..." Tass sighed and deflated a little more. He blinked away wetness. "He told me he was worried about the spiritual health of his town. He wanted me to get involved, to confront his pastor, confront those demonic musicians, and drag them through the pearly gates into heaven."

"Who did?" Jane said, after the six of us just exchanged "huh?" looks for a few moments.

Then we learned Stephen Grandstone had brought Earnest B. Tass to Neighborlee. That explained the sudden change of route in Tass's "mission from God" to cleanse the churches in America. Grandstone money had brought him to our town. All because Stephen Grandstone claimed he wanted to protect his church and cleanse the world of the poisonous influence of rock'n'roll music. With Rev. Earnest B. Tass's divine help.

"So since Pastor Rocky couldn't give him a meet-and-greet with the band, and arrange for a special concert, he brought in Torquemada to stir up trouble?" I waited to see the others' reactions to my statement. They didn't quite believe it, either. "There's more going on than that."

"He was causing trouble for us," Angela said. Her smile chilled when Tass startled at the sound of her voice. He looked at her, and went even more pale than he had been two seconds before.

"What were you looking for, when you tried to bribe those boys to spy and steal?" Ethan said. He stepped forward, pointing at Tass.

From out of thin air, a long, double-edged sword appeared in his hand, as if extending from his pointing finger. It sort of flared softly, silvery-blue with golden flames along the edge, transparent for a heartbeat, then solidifying. Tass gulped and whimpered, and the point nearly touched his bulbous nose.

"That's a pretty cool trick," Kurt murmured.

I was next to Ethan, and I saw the momentary widening of his eyes. He hadn't meant to do that. The sword had just manifested. Maybe it was alive, like other things seemed to be alive in Divine's Emporium, and it had sensed he needed it?

"What were you looking for? It has to be terribly important, maybe … maybe worth your life if you fail to obtain it?" Ethan continued, his voice going dangerously soft. "You were unable to step foot on our land, and you needed to get inside and look for something. What?" He flicked the sword right and left, just a few inches in either direction, wringing another whimper from Tass, and a waterfall of sweat.

"Books," he squeaked.

"What kind of books?" Angela's voice was hard, making me shiver.

The rest of us exchanged looks again. This past spring, thieves had stolen books from Divine's and tried to push Angela through a painting into another world. We knew they hadn't found all the books they were looking for, because when Stanzer and Ethan confronted them, they said the one who hired them had been angry and disappointed. We should have expected another attempt to get at those books. Just not using a slimy self-appointed preacher-slash-con-man.

She repeated her question, and Tass scrambled to reach into his jacket and pull a sheaf of papers from the inside pocket. His profuse sweating had made the ink smear, but there was enough detail of the designs on the covers and the words printed in a strange alphabet, to make her shudder and drop the papers. Ethan dropped the sword and hurried to wrap his arms around her. The sword evaporated into thin air before it hit the ground.

"Fool," Angela whispered, her voice harsh. "You have no idea what evil you have chosen to serve. Did they tell you what those books are supposed to do? Do you know what fools have been caught by the false promises in those books and handed their souls over to be devoured?"

"What do they do?" Ford asked, after giving one scathing look at Tass, and then reaching to clasp Angela's shoulder.

"Do you have those books?" Kurt asked.

"One of the first guarding tasks I was ever trusted with." She slumped a little and leaned her head on Ethan's shoulder.

The look he cast at Tass should have had the sleezoid bursting into flames. Despite how drenched he was in sweat.

"The books promise to bring a soul back from the dead, but the rituals prescribed actually invite a monstrosity to come inhabit the empty body, and offer the bodies and souls of all those involved in the ritual as ... as food for the malevolent forces on the other side of a gate that should never be opened." She took several deep breaths before she regained her usual calm and cool control.

Tass didn't know anything else. He kept shaking his head as the others asked more questions. His voice broke again and again and his shivers grew more extreme until I was pretty sure he was having seizures brought on by terror. Finally, Jane wrapped him in the Ghost field again, cutting him off from our sight and hearing. And smelling. That was an enormous relief, in and of itself.

We couldn't take him to Divine's. We couldn't take him to the church, although I have to admit we were curious to know if Tass really would burst into flame if he crossed the threshold onto holy ground. Well, hadn't we been saying for years that the Grandstones would burst into flame if they stepped onto church property? In all the years they had tried to claim Neighborlee Gospel Church's building and property was theirs, stolen from them, they had always sent their lawyers and other lackeys, and never approached us themselves.

Which brought us back to the Grandstone connection, wondering why Stephen Grandstone, Sylvia's father, had aimed Tass at Pastor Rocky. It couldn't just be because he hadn't gotten his private meeting with Magna Magma. There was something more involved.

Considering what a physical and emotional wreck Tass had become, Jane and Kurt took him to the hospital and had him put into a private room for close observation, under restraints. Chief Tanner was more than happy to oblige, calling the hospital and putting in his recommendation that the patient be kept quiet and examined physically and psychologically.

That evening, once the Sunday school picnic was over, Ford and I met with Pastor Rocky and the deacons and trustees, to make our slightly edited report on what we had learned from Tass.

"Yeah, that sounds like a Grandstone nasty trick," Bo Deverall said.

"The problem is, that's not the usual kind of tactic for a Grandstone," Chief Tanner said. "Especially if that huge chunk of money is real. Since when do Grandstones pay for anything?"

"Maybe he's trying to embarrass Pastor Rocky into running away, close down the church," Fiona Quimby, head of the trustees, suggested.

"Maybe," Ford said. "But I keep snagging on how focused he was on the rock band. He was convinced that some people walked out of that fire unscathed. Making a deal with the devil, according to him. My gut says the band is at the center of this, but I can't figure out how, much less why."

"There are some rumors that there were survivors, but nobody can agree on anything," I had to say. Well, that needed to be considered, no matter how disturbing.

We agreed that we needed to do a lot more research, backtrack the members of Magna Magma and find all the branches of connections. There was a reason out there somewhere, tying Grandstone with Tass with the people trying to steal those dangerous books from Angela. I felt a little queasy, remembering something she had said years ago, to me and to Athena and several others, when asked why she didn't simply destroy dangerous magical articles. Essentially, the form constrained the evil, and destroying it would release the evil, the power, the magic. The burden of guarding a dangerous item was better than the risk of releasing that power or intelligence or potential into the wild.

Speaking of releasing ... Chief Tanner called Pastor Rocky and Ford and my Pop on a conference call some time around 3am Monday morning with the news that Tass had escaped the hospital. No, an angel didn't break down the door and lead him out, invisible to his enemies, as he had predicted in his raving. Chief Tanner requested the hospital record everything Tass said and did while he was under observation. Just in case Tass tried to sue the city or the church. The camera on Tass in his soundproof room died under a suspicious, very limited power outage around 2am. However, the perpetrators of the jail break were caught on security cameras from several different points in and around the hospital, meaning they were rather sloppy in covering their tracks. Or else they just didn't care if anyone saw them. Maybe they wanted to be seen, to instill fear in their enemies -- meaning us?

Four figures in black suits, black hats and dark glasses were caught sneaking into the hospital, coming in through a maintenance door and leaving through that door. They exited with an unconscious Tass, put him in the trunk of an older model black sedan, and drove out of the parking garage.

BoBs? That just confirmed some of our suspicions and theories, but didn't give us any further answers.

Pastor Rocky asked for more prayer warriors, and round-the-clock shifts covering Neighborlee in general, Divine's Emporium and our church, and him and Father Marty in particular.

~~~~~

Sunday night and Monday morning, while the BoBs were breaking Tass out of the psycho ward at the hospital, Felicity and Athena and I had dreams, so murky and shadowed we couldn't make out any details other
~~~~~

than the certainty that Pastor Rocky was in them.

I wasn't able to go to Divine's to talk with Angela before I went to work, and I couldn't go to the church to talk to Pastor Rocky and at least warn him. My sleep was so broken and restless, when I did fall asleep for more than an hour, I overslept. So I was running late for work already when Pop called to let me know about Tass's escape, which just made me even more late. I was frazzled and couldn't focus on my work as much as I should have, but somehow managed to get through three interminable hours of editing work before I felt free to take an early lunch.

Felicity called me about ten minutes before I could clock out, and asked if I could meet her at Divine's. She wanted to talk to Angela about some weird dreams she had, and she needed me to be with her, because she might have to go talk to Pastor Rocky afterward, since the dreams seemed to be about him. While she and Jake had started attending our church in the last year, she didn't feel comfortable enough about going in by herself to discuss what could be a touchy subject.

"Oh, heck … did anyone tell you about yesterday?" I asked.

The silence on her end was answer enough.

"I'm sorry. We had a really weird day yesterday. Get to Divine's and have Angela fill you in, and I'll meet you there. I have one more story to get into the queue."

"Oh, thanks. Just distract me." A shaky laugh escaped her. "I'm scattered enough without a mystery. I swear, my brain doesn't want to kick into gear until afternoon lately. Jake was teasing me …"

"What?" I said it too loudly, and several of my co-workers looked up from their desks.

"If you tell anybody, I will kill you -- no, I will kill all your equipment for the next year." A hiccupping little giggle escaped her. "I think I might be pregnant." Her voice dropped to a whisper as she spoke, so I almost didn't catch the word.

"O -- o -- kay."

"Just okay?" Her voice squeaked.

"Well, don't plan on using that excuse for very long, know what I mean?"

Felicity laughed, then promised she would head over to Divine's and get caught up on everything, and hung up.

Naturally, now I couldn't concentrate very well, but I managed to finish the story I was copy editing. I needed to get out of the office before my empty work queue filled up again.

Coming down the street to Divine's, I saw cars parked in front and in the vacant lot beside it, and they were all guardians' cars. I had the awful feeling I would be late getting back to the office, and probably would have to work late to catch up. Athena came running out to meet me as I got out of my Jeep and debated taking the risk of trusting my unsteady legs and walking. What would take more time, unloading my wheelchair, or tottering up the flagstone sidewalk to the front door, and probably fall flat on my face after ten steps?

She hooked her arm through mine and supported me, and caught me up on everything as we went inside: her murky dreams about Pastor Rocky, Felicity's dreams, and the call Ford got less than half an hour ago, with the details of just how Tass had escaped the hospital. By that time, we had reached Angela and Ethan's expanded apartment. The dimension-spanning magic of Divine's had given them an apartment with the same amount of floor space as the entire house, without a single blip or bulge from the outside to indicate what was crammed inside.

Ford, Felicity, Jake, Kurt, Jane, Maurice and Stanzer were there. I was kind of relieved not to see Daniel. He had been giving me some weird looks lately, ever since Maurice and Holly's wedding. Ethan and Angela were enthroned on the love seat that everyone had silently ceded to their sole possession. She was tucked up against his side, his arm around her, while she held his other hand in both of hers. Neither of them looked particularly upset or worried, which relieved me.

I was grateful for Athena's support getting through the shop and up the stairs. And more grateful to settle into a chair. I couldn't hold back an achy sort of sigh of relief, to get off my legs before they gave in to cramps and started wobbling. I had a huge score to settle with Kerri and her doppelganger friends, for setting me back so far on the road to recovery.

"Can we assume you dreamed about Rocky last night, too?" Ford said.

The hard part of our discussion, sharing the vague details and theorizing what was happening, was deciphering where these dreams came from. Eavesdropping on Big Ugly as he made plans to try to invade Neighborlee again? Or did we have so much exposure to Kerri and her minions that we were eavesdropping on them? Or was there a new nemesis, focusing so hard on Pastor Rocky that we could catch the plans being made? We had so very little to go on, because Athena and Felicity and I had had such nebulous, vague dreams. The next step was to talk to Pastor Rocky.

Lucky me. Since I was closest to him, I got the task of approaching him. I groaned silently. At least, I hoped I groaned silently. Because I was feeling really "off," lately. I had been second-guessing myself, my instincts, my judgments. The worst part was that I kept blaming most of that feeling "off" on Daniel. When he wasn't giving me weird looks, he was avoiding me, and then showing up way too often to be a coincidence, at work or around town, and then avoiding me again, in a kind of lopsided cycle. It was really immature, irritating behavior, totally unlike him. Totally unlike the guy who had been acting like a stalker fan when he first came to Neighborlee, intent on being my best friend despite destroying my sports reporting career to make me the -- gag -- lovelorn advice columnist for the Sheridan empire.

Something was up with him, and I didn't want to think too long, like for more than two seconds at a time, on my only theory. My instincts were on the fritz because I had the awful feeling I knew what Daniel was up to, but I didn't want to figure it out. Not consciously.

Nothing like feeling like a goofy adolescent with hormonal overload when I was on the downward slope toward forty.

Did I say hormonal? Kill me now, please?

Since I had no choice, I agreed to stop in at church after work. If I ever got my work done. We had deadlines to meet, after all. Once that obligation was met, I could fully focus on being a guardian.

~~~~~

Pastor Rocky met me at the door, when I had parked in my usual spot next to the handicap ramp and dropped into my chair. With all the stress of the day, there was no way I was risking walking into the church and not being able to walk out again.

"Thought you might draw the short straw to come check me out," he said, as he stepped out and held the door open for me to wheel through. "Took a couple breaks today and hauled a few scrapbooks and other things out of storage. Lucky I don't have any storage room at my apartment, so everything is here."

We went into his office. "A few scrapbooks" turned out to be four bankers boxes full of old photo albums and five scrapbooks, play bills and mementos like cocktail napkins and coasters, swizzle sticks and other junk with the names of the bars and music venues and casinos where Magna Magma had played.

He gestured for me to take a look. I wheeled around the conference table where he spread everything out. Just looking, reading dates and locations and the notes written by various people who had been there. None of the handwriting looked like Pastor Rocky's square, bold handwriting. So these were all notes and comments and memories written down by other people. It struck me as a little funny, a little ego-centric, that I hadn't really thought about him having a life outside of Neighborlee, even after he talked about running away from the orphanage and living on the road for years. Even though he had talked about his "dark past" to help illustrate any number of sermons when I was growing up, they just never seemed to connect to him.

The pictures and posters weren't in any particular order, but I sort of figured out a rough timeline based on the physical deterioration of the other members of the band. I kept going back to the younger pictures of
~~~~~

the drummer, Frankie Leonides, the one who had started Magna Magma. Something about him kept snagging my attention. I was positive I had seen him before, but I couldn't be sure that Pastor Rocky hadn't shown us some of these pictures before, or I had seen the drummer elsewhere. But where? That was the question.

Maybe I was tired, or maybe I was too intent on not jumping to conclusions that could lead me down rabbit trails. I kind of resisted the notion that maybe the drummer was familiar because I had been dreaming about him, along with Pastor Rocky. Like I said, I had been doubting my instincts a lot lately.

I picked up several posters with the clearest photos of the band through the years and wheeled over to Pastor Rocky. He was sitting in front of his desk, with the bankers boxes spread out in front of him, sorting through bits and pieces, looking like he was trying to find the secrets to the universe in all that memorabilia.

"He keeps jumping out at me. Is there anything special about him?" I spread the posters across the folding table sticking out past his desk, trying not to disturb the piles of napkins and other bits and pieces.

Pastor Rocky's smile turned sad, and the light in his eyes dimmed. "Why is it, your closest friends cause you the most pain, and there's nothing you can do about it without selling your soul?"

"What'd he do?"

"It's what I did. And how he reacted." A long sigh escaped him, and for a moment he sort of sagged in the chair. "I got my soul back, and Frankie didn't like it. Didn't like what my change of direction said about him, actually. He accused me of destroying all of us and then walked out and didn't even try to keep the band together, no matter how much the other guys begged." He scrubbed his face with his palms. "So ... you think you've dreamed about him?"

"I'm not really sure. He just ... snags my instincts." Honestly, how could I answer that question when I couldn't be sure where or when or how I had seen Frankie's face? Or what condition he was in. I couldn't remember the color or style of his hair, or how weathered his face was compared to the younger version of himself.

Besides, did it matter, since everybody in the band had died in the crash?

I flinched, remembering what Tass had said, and the rumors London had harvested off the Internet, the claims that someone had walked out of the fire.

Chapter Four

"Was he playing, maybe? Or in a wanted poster?" Pastor Rocky shook his head. "Forget I said that. Some old wounds don't stay closed. What about your dreams?"

"If it was just me dreaming," I said, "I wouldn't worry too much, because they could be explained away by yesterday's weirdness."

That got a snort and a crooked grin from him.

"The thing is, Athena and Felicity both dreamed, just as vague and hard to remember as my dreams, but they're both sure they dreamed about *you*. Nobody told either of them about yesterday until we got together today to figure out what's going on. Athena and Wallace were out of town with about half his clan, down in Mohican. Felicity and Jake spent the day on the lake yesterday. So there's nothing reasonable and ordinary to trigger those dreams."

"We should just give up using those words in this town," he muttered. Then he snorted and cocked an eyebrow at me. "Reasonable and ordinary." Another sigh. "So, what did you all dream to warn me about?"

"That's the thing. Everything was too hard to see, or if we did see anything, nobody could bring it out of the dreams with them. Other than the certainty we dreamed about you."

"And you think you dreamed about Frankie?"

"I don't know."

He leaned back a little in his chair and crossed his arms over his chest. "I've been praying for the guys in the band regularly for years. Since the band broke up. But I never relived our concerts and some of the good times and bad times on the road, except when I needed an illustration for a sermon." He shrugged. "I never dreamed about them until the reunion tour was proposed and I got that bad feeling. Not just from the fan sites, either."

We agreed he would think about the dreams he had been having and try to figure out which ones were truly memories, which ones varied from memories and how, and make notes. Then I would have to read through them, to see if they triggered any memories of my dreams.

~~~~~

Felicity, Jake, Jane and Kurt invited themselves over for dinner. They brought the food, and left me free to make sure the house was clean, and then scramble to write up my report on what I had found out from Pastor
~~~~~

Rocky. I attached all the photos I had taken of the memorabilia he had spread all over his office and sent the report to the rest of the guardians.

One nice thing about being a semi-pseudo-superhero was that we had the metabolisms to fuel our unusual talents, meaning we could eat anything and everything we wanted. Within reason, of course. A healthy diet was always the sensible approach, but we had leeway to indulge without that indulgence coming to rest permanently in our bellies, thighs and backsides. That night, we did an ice cream bar. Like a salad bar, with every kind of topping we could think of to take ice cream to the edge of insanity.

We gave ourselves time to relax and catch up on what each other had been doing in what passed for our "normal lives." At the top of the list was the progress on planning for Jane and Kurt's wedding in the fall. With all the foster brothers and sisters and aunts and uncles Jane had, growing up at Hoax headquarters, we had all anticipated some complications from such a large extended family. So far, the only tension came from Demetrius and Beau wanting to walk Jane down the aisle, and neither being willing to defer to the other. She planned to have both men walk with her, but she and Kurt were having too much fun watching them maneuvering around each other and trying not to suck up to her while sucking up.

Eventually, the conversation did slide back to what threatened to be our newest crisis. Jane suggested that Felicity and I spend some time with Bethany. She was not only a good artist, but her emerging Fae talents included being able to pick images from people's mind if they focused hard enough. If she could draw the bits that were poking out of the shadows in my mind, then maybe the memory would come further into the light, and I could figure out what Frankie had been doing, where he had been, how exactly I had seen him and why he caught in my dreams. A clear image from my dreams might help Felicity clarify things. Especially since it didn't make any sense that I was dreaming about a dead man. Unless the dead man had done something, set something in motion, that was going to eventually bite Pastor Rocky?

"I wish all my dreams lately were vague," Felicity said, after we had chatted a little bit about how dreams in the past had alerted us to Big Ugly's schemes. She glanced at Jake, and he put his arm around her.

"What?" Kurt immediately sat up, that big brother alertness visibly slipping into place. He didn't do it very often, and he had the sense and tact not to play the big brother, we-grew-up-together-I-know-you-better-than-you-know-yourself card. Sometimes it was really comforting to have him go all protective.

"I've been dreaming about Emilio." Felicity shrugged. "Not very often, but enough that I recognized him after the second dream.

"Problem?" I looked at Jake. He wasn't quite in his security consultant mode, his expression still relaxed and sociable despite his concern.

"Not like I'd get jealous." Jake shrugged. "The last two times, she's talked in her sleep, telling him to go away."

"How often?" Kurt said.

"Oh … " He looked at her and they locked gazes, with that sharing of thoughts that had nothing to do with semi-pseudo-superhero talents. "The dreams have been three or four days apart each time they come."

"But they've been coming regularly?" I asked.

"Patterns aren't good," Jane murmured. "If you have recurring dreams, either Emilio is … come to think of it, I have no idea who this Emilio guy is. Problem?"

"Bozo exchange student I fell for in college," Felicity muttered. "I changed my plans to be roommates with Lanie, so I could be closer to him. He was going to be a vet, I was going to work with him. It was like those shows on NatGeo about the married vets. Only it didn't end up that way."

"The jerk went back to Greece for the summer, and never came back in the fall, and then it turned out he wasn't from Greece, and his name wasn't Emilio," Kurt said.

"Uh huh." Jane smiled and leaned over to hook her arm through his and draw him closer to her. "Have I mentioned lately how lucky I am you belong to me?"

We all laughed when Kurt gave her that "huh?" frown that dug deep ridges across his forehead and around his mouth and scrunched up his nose for a few seconds. It didn't last long, and he laughed with us.

"Gotta love a guy who looks after his sisters and wants to pound anyone who hurts them," she said with a sigh, while we were still laughing.

Fortunately, Daniel hadn't crossed the line from just irritating and confusing me to irritating and confusing the people closest to me. I did not need Kurt having a big brother talk with Daniel and really tangling up everything. Not with the weirdness threatening to crash down on us.

~~~~~

That night, no surprise, I had a disturbing, recurring dream. The worst part was that I forgot what I was dreaming each time I yanked myself awake, gasping and holding up my arms to ward off something. Judging by the racing of my heart and the stink of fear in my sweat, the dream itself was pretty disturbing on its own.

The fourth time, I remembered it all when I woke up.

I was at the Agora, an old live performance venue down in Akron when I was in high school. I only went there once. The details were blurry to the point that I shouldn't have recognized it, but I knew, the way I always "knew" things in dreams, that I was at the Agora.
~~~~~

Magna Magma from the old days, not the reunion tour group, was on the stage. That was no surprise, considering how intently I had studied all those pictures and posters and had been thinking about them.

The press of the crowd pushed me closer to the stage. Everybody was either shadows or entirely invisible, but I could feel them and hear them.

I got up in front of the stage, with nothing between me and the performers but a deep, inky, churning black pit that looked about a thousand feet wide when I focused on it, but vanished when I lifted my head to watch Pastor Rocky and his band.

Only there was nobody on the stage now but Pastor Rocky and Frankie Leonides. The other instruments were playing, I could hear them, and hear the voices of what sounded like a dozen people singing, but there were no other people and no instruments. Other than three different versions of Frankie Leonides, different ages, and Pastor Rocky, as he was when his retro band played. All three Frankies looked pretty vicious, in a snarly bad mood as they slashed at the drums with their drumsticks. I couldn't hear what they were saying, but I had a pretty good guess they weren't singing the same song as the invisible band members. The one on the far left threw his drumsticks to the one on the far right, and he threw them to the one in the middle, who threw them back to the left, on and on, around the circle.

I got an ache in my neck from trying to turn my head fast enough to watch them. My eyes hurt, and I couldn't figure out what I was supposed to be watching. My head snapped back and forth, trying to keep up, as the drumsticks kept flashing through the air like guided missiles.

Or like knives.

After about ten rounds of this, the drummers on either side moved up closer to the front of the stage and the one in the middle moved up closer to Pastor Rocky. A sick, chilled feeling moved through my gut, and I couldn't move. I tried to call warning, but I had no voice. While I nattered over my inability to call out, the drummers moved even closer to the front and to Pastor Rocky and each other.

Then the middle drummer, the slickest of the three in looks, in a three-piece suit and fancy styled and gelled hair, suddenly had no drums in front of him. He was standing up and holding the drumsticks like daggers, poised to slam them downwards.

I screamed.

The drumsticks slammed down into Pastor Rocky's chest as he turned to look at me.

I woke up.

Of course.

I was sweating and shaking and positive I really had screamed, loudly enough to be heard by Harry in his garage apartment, if not my neighbors on either side of my house.

I sat up in bed, wishing Cerb was at least there to come whining into my room and jump up on my bed and let me hold him while I finished shaking out the nauseated feeling and get the smell of blood and my own sweat out of my nose. Instead, I huddled in on myself and tried to take deep breaths and tried to pray. Basically saying, *Okay, God, was that from You? And if it was, what does it mean? What am I supposed to do? And if it isn't from You ... protect me from whatever nasty is trying to get my guts tied up so tight I'm useless.*

~~~~~

The next morning was Tuesday. I did not want to go to work, but I also didn't want to spend the day in bed to catch up on my lost sleep, because nope, didn't want to risk living through that dream a couple more times. I called Bethany and left a message, asking her to meet me at the newspaper office at lunchtime. I needed her help getting something I had dreamed onto paper, for others to see. Honestly, I was relieved to be able to leave a message instead of having to talk to her while I was still headachy and trying to force down some breakfast. I had gotten up early because I couldn't sleep, so I headed into the office early. Maybe I could get most of my work done, take off early, and go to Angela with whatever Bethany produced.

Bethany and Harry were both waiting for me, sitting on the park bench next to the newspaper office's front door. I was an hour early for work. How did she know to get there and wait for me? It had to be the Fae side of her heritage, and all that time she was spending visiting the Fae Realms with Harry, meeting her distant relatives and taking lessons to prepare for the treatment to make her a Changeling.

"Wow, really bad dreams, huh?" she called out to me, when I opened my door and got out to reach into the back seat and get out my wheelchair.

No way was this one of those good, energetic days when I could dare going without my wheels. I was surprised my legs didn't fold up while I was transferring from chair to Jeep, and drop me to my driveway.

"How bad do I look?" I mean, I had washed and dressed in clean clothes and brushed my hair and put on makeup, and I thought I looked pretty calm. Not that I spent a lot of time studying my face in the mirror. Just enough to make sure I didn't terrify small children on a regular basis.

"You don't," Harry said as they crossed to my handicapped parking spot. "Bethany's been focusing on non-sensory perception exercises for the last week, so the volume is kind of turned up high for her. Plus, she had a dream about you, and when you called, we figured the best choice was to get it over with while your memories were still pretty clear. You know, not contaminated by thinking about the dream for hours."

"Yeah, makes sense."
~~~~~

"Bad?" Bethany said. She held out a hand to help me steady myself as Harry pulled out my chair. She had the guy well-trained by now.

I looked around, to make sure we were as alone as I hoped. "I saw some guy stabbing Pastor Rocky."

"Have you told him yet?"

"Too early in the morning for that kind of news."

"Uh, yeah, that makes sense," Bethany said, trying not to laugh.

"The thing is, I can get you pictures of what this guy looks like, but he changed in a few details, maybe what he looks like now, so I really need you to alter the image, if that makes sense?"

"Perfect sense," Harry said. "Let's get inside before people see us and start wondering what happened now."

He had a point. The best way to warn people that something odd is yet again happening in Neighborlee is to stand around in public having a conference that you really don't want anyone else to overhear.

We unlocked the office, went inside and headed for my desk. She settled at Franny's desk, and the back didn't try to collapse, like it always did when Daniel sat in her chair. Huh. Fae magic did have some advantages. Bethany pulled out her sketchpad and pencils while Harry went to the office kitchen to get us glasses of ice and water. I tried a few deep breathing and calming exercises, to help me focus on what I could remember of the dream.

Bethany really had been practicing her sensitivity and her manifesting ability to reach into people's minds and touch the images there. Especially if someone with some non-traditional abilities, such as *moi*, focused on sending those images to her. She was also a very good artist. By the time Harry came back, maybe not even ten minutes for the round trip, she had the first sketch done. This one was the middle drummer, the fierce, exultant expression on his face, and the drumsticks raised high and ready to slam down into Pastor Rocky's chest. Then she produced sketches of the band at the start of my dream, and the changes in the drummers as the nightmare progressed. Her hand had to be aching by the time she was done, because she had been sketching so quickly. And not a smudge of pencil on the side of her hand. That was some useful magical talent.

I put the sketches between sheets of layout paper, and then protected between two pieces of cardboard, to protect them from smudging and make sure no one saw them. We didn't want to panic any of the people who knew and loved Pastor Rocky.

I was praying for help, and there must have been people praying for me, because I got through my day of work without any glitches or necessary do-overs, and no delays, no last-minute calls or problems. I left work early, which was nice, and headed right over to the church.

On the way there, Sherwood called me, and didn't even wait for me to answer the phone. He made it accept his call and started talking to me. Kind of freaky. Especially when he gave me the information that he thought was important enough to risk causing an accident.

Now I had even more reason to talk with Pastor Rocky ASAP. This was getting more seriously weird, in a negative way, as the hours ticked by.

Pastor Rocky was taking a break, sitting at the picnic table outside the back door of the church, leaning against the wall, eyes closed, and actually looking like he had had a good day. Despite the loads landing on him lately. He opened his eyes as I parked my Jeep in my reserved spot. Gimp parking does have its privileges. He cocked an eyebrow at me high enough to make Spock jealous and waited until I got my chair out of my Jeep and was wheeling up the ramp. With a nod to me, he got to his feet, moving a little slower than normal, opened the door and held it for me, then followed me into the church. He led me down the halls to his office and stood aside to let me go in first. While he shut the door, I went to the conference table and spread out the sketches Bethany had made. He looked at them, frowning a little more than usual.

"Frankie isn't a suit kind of guy. Or at least he wasn't when I knew him. So who gave you these pictures?"

"I dreamed him stabbing you. He looks like he's prosperous, considering his three-piece suit. And there's something different about his face, that isn't in any of your pictures." I took a deep breath. "I'm scared this was a warning dream."

"Problem. As far as I know, Frankie is dead."

"Yeah, but there are the rumors and weird stories going around, and with our luck, some of the guys survived and they're pissed at you, maybe at Father Marty. And London and Sherwood were doing a lot of backtracking of the guys in the band. It looks like someone has been doing some heavy-duty erasing of Frankie's footprints, between the band breaking up and now. Kind of suspicious that it looks like the guy just vanished, and maybe was never born."

"Well, he didn't hatch. And I know his birthday. He always made sure we celebrated. Granted, we wished we were dead the next day, but ..." He sighed and finally sank down in the nearest chair. "You'll send me the basics of what they found out, where they got the information?"

"Already on its way."

"Thanks." Another sigh. "I hope you aren't going to ask me to go into hiding or lockdown or something."

"Living a normal life is the best revenge. Besides, it drives the creeps crazy if they think you don't care."

"Or they think we don't know they're there, and they're feeling superior."

Was the guy trying to cheer me up or depress me?

"Just make sure you don't go out of town, where someone can get hold of you."

"Hey, who's the murderer here?" His grin was almost convincing.

"I'm worried about someone sneaking up on you where there's no one to watch and defend you. You're one of ours."

"And I appreciate it." He sighed and leaned over the table, his hands flat on the surface, arms stiff, and stared at the images. "You know, now that you mention it, now that you put Frankie in a fancy suit ... there is something about him. Something I've seen, and recently. It could just be I've seen someone who looks like him, but the man I saw certainly didn't have that fierce, going nasty nuts expression."

"The important thing is that we never do see it live and in person."

"We?" He turned his head to look at me, and his expression softened.

"Like I just said, you're one of ours. Neighborlee takes care of its own. Who knows? Maybe ..."

I suddenly couldn't breathe for a moment, and there was this sensation of standing in two places at one time, or maybe more accurately, two different times. I was back in my hospital room, just days after the accident, when I was numb from the shoulders down and my telekinesis seemed to be dead. Pastor Rocky had come to see me, and I spilled a lot of my confusion and frustration and my questions about God on him. He hadn't blinked when I told him I used to be able to fly and told him some of the things we had done to protect Neighborlee. Especially that one fateful night at the quarries.

"Maybe this is the reason I didn't die that night I broke my back. Well, yeah, I did die a couple times, but they brought me back. Maybe keeping you alive, protecting you against this wacko, is the real reason God gave me my crazy powers and let me live despite all the damage and ..." I shook my head. Too much speculation, and it sounded more far-fetched with every new detail I added to the idea.

"Don't take this the wrong way, Lanie." Pastor Rocky reached out and rested his hands on my shoulders. "But I really hope you're wrong. I hope I'm not the reason, I'm just a beneficiary of all the amazing things our Lord has entrusted to you as tools."

For a second, I had this shout of protest pressing hard in my chest, and yeah, some hurt feelings. Then a heartbeat later I understood what he meant, and it made sense. Too much sense.

"What keeps sticking in my head is if Frankie is dead, then why are you dreaming his face?" Pastor Rocky mused, studying one sketch.

"Maybe just to get us to ask questions?" I shrugged. "Maybe it's a member of his family, a younger brother who looks a lot like him? And he's out to get you because you didn't die in the bus crash?"

"That's a possibility, but I just didn't know that much about his family. None of us really talked about our families. Most of us were rebels, or castoffs or ..." He shrugged. "Someone else needs to be asking questions. I've come to the end of what I can do. Except call the last numbers I have for everybody and see if anyone knows anything."

We agreed he would do that. And I decided if I had to, I would nag London and Sherwood, and if Athena and Wallace weren't too busy preparing for their wedding, I'd ask them to help out. These were questions that had to be answered before something awful happened. I was positive I had seen Frankie somewhere, involved in something, other than that dream of him stabbing Pastor Rocky. Whatever he was doing, I didn't like it.

Then ordinary life interfered, when I wanted more than anything to just head home and crash. I had to do some banking, and then pick up some groceries so I could eat healthy rather than giving in to some stress eating junk food binging. By the time I got home, I was wiped out. I was grateful I didn't have to make calls and update people, and nobody was going to call me to ask for verification or clarification. What had we ever done before London and Sherwood were born and joined the guardians?

Maybe I spoke, or thought, too soon. London pinged me while I was wracking my brains, trying to come up with something that sounded good for dinner. Something I would enjoy, rather than just eating to put something in my aching stomach. I figured whatever she was contacting me about, there would be documents involved. Plus, my eyes were tired and I didn't feel like dealing with the tiny images on my phone screen, so I headed down the hall to my office to wake up my computer.

"Paydirt. At least a little," London said, when I told her to go ahead. "Thought you might want to see this first. I'm copying the others on everything. It's all Frankie Leonides," she added, before I could think of a semi-snarky response about how the interruption hadn't helped me figure out what to have for dinner.

"Thanks. Is it bad?" I had to ask.

"Read it, first." Then she blipped off the screen and the download links and URLs for videos and other data she had found appeared on the screen.

Pastor Rocky's former drummer friend had essentially vanished from the public record about four years after the band broke up. There was no documentation anywhere, other than a few newspaper articles about him being a witness to an accident being investigated by federal authorities. The fact that the newspaper articles didn't get any follow-up was suspicious. Sherwood had attached the condensed version of an analysis he had done. He took the theory that the accident was something having to do with the FBI or maybe even foreign espionage, and Frankie was in Witness Protection. He went off on that tangent while London followed all the other branching possibilities and theories and leads, such as people showing up in surrounding towns, then counties, then states with amnesia or massive injuries requiring plastic surgery. Sherwood had worked with Wallace and Cosmo to develop an algorithm for patterns used in creating new identities for people hiding from the authorities and criminal organizations, or domestic abuse or nasty relatives or insistent creditors. He had followed that trail and admitted there was still a lot of work left to do. He and London were using the sketches Bethany did for me, along with the old pictures Pastor Rocky had of Frankie, to try to match features to people caught on TV and the Internet, security cameras and even satellite surveys. He estimated days to go before they could start ruling out many different options.

Bottom line: so far, there was no documentation that Frankie Leonides was still alive, or even that he had existed beyond that day he stepped out of a seedy diner on a bad side of town at 2am and was nearly smeared across the pavement by a car that had flipped over onto its roof at a high rate of speed. No documentation. No hospital records. No credit cards. No bank records. No traffic tickets. No criminal court appearances. No performances with other bands. The guy had evaporated. Except that he had initiated the Magna Magma reunion. So if Frankie no longer existed, was it another lookalike, maybe a doppelganger, who had put everything together?

The really suspicious thing in all that data and the reams of follow-up work? No one made any effort to erase his trail leading up to the day of the accident. Which led to all sorts of questions of who had made him vanish, and why, and why didn't they care about totally erasing his existence?

Had I totally misinterpreted the dream that warned me about the threat to Pastor Rocky? Maybe I just saw a small similarity to Frankie in the man who stabbed him with the drumsticks and warped the images from my dream when I woke up.

~~~~~

Wednesday was a half-day, and I was glad to head home early to relax. Not that I really knew how to do that. I needed to get my brain off the Magna Magma puzzle for a while. I could be virtuous and work ahead on my next *Talk to Terry* column. Or I could just go into cave troll mode and binge watch one of my TV series on DVD. The question was which one.

Before I could do more than open the cabinet and look at my collection, Felicity called. She wanted to come over. Jake was out of town on a job, and she was alone when she got an instant message on her phone.
~~~~~

She was surprised, but not so flustered she made the mistake of responding or even acknowledging she received the message. She needed to talk about it and get my input.

"Emilio is back in town," she said, as soon as she opened my back door and stepped in. "The thing is, he's not Emilio. That was just the name he was using." She grabbed handfuls of her hair and yanked as she dropped into the nearest seat at my kitchen table.

I did feel sorry for her, because it was clear she was upset, but I really hated it when Felicity got dramatic. Any second, she could lose her self-control and maybe let off an EM burst, even though it had been several years since she didn't have control over her power surges.

I should have worried more when she said she had been dreaming about him. Another warning we didn't take seriously enough.

"Want me to pick him up and fly him over the quarries and let go?"

That got a snorting giggle out of her.

"No. Much as I'd like to. I don't even know what his excuse is."

"Do you feel like you owe him anything?"

"No, not really."

"Then don't respond."

"It's not that easy!" She leaned forward, propping herself up on the table on her elbows.

"Never is."

"How would you know? Other than that wannabe molester trying to use you as a pipeline to your students, you haven't ... sorry. That wasn't nice."

"You're justified. So, what do you want to do about Emilio the silent?"

"He says he wants to explain, and he wants to make things right, and he hopes I'll give him a second chance."

"Whoa. Whoa. Warning, warning, danger, Will Robinson!"

Felicity's face twisted a few times like she couldn't decide whether to laugh or be annoyed. She sat back and slouched a little in her chair and crossed her arms over her chest. At least I didn't have to worry about inadvertent EM bursts frying my kitchen appliances. However, push her too far and she just might do it accidentally on purpose.

"You've read a whole lot more romances than me," I pointed out. "Any book that starts out with a long-absent boyfriend showing up and asking for a second chance --"

"Usually leads to a big reunion scene. Yeah. I know. Don't assume I haven't thought about all those books and wondered if those writers had any idea what sort of a mess that supposedly romantic setup creates for the real people involved."

"It's the Hallmark Channel curse."

That got her laughing. I had lost count over the years how many movies we had started watching on Hallmark, where the story started with the heroine planning her wedding, or officially getting engaged to a guy she had been waiting on for years. It was a sure sign that the relationship she had invested years in was doomed, because no matter how wonderful she considered the guy she was currently with, he would be yesterday's news by at least halfway through the movie, if not the first commercial break. We usually turned off the movies that started out with a girl in a relationship. Unless, of course, the guy was a real scumbag loser. And then we really couldn't feel sorry for the imminent broken heart, because she should have been smart enough to break free of the guy months or years ago.

The thing was, it really wasn't funny when those awful tropes showed up in real life. They were tropes because someone, somewhere, decided it was a reliable story pattern. Excuse me? Breaking up a couple that was generally happy together just to put the heroine through seventy-five minutes of angst for entertainment purposes didn't sound like a good time to me. How much time did that translate into for real life people like Felicity? Besides, I really liked Jake. She had waited long enough for him to show up and prove himself her knight in shining Kevlar. The guy was firmly grounded and didn't freak out and run for his life or go for the garlic and holy water and silver crosses when he found out she was a semi-pseudo-superhero. Had to love a guy like that.

"Nothing and no one could ever convince me to trade in Jake. I can't think of anything Emilio could offer me that would make me even waver for two seconds." Felicity sighed. "The thing is … I'm curious. I want to know if he was always a lying jerkface single-cell slime-dweller with a talent for fooling people, or I was an utter idjit who fell for the first cute guy who flashed a dimple at me."

"Emilio had dimples? Where? Sorry, but dimples are usually in cheeks, so …" I grinned. "How did you get to see them?"

Chapter Five

Felicity snorted and tossed a cookie at me. "He didn't, but the guy was utterly charming."

"And you were a college freshman and you two had so much in common, with the critters and all that. Give yourself a break. Or better yet, let me break something on him."

That remark only got a crooked smile.

"I just want to know why, y'know? Was it something I did that scared him? Did he get hints of what we were, what I could do, and that sent him running?"

"Or was it something back home?" I suggested. "Some problems that he had to take care of and he didn't want to get you involved or hurt you, so he figured silence was the best tactic for everyone."

"No, don't get started making him a hero or a martyr or whatever." She snatched up two cookies and slouched back even further and started doing her beaver buzz saw routine on them, nibbling off little bits in rapid succession and nearly inhaling them. Instead of making me laugh, as the trick had done when we were kids, it worried me. Felicity hadn't done nervous energy eating like that for years now.

"You should consider the fact that the guy made contact because he wants something. Besides forgiveness. How did he find you? How did he make contact?"

"I have the same email from college." She shrugged. "It's not like it had my last name and I needed to change it when I got married."

"He could have contacted you long ago. Why did he wait until he came back to town? They do have email in Greece, don't they?"

She tossed half a cookie at me. I snagged it out of the air with my telekinesis. I lobbed it back to her, making her giggle as she ducked and tried to catch it. She wasn't so good and ended up making a spray of crumbs. I decided to save cleaning my kitchen floor for tomorrow.

"Go into it with the attitude that the guy might just be playing you, he wants something, and he's going to lie. Then all your surprises will be nice ones."

"Yeah ... that's about what I was thinking of. I just needed some feedback from you, make sure I got it right, I wasn't being too cynical."

"Have you thought about what you're going to tell Jake? You aren't going to face the guy on your own, are you?" I hurried to add, when

Felicity went very still. The utter lack of reaction in her flashed warnings at the back of my brain. "Hey, the guy adores you. Let him earn his keep playing guard dog and keep him thinking you need more protection than you really do."

"I know, I just ... it's stupid, but I don't want him knowing I was such an idiot to let the eye candy trick me into thinking the package inside the wrapper was worth the trouble. You know?"

"No ... you don't want Jake thinking for even two seconds that you were rejected."

Felicity scowled at me, and reached for the plate of cookies, probably to lob them all at me. I mentally yanked the plate out of her reach, with enough force that three cookies slid off the plate. We sat there for a few seconds, then she grinned and rubbed at her face and groaned and slouched a little more.

"When did you get so smart about people?"

"Occupational hazard, dealing with all the clueless twits who keep writing to Terry for advice. You see enough stupid mistakes people make, you pick up patterns and you try not to let them happen in your own life. Or your friends' lives. Honestly, Felicity, you are my sister and I love you to pieces, but if you can't see how much Jake loves you and he'd take a bullet for you, and if you don't do everything in your inhuman power to protect what you two have ... I will shake you until your eyeballs rattle out of your skull. And that's just for starters."

"No need." Now she just looked tired. "I want some research done on Emilio before I meet him. I'm just trying to decide now if asking Jake to come with me will be a sign of weakness or fear, or scare the guy into lying instead of telling the truth."

"The research, I can help you with. Or rather, London can." I wondered if that had been the main part of the reason for her coming to see me, since she had pretty much admitted that she was already planning to do what I advised. Felicity usually avoided contacting London and Sherwood. The residual energy field around her, that used to fry her cell phones and other equipment before she learned to control the EM bursts, usually prompted her to limit contact with our AI friends.

Felicity came prepared. She had pictures of her and Emilio from college, his contact information when he was attending Willis-Brooks College, his student ID number, and other information. She had no contact information for his home and family in Greece, other than a general area. When he went home, he had told her he wasn't sure which members of his extended family he would be living with, in which towns, which island in Greece. When Emilio didn't return to WBC in the fall, we realized that should have been a warning sign about their relationship.

We didn't have friends with powerful and fast links to the Internet back then. Now, we did. Not only did I send the information to London and Sherwood, including the pictures I loaded into my tablet, but I suggested they start with digging through airlines records to track Emilio's flight path when he left Ohio. London and Sherwood were kind of busy with several dozen other research tasks, along with constantly updating our defensive shields, tracking the activities of the Rivals and Grandstones and trying to find Kerri. Athena and Wallace were visiting his family out of town this weekend, so I contacted Cosmo.

Doni came with him. She had a lot of smarts and often came up with ideas and suggestions that nudged the three computer geeks into finding brilliant solutions. She already had some ideas of where to start by the time she and Cosmo got to my house.

We settled in at my kitchen table, with all the leaves pulled out, to talk and brainstorm and snack through the afternoon and into the evening. Cosmo took all the information Felicity had brought and got to work. It helped that he and Wallace and Athena had designed several search engines they were beta testing before putting them out on the market. The first search, tracking Emilio's path from when he left college to head home to Greece, took less than an hour. Cosmo used most of that time to find the back doors and gaps in fire walls to access the college's database and then search the airline ticketing records from nearly fifteen years ago. There had been several consolidations and changes in databases and software in the airline industry in that time, and new regulations and security precautions. He had to work his way through all the barriers and skip over gaps and figure out which forks in the road were legitimate and which were just big glitches and mistakes and sabotage inflicted on the airlines over the years.

Our first answer was something of a non-answer. Emilio Santori, according to all the airline records and visa authorities and anybody else involved in tracking the activities of non-citizens going to school in the United States, had never left the country. There were no airline records of tickets issued in his name.

Even worse, there was no Emilio Santori with a green card or any other official paperwork allowing him to be a student and reside in the United States. According to the registrar's records at Willis-Brooks College, he did have the proper paperwork, but the numbers were wrong and didn't have corresponding paperwork and permits and other records with the state or federal authorities overseeing such things. Emilio Santori had indeed flown out of Cleveland Hopkins Airport on the day that Felicity took him to the airport for a flight to JFK, where he was supposed to get on a flight to Greece. What Emilio did when he landed in JFK was a complete mystery. At this point in time.

"So basically the guy is a lying scuzzbucket," Felicity said, with a much lighter tone of voice than I would have expected from her.

"Here's a theory you probably thought of, just not consciously," Doni said, while Cosmo sent the data to my printer. "Maybe the guy wasn't from Greece. Maybe he wasn't Greek at all. He was just playing a game and maybe he got caught and had to run for it."

"What good would it do him to romance an orphan college girl with nothing but ..." She paused with her mouth open, her eyes narrowing so I couldn't see reflected in them all the awful thoughts swirling through her mind. But I could guess.

"Maybe the Rivals or agents of the Grandstones had you picked out that far back, they just couldn't figure out what you did, if you were worth the effort, and how to get their hands on you?" I offered, making my tone soft and iffy.

"Considering how much bad blood there was between us and Sylvia by then?" She shook her head like she was trying to shake off something stuck in her hair. That changed into a shudder. "They guessed, they put the clues together, but knew they couldn't get at me because I was so erratic. No controls. I was more likely to zap them than get converted to the dark side."

"And maybe someone has been watching you closely enough to know or to guess that you have control now, and you're useful or profitable or whatever," Doni added. "Major problem with that scenario, though. Grandstones have sabotaged themselves so much in the last few years, they're not a threat to anyone. I've been hearing rumors they're facing some pretty big money problems. And the Rivals are still pretty much limited to a few stragglers who can't get along well enough to survive, forget about becoming a threat."

"So what does Emilio hope to gain from romancing me?"

"Maybe he isn't. Maybe he's scared to death and he wants to come in from the cold?" I said, more thinking aloud than really offering an answer.

We kept playing with that question and coming up with variations of what Emilio wanted from Felicity. Cosmo kept digging, trying tactics such as looking for people named Santori in the various towns in Greece where Emilio claimed he had relatives. Half the towns didn't exist, or if they did, the names were spelled differently. There were plenty of people with variations of Santori as their names. Getting into public records and finding out if there was anyone who looked like Emilio among their sons and grandsons and nephews and cousins would take a lot more time and patience than we had that day.

During all this, Jake came home from his business trip. When he found Felicity wasn't home, he came straight over to my house without even calling. That just proved how well he knew her. Since she didn't leave a note for him, he put a few other clues together and figured something was wrong. He stopped for ice cream and Hunky & Dory's barbecue buffet carryout party pack before coming to join us.

We plowed through the barbecue buffet and were starting in on the ice cream by the time we caught Jake up on what we had discussed and theorized and the data Cosmo and London had found so far. He agreed with us that the next step was to respond to Emilio's request for contact and agree to a meeting. In a very public place, in broad daylight, with lots of backup. Then we worked up a script for various possible responses on Emilio's part and Felicity's.

"We're forgetting something really important," I said, as Felicity picked up her phone to respond to Emilio's message. "Kurt will kill us if we don't let him play big brother." That got a big grin from Felicity. "And Jane will insist on being ready to encapsulate the guy if he turns out to be trouble."

"Makes a lot of sense to me," Jake said, nodding. "If the guy has gone over to the Evil Empire, then we might need a lot more than the usual firepower."

I texted Kurt and Jane to see if they were free to talk. The delay in answering should have been answer enough. I assured them it wasn't an emergency, but we would need their help with a possible mission, and I would send over the details. When that was done, Felicity contacted Emilio. He didn't respond, and Kurt's only response came after everyone had gone home, and consisted of, "We'll be there."

~~~~~

Sherwood woke me just shy of 5am Thursday morning. Bethany's sketches of Frankie Leonides had triggered a match. The first one triggered a cascade of matches, although not as many as we would have wanted. And they were just plain confusing, quite frankly.

The images of Frankie showed up in the files of the security system from Eden.

He was one of the Blues Brothers wannabes that Harry and I had spotted on New Year's Eve, just before all the weirdness with the doppelgangers splatted down on us. The BoBs again. Not a good sign.

Sherwood had gone through the security videos frame by frame, following the progress of the black-suited gang during the short time they were within pickup range of the cameras. Several details were important enough to create a pattern and for him to wake me up to report right away. To be fair, he woke up Kurt and Pastor Rocky and Ford, too.

First, the BoBs kept Frankie surrounded. No matter where he turned, he was always at least three deep in black suits and sunglasses.

Second, he was focused entirely on Pastor Rocky, who was on stage with the retro band, the whole time his gang stood there in the doorway.

Third, the gang hurried him out of there when Pastor Rocky stepped
~~~~~

down from the stage and looked like he was heading for the doorway where they were standing.

When we met at the church to go over this information, Pastor Rocky had to think back to the events of that night. As far as he could recall, he didn't see the Men in Black/Blues Brothers gang, and the only time he remembered leaving the stage while his retro band was performing had been during a break, when he had gone to use the bathroom.

So if that really was Frankie Leonides, was he afraid Pastor Rocky would blow his cover and ruin whatever his purpose was for crashing the New Year's Eve party?

And the fourth item, which turned everything from puzzling to creepy: most of the faces in the Blues Brothers gang were caught on other security camera recordings after the entourage hurried Frankie out of Eden. But none of those images were around Eden -- they were security video for our church. Three-fourths of the BoBs were the ones who had managed to get through the shield during the low energy points. Even worse, they had shown up on security cameras that "just happened" to be covering the edges of Neighborlee Gospel Church's property. They never stepped foot onto the property itself, but were constantly lingering in the trees, across the street, loitering in shadows. When they left their vigil, they got in their vintage black sedan and followed Pastor Rocky when he left the church. Creepy enough?

"We've set up a search program for security cameras all around town," Sherwood said, once we had gone through that really disturbing information. "The different stores and the police surveillance system don't hold onto videos for more than a month, but maybe we'll get lucky and catch them following Pastor Rocky around town."

"Not what I would call lucky," Pastor Rocky muttered.

"Sorry."

"No, don't be. I'm grateful you're looking out for me. It's just ... I guess this is why his face looks familiar. You saw him at New Year's, Lanie."

"No. I'm sure it was somewhere else, something else," I had to say. The more I thought about that image from my dream that Bethany had drawn for me, the more sure I was that I had seen the slick, fancy-dressed Frankie, not the sweaty, decades younger drummer, and not the fierce, twisted face just before the drumstick knives slashed down at Pastor Rocky.

"So why would that Kerri woman send her people to watch Pastor?" Ford said, when all of us were settling down into a thoughtful, worried kind of quiet. "Why was Frankie or his lookalike with them? What does she want from him?"

"Maybe they aren't hers," London offered. "Lanie and a couple others mentioned their clothes, and how Kerri's minions looked more like Men in Black, stylish, as opposed to ragged and Salvation Army Classic, I think the phrasing was, like the Blues Brothers."

"She's right," I said, wanting so much to be able to laugh.

"Standard minion uniform." Pastor Rocky shrugged and looked like he wanted to be able to laugh, too. "So two different groups of problems?"

"Here we go again," Kurt muttered.

"So what happened to Frankie after the gang hurried him outside and kept him from running into Pastor Rocky?" I asked.

"Sorry, but the security cameras in the parking lot were on that rolling program where they just clipped ten seconds at a time, taking turns all around the lot. We gleaned a few images of them hurrying into a few dark cars, parked out of the reach of the lights, and that's it. No license plates were visible," Sherwood reported.

"We were kind of tied up with other weirdness at the time," Kurt said. The rest of us groaned, each busy with our own memories of that night when the doppelgangers landed on us and kept us busy for several months afterward.

"So, the really big question is if that really was Frankie Leonides at New Year's, and if so, why was he there, what did he want or not want from Pastor Rocky, and what are his people looking for now?" Ford said.

There was no way to get those answers until we had cornered some of those BoBs and questioned them. Sherwood and London promised to put together a report for Gordon and leave it in his hands how to report the situation to Chief Tanner and get the Neighborlee Police Department on the lookout. Our friendly resident AI's created an active link to the security cameras throughout town, to be on the lookout for the BoBs next time they showed up at the church. For all we knew, they were hiding in the shadows or trees across the street right that moment, having followed Pastor Rocky from his apartment.

"Nope, nobody there," London said, as soon as Kurt thought of that and mentioned it. "They haven't been able to cross through the shield since more people signed up for prayer shifts and coverage became 24/7. The energy doesn't have those little fluctuations, and it isn't doing them any good to have those few remaining 'Welcome to Neighborlee' signs, because the weak points aren't weak enough for them to penetrate."

"You know, if there weren't so much other freaky going on, that would freak me out," Pastor Rocky muttered. Then he snorted and grinned, but that bit of amusement didn't wipe away the weariness. "The funny thing is that Marty won't be disturbed by that detail, if I tell him. That's something he'd understand. The power of prayer and the Holy Spirit to keep enemies away from us."

~~~~~
~~~~~

Meanwhile, Emilio responded to Felicity's response. He agreed to meet her Saturday by the gazebo in the park, as public a place as we could arrange without going to Public Square in Downtown Cleveland. But honestly, when you think of it, people are so trained not to get involved or notice things in big, busy, public spaces, an alien could land in a spaceship in that big, paved space in front of the Terminal Tower, and nobody would react. They'd just keep hurrying about their business, ignoring the monsters just like they ignored the beggars, until someone started shooting. Not like that iconic scene between Loki and Captain America, which was filmed right there on Public Square, by the way. (Would they have let me be an Avenger if I showed them I could kinda-sorta fly at that time?)

Felicity and Jake were waiting when Emilio showed up.

Of course, Kurt, Jane and I were waiting, too, but we got there a good hour before them and settled in to wait, floating just above the roof of the gazebo, invisible in the Ghost field. We wanted to make sure Emilio didn't set up a trap ahead of time, then go away, maybe leave some nasty friends waiting to ambush Felicity when she arrived. Not that Jake wasn't up to dismantling traps, but even he had his limits when it came to things like tasers or tranquilizer darts. Jane took care of searching for any kind of spying gizmos, like cameras or motion sensors or microphones or super spy gadgets. For instance, to shoot poison or tranquilizer mist into the air or release a net to fall from the roof of the gazebo, or a dozen other scenarios that quite frankly struck us as a little melodramatic and uber-Bond, even if they were possible. It all depended on whose side Emilio was on and who he was working for.

It turned out the guy wasn't working, period, in several different meanings of the word.

He looked a lot older than expected. Lines around his eyes and mouth, and none of them were from smiling. I remembered him as smiling a lot, always cheerful, and the animals he worked with had seemed to love him. I had to wonder, knowing how animals were such good judges of character, if Emilio had been corrupted once he left Ohio. Maybe he had access to a body spray that covered his real scent or drugged dogs and cats and other animals into loving him instead of barking and biting and hissing? I admit, I was primed to consider him a bad guy because of what he had done to Felicity, rather than giving him the benefit of the doubt that he had actually planned to keep his promise to return, and later something had changed him into a creep.

He had gray in his hair and had lost weight. Back in college, the guy had the typical Greek god physique, if slightly on the chunky side. Felicity had never really been shallow, and there had been a lot of good aspects to him that made her fall in love. Supposedly. The extra thirty pounds were gone, along with a lot of his definition and the six-pack that he had never needed a size-too-small shirt to show off to advantage. He was a snappy dresser, more stylish than his college days, when faded jeans and T-shirts and work boots were "in." Lavender, open-collar sport shirt, pale sage-colored jacket and darker sage pants. Everything looked a little too big on him, like he had lost weight after spending a lot of money on his clothes. Either that, or he had misjudged the size of who he mugged for a set of new clothes. Kurt just shook his head when I made that observation and gestured for me to hush. Hey, it wasn't like anyone outside the Ghost field could hear us.

"Sweetheart." Emilio held out his hands as he stepped out of the sunshine, into the shade cast by the gazebo.

He stopped short, meaning he had seen Jake standing there in the shadows, leaning against the gazebo, while Felicity was sitting on a bench outside the gazebo. We couldn't let them meet inside, could we? Otherwise, we wouldn't be able to see anything. Granted, Jane could have lowered us through the roof, thanks to the Ghost field, but that took up energy. If Emilio had nasty semi-pseudo-superhero friends, we couldn't take the chance that someone could shut down the Ghost field while we were only halfway through the roof and dropping to her rescue. Not a comfortable place to be.

Besides, there was the lesson we had been learning the hard way of not inviting people "inside" and over thresholds and barriers. Meeting outside the gazebo wasn't the same as welcoming Emilio completely. We had gotten a whole lot more cautious and aware of ancient traditions and protections and precautions in the last couple years.

I had passed on the word to our praying friends to keep Felicity in mind that day, because a dark splotch from her past had made contact and we had no idea how the meeting would turn out. That prayer shield, and a good dollop of animosity toward Emilio for hurting her all those years ago, would be working in our favor. I was all for stacking the deck against the enemy and the unknown.

"Uh ... who's this?" He offered Jake one of those smiles that clearly said, "Hey, I'm being civilized, but you're pushing things, bub. Make like a tree and leave."

"Hey," Jake said. He stepped up behind Felicity's bench and rested a hand on her shoulder. The hand he normally would have held out to shake with someone he was meeting for the first time. "I'm Jake, Felicity's husband."

"No." Emilio's smile cracked and he took a step back. Even in the shade, he clearly lost a few degrees of color. "You're not. Nobody told me. They should have told me."

"Interesting," Jane said. She didn't keep her voice down and Kurt didn't hush her.

"I see it," Kurt said.

"See what?" I whispered.

He pointed. "It was there a second ago. Just a pulse. Like black light, shooting into the creep, and then shooting out again."

"Along the same path," Jane said. "Like ... he's connected to something, maybe?"

"Okay, it's official," I said. "The guy is here for no good. I don't suppose we can zap him now and avoid the mess?"

"I wish," Kurt said, with a growl at the back of his voice. Yeah, he was in big brother mode.

While we had been conferring, Emilio was stammering through an explanation. He had been trying for a while to build support for returning to Neighborlee, contacting classmates from his college days. He tried to make a joke about a conspiracy that nobody had stayed in town. While it was easy to find people through the WBC alumni association, he had difficulty connecting with people still in town who remembered him. Those who did remember him didn't want to reconnect because he had hurt Felicity.

Emilio couldn't contact Felicity through the alumni association because she hadn't finished college, so she didn't graduate, so she wasn't considered an alumnus.

"What was so hard about letting bygones be bygones?" Emilio said with a shrug and a crooked smile. "Why did they all think it so weird, like I was asking them to donate a kidney, when I asked them to welcome me back to town?"

"Gee, I don't know," Jane murmured. "Maybe because it's a little weird that he would need a formal welcome?"

"Oh, I agree with them," Felicity said. "It seems a little weird to me, too." She glanced upward, to where we were hovering inside the Ghost field and invisible. Learning to control her EM bursts enabled Felicity to locate hovering balls of energy.

"I was hoping for some help from them, maybe to act as go-betweens, you know?" Emilio said.

"Hey, didn't he have more of an accent when he was here before?" Kurt said, turning to me.

Chapter Six

"Yeah. He sounded more like Deanna Troi back then. Now ..." I muffled a snort of laughter. "Remember when I played that crazy river woman in the VBS skits, set in the rainforest, and I couldn't hold onto my Spanish accent? I kept sounding like really bad Jamaican."

"Yeah, the guy has been watching *The Pirates of the Caribbean* too much." Jane looked away from Emilio for a second to exchange grins with us.

"You were the last one I contacted," he was saying, in response to whatever Felicity had said. "I didn't want to. I felt so guilty. I mean, I know I hurt you, so it isn't right for me to ask for your help, but ... sweetheart, you're my last chance. I'm close to desperate."

"Why? For what?" she said. Felicity did an admirable job of sounding like she really didn't care, she was just asking to be polite.

"There it is again." Jane pointed, and this time I caught the flash, a blip of something dark leaving Emilio, shooting out of his back, vanishing in the sunshine.

He shuddered and wiped at his face. The guy was sweating, and it wasn't that hot of a day.

"Could we go back to your place to talk? Get out of the sun, some place private?"

"I don't think so," Jake said.

Emilio flinched and gave him a surprised look. Maybe he had forgotten Jake was there? That wasn't a good sign. I wasn't ready to feel sorry for the guy and give him the benefit of the doubt that maybe he was sick or in trouble. Gut instinct kicking in. I had learned the hard way to listen to my instincts. That niggling sense of something wrong said not to trust someone who otherwise seemed trustworthy or pitiable.

"You know, I took so long contacting you because I was scared you had left town."

"Oh, that's logical," Kurt said, again with the growl in his voice. Jane didn't hush him, either. It really was a good thing we were inside the Ghost field.

"I didn't realize you were married."

"That's obvious," Felicity said.

"Can we go to your place to talk? In private?" He looked at Jake, a brief glance that clearly said he meant no one but him and Felicity.

That was not happening. Even if Jake allowed it, which I knew he wouldn't, we weren't going to allow it.

"Why do you need to be in private? There's no one within fifty feet of us, nobody to listen in." Felicity smiled all innocent. One corner of her mouth twitched, her usual "tell" for when she was lying. I hoped she was enjoying herself, giving Emilio a hard time. "Why can't we talk here?"

"The animosity is pushing me away." Emilio tried to chuckle, but he made a choking sound and lost a few more visible degrees of color. Sweat popped out all along his hairline, and I honestly expected it to wash off makeup, revealing he was all pasty. He trembled a little.

Another blip of that black light effect shot into him. He flinched. Then he hunched his shoulders as a responding blip of light left him. That was just too freaky.

"Animosity?" Jake said.

"He never would have used a word like that in college," I said. I got another one of those warning shivers. The familiar clues I expected weren't visible. This was a strangeness we hadn't faced before.

"I'm not getting that weird vibe we got when the doppelgangers were around," Kurt said.

Which just proved that even if we didn't have telepathic links, we could read each other's minds when it really mattered.

"I know I'm not welcome," Emilio continued, his voice rising a few notes on the scale. "It's one thing to ignore me. It would have been smarter to just come in with no one remembering me, recognizing me, but no, we had to do it the hard way."

"What?" Felicity stood and sidestepped the bench, backing away. Jake put his arm around her and turned, putting himself partially between her and Emilio.

"I'm not welcome. There are eyes on me, hating me, willing me to leave. It's not fair. You need to listen to me, let me explain, before you judge me."

"Since when did you get all metaphysical and spiritually sensitive?" Her voice cracked a little, and she turned to look up at us.

Emilio looked up too, and for a second I had the awful feeling he could see us. That frown turned into a typical "the girl is kinda crazy" look. We sometimes got that when we were kids and talked about things that other kids around us never could have understood.

"That's not it." He tried to laugh. "Just please, for all that we meant to each other. Say you welcome me back anyway? You forgive me? Say you'll give me a place in your life again?"

"Why is that so important?" Jake said.

"Please tell me I still have a piece of your heart?"

"Emilio, you're a little freaky." She took a step back, and Jake let her slide out from the circle of his arm so he stood completely in front of her now.

"You wouldn't be so angry with me if I didn't still matter to you, right?" The sweat poured down his face and darkened his collar. I imagined a dark stain spreading across the back of his jacket. "Look, you cast me out. I couldn't even get back into town until you agreed to meet me here."

"Okay, that's a bad sign." Jane moved the Ghost field bubble downward.

"Go for it," Kurt said.

The Ghost field shut down with a nearly audible click and we dropped down hard on the grass. Emilio shrieked and his eyes rolled back in his head. I thought for sure he was going to faint. Another blip of that black light effect shot into him, making him spasm so he threw out his arms and his legs stiffened. Kurt and Jane moved around to surround him. An even bigger blip of light shot out of his back. Where I was standing, about ten feet away, I saw the path of that light. A straight line course down through the center of town, toward the Metroparks. On a hunch, I envisioned that blip going straight to that freaky house that had been so much trouble all those years ago, on the border of Darbyville and Neighborlee.

I was proven right, of course. Not that it did us much good then or later.

Kurt caught Emilio as his legs folded. Jane wrapped him in a separate Ghost field bubble and he went transparent.

"Okay, that's pretty cool," Jake said. "Where did he go?"

"You can't see him?" Felicity was back inside the protection of his arm tight around her. "Can you see him?" she asked me.

"Yeah," I said. There were some benefits to getting scorched in that tug-of-war with the doppelgangers back in the winter. I had increased sensitivity to energy and could see "sideways," as we called it. "The guy looks kind of sick."

"Something was draining him as we were talking," Jane said. "Something wanted ... okay, I'm just theorizing, moving on hunches or whatever ... he was pretty insistent on getting a *welcome*. Did you notice what he said about animosity pushing him away? Who talks like that?" She nodded to me. "Other than writers or the daughter of writers?"

That got a small smile from all of us, a loosening of the tension. We needed it.

"Okay, good point," Kurt said. "Definitely we don't take him to Angela. If it's all about being welcomed, then we don't want to take him over the threshold, inside our safe place."

"Oh, heck," I whispered, as epiphany flared so bright inside my head it hurt and threatened to blind me.

"What?" Jake said.

"This is more of that thing with the doppelgangers and when Ethan came to town. Those things need anchors, to be allowed inside the border. To be welcomed. Something figured out Emilio's tie to Felicity and is using him, just another angle to getting a foothold in town."

"Big mistake, expecting me to welcome him back." Felicity frowned. "Hey, whoever they are, they don't do their research. Anybody asking could have found out I was married."

"Lots of flaws in his story," Jane said. "It could be Emilio is a puppet, an unwilling player. He has enough awareness of what is going on that he resisted using his connection to you, until there were no other options."

"Our enemies are idiots," Kurt said. "Why doesn't that make me feel any better?"

"Or they're brilliant tacticians, and lulling us unto a false sense of superiority, so we relax and make mistakes. Trick us into false assumptions about them and their plans. Maybe distract us so we don't see the real point of invasion until it's too late."

"You're kind of depressing," Felicity said. She leaned in closer to Jake and shivered a little, like she was cold. "You used to be such fun. Kurt, what did you do to her?"

Kurt just shook his head and didn't play along with her teasing. At least, I hoped Felicity was teasing.

We ended up taking Emilio, inside the Ghost field, to Stanzer and Ethan's P.I. office. We didn't dare take him inside Divine's, and honestly, we didn't want him getting anywhere near Angela. Asking for help from Stanzer, and through him, the Hounds, was our next best tactic. I called ahead, riding with Felicity and Jake in their car, while Kurt and Jane flew with Emilio. Considering the potential of the Hounds, and abilities Stanzer hadn't revealed yet, we didn't want to generate any knee-jerk defensive reactions to the presence of that much energy at work. Like maybe a semi-nuclear explosion in downtown Neighborlee.

We didn't have much of a plan, other than needing a secure place to keep Emilio until we could figure out what to do next. There were two entirely empty floors in Stanzer's building, waiting to house other members of the Hunt when they were found. Dawn and the girls had the top floor, the three boys had the floor under them, and Stanzer lived on the second floor, with the PI office on the ground floor. Those two empty floors would make good prisons, with a little help from some un-Earthly talents.

As soon as we were all in the office and Kurt explained the first step, Stanzer hooked his thumb upward at the next floor of his building and said to make ourselves at home.

We got Emilio settled. We discussed a little how we could get answers from him, different tactics. The Hunt did have some talents that might be useful, but there was the inconvenient little detail that most of them were kids, teenagers. Yes, they were warriors, and yes, they had gone through an awful lot of their own weirdness and danger in the last year, but was it right to ask them to get involved in this new problem, including rummaging around in a guy's mind?

While Stanzer went up to talk to Dawn and the other kids, Jake kissed Felicity and headed off to an appointment he had on the East Side. Kurt had an appointment, too. He volunteered to stop at Divine's and update Angela and Ethan before he went.

I had been on the edge of the park when the Hunt faced down Wolcott and he got his comeuppance. Now I had a front row seat to see them work. They had been hurt when Wolcott subjected them to falsely labeled memory treatments, when he was still pretending they were his kidnapped grandchildren. The treatments forced their talents to mature ahead of time, so he could use them for his own profit before turning them over to Gahlmorag. There was no way of knowing exactly what damage had been done to them, or what kind of price the kids would have to pay for that forced maturity when they were older. I was just grateful they were willing to help defend Neighborlee and use their talents to help us right now.

Cinden was a healer. She did Emilio a favor when she knocked him unconscious with just a tap of her thin fingers on his forehead. Funny, but he looked kind of relieved to go limp and close his eyes. Cinden and Serena teamed up and did a full scan of him and determined that yes, something was draining him. Those blips of black light we saw were regular "sucks" on what was essentially an open wound in his mind and spirit, kind of like a lamprey. She theorized they were punishments for messing up, and regular bursts of instruction, guiding him. As far as she could tell, the Ghost field had broken the connection with his puppet master.

That was kind of a relief that Emilio wasn't a completely willing partner in this new attempt to get a foothold in Neighborlee. It looked like he had been resisting somewhat, maybe even trying to protect Felicity. However, he had sold his soul in a lot of ways, so he wasn't exactly an innocent victim or an oblivious dupe who didn't realize what he had signed on for. The guy had fallen in with some people who promised him power and protection, as long as he acted as their spy and point man, infiltrating territory they wanted to soften up and corrupt, to make it ready to fall.

Searching his memories and healing his body and mind would take time. The girls only had so much energy to use. We all agreed the best course of action was to leave Emilio unconscious. It was merciful to him, and it made controlling him and keeping him hidden easier. And if he wasn't awake, he wouldn't be resisting the Ghost field keeping him cut off from the puppet masters.

Over the course of several days of healing Emilio from the years of draining and punishing, Serena got most of his story, which boiled down to several important points. First, he had been sent to Neighborlee as a college student to investigate and pinpoint the power source in the town. He didn't know it at the time. At least, not consciously. His job had simply been to use his natural charm and friendly personality to make lots of friends. Then he made the mistake of falling in love. He decided he wanted to retire from the spy biz, settle down, and be exactly what everyone thought he was, a veterinary student.

He blacked out when he called his contact, in that house in Darbyville that tried to take a bite out of Angela years ago. When he woke up, he was in a shadowy meeting room. This was his second meeting with his boss, who spoke softly, but with a tone that threatened to separate his skin from his flesh as she told him just how disappointed she was, how much he had failed her, and reminded him just how binding his agreement was with her.

Yeah, *her*. His boss was a woman. A scary, pale woman who wore all black and had piercing cold eyes. He could never see her clearly, surrounded by an icy fog. Her minions were always silent guys in dark suits, and they had a talent for appearing out of nowhere, with no warning. The really weird thing was that the black suits couldn't seem to cross the border into Neighborlee. They always had him meet them in Darbyville.

Emilio was in terror for his life when he signed a new contract with the boss lady, and had been living in terror ever since, because now he knew they could summon him no matter where he was.

Yeah. A contract. Kurt was there, maintaining the Ghost field around Emilio, and he caught that piece of information. It reminded him of the contract Kerri and Pi Surprise had tried to trick Pete and me into signing, giving them access to Neighborlee through us.

After Emilio signed the contract, the boss lady put a band of braided metal on his wrist. She claimed all her higher level associates wore it. He said he felt like a dog with a microchip for tracking. Things changed drastically for him. He was supposed to meet Felicity at Divine's a couple days before he was supposed to pretend to go visit his family in Greece, but he couldn't find the shop. He went to the dead-end street, but the building wasn't there. Then the next day, he couldn't even find the street. That scared him, and it angered the boss lady. She ordered him to leave town. He was useless. He had messed up his assignment.

For the next few years, he was traveling the world, following in the trail of different people who were into "all sorts of freaky stuff I don't even understand," in his words. Emilio was mostly a spy, getting close to people who possessed all sorts of odd objects with designs in silver or made of precious gems, or things that had been buried for decades, maybe centuries. He never got close enough to catch any details. His job was to get close to people, charm them, make friends with them, get them to welcome him into their homes and businesses and places of worship. He crossed all boundary lines of belief and was all things to all people. Once he got the welcome, he opened the door to the boss lady's minions. They came in and did the dirty work, removing the objects and dealing with anyone who resisted them.

At that point, Bethany came in to work with Serena and Cinden to search Emilio's memory for images of the boss lady and her minions. None of them looked familiar, none of them looked like the BoBs spying on Pastor Rocky. She didn't look like Kerri, as we had theorized, along the lines of "better the enemy you know than the one you don't." After all, we had beaten Kerri a couple times now. The last thing we needed was a new nemesis joining the fight.

Then Ethan saw one of the sketches. The boss lady was none other than scary Mrs. Von Helado, who had hired him to come to Neighborlee and trick Angela into accepting a talisman intended to drain or enslave her.

This roller coaster of suppositions and theories and possibilities and more enemies to deal with was starting to get really old, and really nauseating.

Keeping Emilio in the Ghost field, to maintain the break in his connection with the boss lady, was draining on Jane. She and Kurt ended up flying him to Hoax, where several of her teachers could put him into a different isolation field, and keep the connection severed. Considering how much Mrs. Von Helado and her black-suited minions wanted to get into Neighborlee, we didn't dare keep Emilio inside the borders of our town. If we held onto him too long, it might be considered "sheltering" him, and that could translate to welcome, and then they could get through our defenses. We didn't want that.

"Okay, at least we have a better idea of who or what we're up against," Stanzer said, when we had gathered at Divine's to have another war council.

Everyone was there. Guardians. Support team. My folks. A lot of the Sheridans. And Hoax attended by conference call.

"Uh, not really," Ethan said, raising his hand like he was making an objection. "We just know they're bad news, they keep trying, and now we have more proof they were involved in that twisted social-psycho experiment back when Lanie was in college. Something has to be done about that house, and something has to be done to permanently break the link with Emilio. The guy is greedy and kind of stupid, but he doesn't deserve to be a crowbar and possible food source for that hag. Both end up on the short side of the deal."

"And breaking the link between them will deprive our enemy of one more weapon, and perhaps cause them some pain," Angela added.

Like always, the two of them managed to sit together and hold hands. In this case, they were snuggled together in the wide swing seat, with Ethan's arm around her. They had centuries of separation to make up for, but doggone it, I got twinges of jealousy every time I saw them acting like newlyweds. They radiated contentment even when we were discussing enemies and strategies and trying to figure out what was going to get thrown at us next.

Pop brought up the contract that Kerri had tried to foist on Pete and me.

"The contract disintegrated when it got to the fence around Divine's, according to what the kids told us," Pop said. "Is there any way we could get him to sign another contract that would overrule the first one? What would happen if we found the contract this boy signed? Could we just burn it? Would that set him free?"

"It's worth trying," Maurice said. "The trick is determining how strong the magic is, woven through the contract, and how crucial it is to doing the puppet thing on the loser."

"I don't know if it does us any good," Ford said, speaking slowly, his forehead wrinkled in very visible thought, "but can you remember anything from your two encounters with that bad magic? You touched the contract, and you were stuck to the coin that was meant to drain Angela. Anything you can remember that might help us? Any sensations, any clues to the magic involved and maybe the source?"

"Hey, most of the time, I wish I could forget. Scorched my wings both times." He twitched his shoulders, like he could still feel the effects. "Sorry. That's a good idea, but all I was feeling was the burn." He nodded, lips pursed. "But you know, maybe I could talk to the girls, have them try to dig through my memories, see if anything comes through. Muffling the pain in my memories might muffle other sensations, though."

We went through other ideas and theories. London reported on the progress she and Sherwood were making in not only monitoring but strengthening the field protecting our town, and their search for information. Then there was the search to match the face I had seen in my dream with someone else I had seen. Or at least determine if Frankie Leonides was alive and well and causing trouble, or someone was using his face.

Stanzer had an idea. Maybe if Serena and Cinden worked with me to explore my memories of the dream more, Bethany could draw a larger scene, get more background details, find out where the stabbing took place, and if it predicted an actual event. This could be another case of dreams eavesdropping on plans of the enemy, with nothing solid yet. We needed more details.

So that was how I ended up going to Stanzer's building after work on Thursday. We set up in one of the empty apartments. The girls hauled a mattress down from their apartment, so I could be more comfortable, and relax fully while they took me backward in my memories. Dream exploration was never as easy as it might sound to those who had never done it. Not even those who were used to regression hypnosis and other methods to plumb the depths of memories.

For one thing, there's a very fine line between letting the remembered events unfold as they really happened, and influencing the memories, adding details, maybe changing the sequence of events and emphasizing the wrong things. Or worse, changing details so nothing was as it happened. Too many people who went through regression therapy to investigate childhood traumas have been influenced to "remember" things that never happened, placing blame on people for crimes they never committed, shifting responsibility from guilty parties to innocent victims, and destroying lives and careers and relationships. I could influence what I saw and remembered so I would see what I wanted and needed to see. That wouldn't help us at all.

The girls put me to sleep while talking to me about what I had seen and done and discussed with people that night. Serena and Cinden were there when I opened my eyes in the auditorium of the dream. They stayed with me, out of my line of sight, but I could feel them there, watching.

Or rather, watching *me*, but not watching the events on the stage. Everything was blurry for them, as they reported later. They couldn't hear the voices or the music, if that discord and banging and shrieking could be called music.

When I woke up, that banging was still throbbing an ache through my head. I managed to push the discomfort away thanks to a new revelation: there were other people in the vision. People who weren't in the band, which went invisible after a short time. Meaning there were more people on the stage than Frankie and Pastor Rocky.

Bethany had been pulled into the dream with me, thanks to Serena and Cinden, but she hung back at the edges. Only time would tell if she had seen the important details. When I woke up, she got to work, sketching with colored pencils this time. That made a difference. Frankie the drummer, or whatever he had morphed into, or his lookalike, was now revealed as a dirty blonde with shaggy hair that changed, slicked back and gelled during the course of the dream. The sharp angles of his cheekbones got sharper, and the five o'clock shadow melted away and the earring vanished, including the piercing hole. His ragged T-shirt and jeans turned into a slick three-piece power suit that probably cost more than my Jeep when it was new. There was just this feeling of power and expense and elegance that came through the dream.

More important, a man stood in the shadow cast by Frankie or whoever he was. When Bethany sketched him, some of those long shadows dripping off of the drummer's arms merged with the man's arms. As if he guided the arms that stabbed Pastor Rocky with the drumsticks.

While Bethany was finishing the sketches, Dawn and Pendry came in with dinner for us. I needed it. Traveling memories is an exhausting and physically draining business. If my head wasn't still throbbing like those drumsticks were slamming against the base of my skull, I might have reached with my mind for that big tray in Pendry's hands and yanked it across the room. Probably would have made a big mess, and the last thing I wanted was to waste all that incredible, delicious-smelling food. And yes, these girls proved how smart they were by serving chocolate first.

We settled down for a nice picnic sitting on the floor. Bethany put aside the sketch pad to pick up the big bowl of chili that had a nearly visible cloud of spices wafting up from it. Cinden sure knew how to cook. I was reminded of a remark in a first season episode of *Roswell*, when the alien kids were in the diner late at night. They lifted the lid on the cake stand holding a chocolate cake and sprinkled tabasco sauce over it and dug in. They were addicted to spicy-sweet because of their muted senses when they first emerged from their artificial wombs.

I started telling the girls about *Roswell*. It turned out I didn't need to. The members of the Hunt tended to gravitate to a lot of TV shows and movies that reflected a little bit what they were. I could relate to that. Hadn't Kurt and Felicity and I dove into comic books about superheroes and all the TV shows and movies about super-powered people, mutants and meta-humans and other terminology made up for those who had un-human and extra-human powers?

Pendry gasped. Her bowl slid from her hands, and she scrambled to catch it before that incredible chili spilled across the floor. Several words escaped her, muffled, but clear enough to get shocked looks from Serena and Dawn and Cinden. At a guess, those were curse words from their homeworld. Pendry put her bowl down and scrambled forward a few feet, to snatch at Bethany's sketchpad, which she had left open.

"Why wasn't this in the first sketch?" She pointed at the man standing behind the drummer.

Bethany had made more than a dozen sketches as the dream progressed and Frankie the drummer had turned into Mr. Slick with the drumstick knives. The man who had joined the scene, turning from shadows dripping off the drummer's arms into an active participant in the stabbing, changed only slightly. His clothes changed from a dark jacket and jeans to a power suit also, but his face hadn't refined or aged. If anything, he looked darker. There was a vicious light in his eyes and the way he partially bared his teeth by the time we got to the final "frame" of the image, with the drumsticks going into Pastor Rocky's chest.

"I didn't remember him. All I was focusing on was the drummer doing the stabbing," I said, after thinking for a few seconds. I shivered a little as an idea formed in my mind. "You know this guy?"

Pendry nodded and put the sketchbook down, and shoved it across the floor a few feet, back toward Bethany. Her mouth flattened and I had the feeling she was fighting for words that didn't reflect the fire I glimpsed in her eyes.

"He tried to take me from my folks. There was just something really cold and dark about him, and it didn't make sense, because my impression of him is fire. Burned stuff, actually. All scorch and ashes and heat, but ... cold." She shook her head. "I didn't see him, but I swear, everything inside me says he was involved when my foster parents were killed. He's why I took off and ran, instead of letting them put me back in the system."

"What did he want? Why did he want you?" Cinden asked.

Pendry flinched and looked down at her clasped hands, so tightly wound together her fingers were either white or dark red with trapped blood.

"You did something that got attention," Serena said, her voice soft. "Something that made people, the wrong people, start asking questions." She got up on her knees when the other girl nodded, and scooted a few steps closer, to wrap her arms around her. "It's okay. We all messed up. We're just kids, and a lot of us expected to be sent to allies who understood and could train us. It takes all of us a while to figure out we need to hide what we are."

"What did you do?" Bethany asked.

Pendry had strong telekinesis, sometimes teleporting things under great stress. Stanzer had asked if I would be willing to mentor her since we shared that talent, once she was ready to start going out in public and meeting more people than the Hunt and the guardians.

"You moved something from too far away, so you couldn't convince people they didn't see what they saw," I guessed.

"Someone." Pendry took a deep, loud breath. "There was a little kid running across the road and she ran out between two cars and there was a truck coming and I was on the other side of the street and I just made her ..." She shrugged and held out her arms. "Come to me."

"With no flying from there to you," Cinden said.

"And there was a traffic camera that caught all of it."

"Oh, lovely. I have gotten to the point that I loathe cameras, period," Bethany said. "So how much press did you get before this guy showed up?"

"Press?"

"Newspapers, TV, radio, reporters, people asking really dangerous questions," I filled in.

"Oh. About ... two weeks. My social worker was worried and talking about moving me to another state, because my picture was on social media." Pendry snorted. "I didn't even know what that was. I was still learning English. People were showing up claiming I was their daughter or granddaughter or niece. Either I ran away or I was kidnapped. My social worker was smart. She made sure important things were kept out of the reports. Like I couldn't speak much English and how I was found unconscious in a storm and nearly drowned in a flood, and the scars from the Hounds. People were asked to provide birthmarks and information on how and where I was lost. There was a lot of noise. Especially when they were proven wrong, and they kept insisting I belonged to them. Then he showed up." She shivered.

"What did he do?" Then I knew, by the misery and fear darkening her eyes. "He knew everything, or he knew enough that it was too perfect?"

"He didn't even try to lie and say he was a relative. He just came right to the house. Nobody was supposed to know who my foster parents were. The whole thing happened two counties away from where I lived. I was with a school group on a field trip, and the school was supposed to hide that information and protect our identities, but someone figured out one thing and talked to someone and that led to another person and he --" She flicked her hand at the drawing sitting on the floor between us.

"He put the pieces together. Two months after the mess started, he came to our house. He never even contacted my social worker. He just knocked on the door and told my foster parents that he was going to take me to a place where special children like me could get the training we needed. He didn't ask, he just said he was going to do it. He never got angry when they said they wouldn't and couldn't just hand me over to him. He didn't even care about the legal problems. He was just so cold. He told them he came with a higher authority, and they had no right to say no and he wanted to talk to me."

Chapter Seven

"They wouldn't let him talk to me," Pendry continued. "I was upstairs, listening, and there was a mirror by the door that let me see everything. He just turned and looked right in the mirror, like he knew I had been there the whole time, and he told me it would be much easier on everyone if I just packed what I wanted to take with me, and I came with him right away. He said we didn't have any right to say no to him. He didn't get mad and he didn't laugh or anything when my folks said they were calling the police, and he had to go away, and he wasn't allowed to come back unless he had permission from my social worker. He said they were making a big mistake, and he told me if anything bad happened it would be all my fault. Then he just walked out the door.

"Then I got a letter, with instructions to call him when I was ready to be smart and turn myself over. When we gave the number to the police, they said the number didn't work. And the business card he left with my foster parents disappeared. And they got phone calls, every day for five weeks, asking if they were finally smart and they were ready to give up and stop acting like stupid children, that they had no right to say no to higher authority and superior wisdom." Pendry rubbed at her eyes and managed a crooked smile that didn't last very long. "It's crazy how clearly I remember all that."

"Trauma digs deep trenches in our minds, so it's easy to hold onto details like that," I offered.

"Do you remember what the business card said?" Bethany asked.

Pendry started to shake her head, then she looked to Cinden and Serena. The three exchanged grim smiles. In moments, she was lying down where I had been while they searched my memories and reawakened the dream. This time, Bethany's artistry wasn't needed. The name and phone number and business name and website were easy enough to write down.

"Lightning Pathway Ministries?" My voice cracked a little as I read that. Great, just what we needed, another crackpot New Age revelation guru. "This guy claims to be a minister?" I flashed back to that wacko preacher, Earnest B. Tass and how he publicly attacked Pastor Rocky on the word of Stephen Grandstone and his own self-righteous, self-appointed "mission from God."

"He works for them," Pendry said. "My foster parents said they wanted to know more about this place he wanted to take me to, the people I would be working with. He got upset, like they had insulted him by asking for information. And no one ever said no to his boss. Then he said they weren't worthy to speak to his boss, and idiots said he had something to hide because he didn't go outside and he didn't talk to people."

"So basically he sent his hatchet man to come talk to you," Bethany said. "Why does this sound like the plot to another really bad SyFy Channel movie?"

"I wouldn't know," I said. "I stopped watching after they cancelled *Warehouse 13*."

Poor Pendry. She looked completely lost. The show was before her time. Definitely, she needed help relaxing, we all needed a break from the grimness, so I suggested all the girls come over to my place and we would have a *Warehouse* marathon. The other three jumped on the idea. Before we left, all of us in my Jeep, I sent the information to London to start investigating. I considered calling Gordon, to ask him to access a police or FBI database to see if this Lightning Pathway Ministries had set off any alarms or at least garnered some complaints over the years.

By the time everyone had settled in at my place, and the pizza delivery service had left a feast in my kitchen, Pendry had told us more of her story than she had told the Hunt since the Hounds dragged her out of the Metroparks to join them. The months of fear before the fire that killed her foster parents. Her decision to escape the system and strike out on her own. Not just in the hopes of finding more members of the Hunt, but to stay free of the man, according to the business card, named LaRiche.

London popped up on my cell phone with the information before I started the first episode of *Warehouse 13*.

Lighting Pathway Ministries was indeed what I had feared, just from the name. An organization promising enlightenment for mind and body, a pathway lit by the cosmic powers and built by visitors from another world, another time, and another dimension of reality.

I would have laughed, but I had come up against enough weirdness from other dimensions and places, I had lost my sense of humor about it. All this was hitting too close to home. What if the people behind this so-called ministry had gained real access to not just other dimensions and realities, but to the inhabitants, who were sharing their technology and philosophy? What if those inhabitants were the nasty kind and they were only *pretending* to be helpful, to trap the Human race and enslave us? Or, according to the *Twilight Zone* and other shows, they were preparing to turn us into alien chow?

Bethany had her tablet with her, and we sort of divided up the website between us. I had my computer open and searched pages with Pendry and Serena sitting on either side of me, while she had Cinden and

Dawn with her, searching other pages. We found photos of the high-level minions of this self-appointed guru, who wanted to help ordinary Humans refine their minds and bodies to prepare them for transition to a higher plane of existence. For all the accolades for their enlightened teacher, they were very stingy about giving his name or posting any photos.

All this time, London was searching the site too, and she found what we were looking for. Sort of. She sent links to us.

The titles this guy claimed for himself got me irked and a little steamed, the longer I thought about it: His Lowly Holiness of Servitude in Suffering, the Humble Reverend Ambrose Lux.

He was appropriating one of the most important titles for Christ -- the Suffering Servant. Not cool. Common sense says to never, ever trust someone who proclaims that he's humble. Worse, this guy knew the Bible well enough to steal, and warp what he stole.

Besides, Ambrose and Lux both meant light, in different languages. Definitely a made-up name.

London found one photo among more than forty pages. It was dark, with low-level contrast. Lux was standing in a dark place, in dark clothes, and only dimly reflected light highlighted the long planes and sharp angles of his face, his long hair and receding hairline. It was hard to tell the color of his hair in the shadows, and the angle was a side shot, so only one side of his face was partially visible. He wore a suit, which sort of relieved me a little, because it would have been a cliché if the guy was wearing robes, ala bad Bible-themed drama, or Star Wars Jedi attire.

Something about the planes of his face made me shudder, then that shudder changed to a cold sort of tingle. The kind of chill that warned me I really wanted the idea trying to force its way up to my conscious mind to be wrong.

Bethany asked London if she could send that photo to my printer, then before I could ask her what she was thinking, she changed her mind. She asked London if she could do a comparison between what was visible of Lux's face to the first sketches she had made. London came back with her answer before Bethany could even finish asking.

Lux bore a strong resemblance to Frankie Leonides, the long-lost drummer from Pastor Rocky's band.

We gathered up the food and moved back to Stanzer's building, to use that empty apartment for a secure meeting. Before we left my house, we called Angela and Ethan, Kurt and Jane, the rest of the guardians. Then we had London send them emails containing a summary of what we had found out. Just so we could get the preliminary information sharing out of the way and not waste time getting down to the biggest concern.

Nearly all of us had arrived when London alerted us to something we needed to see. She said it aloud, speaking through all our smartphones, which was kind of freaky. Especially since there was a delay of as much as a second between some of our phones, depending on the service we were using.

Only people who were part of the inner circle of the Lightning Pathway could find the page she had uncovered, because there were no links to it anywhere else on the website, nothing about it in the menu. This page stated the new, revised goals of the inner circle of disciples, after a grand, new revelation that had come to Lux more than a year ago. It gave the specific date, and Stanzer and Dawn caught the significance first.

It was the date the first blue storms struck, awakening the memories of those members of the Hunt who had managed to forget their heritage and their journey across dimensions to Earth.

Coincidence? Not likely, after what we read.

First of all, the page described blue lightning storms and dreams of children falling from the sky, through a vortex from a higher dimension. These children had been sent by the Mother of Celestial Destiny, who had torn the sky open with her purifying lightning. Their transition from pure energy to flesh was marked by the blue lightning.

They had been sent, one by one, arriving as children and infants. It was the holy duty of the inner circle disciples to find these children and bring them to Lux, so he could awaken their memories and help them return to their pure and true state of energy. All those who aided in the quest would be rewarded with shares in their power, and insight into the pathway marked by lightning through the skies, to another dimension where the purifying energy of the Celestial Mother would refine and renew the entire planet.

Other linked pages detailed sightings of these lightning children over the years. Pendry was the most recent, with pictures of her. The page denounced her foster parents as agents of the darkness, who blinded her to her destiny and blocked her remembering her duty and heritage.

Dawn hurried to retrieve her computer and settled down at the far side of the room, so she could hear what we were discussing but not distract us. I heard her tapping away furiously on her notebook. Later, we learned she had been comparing the sightings of the lightning children to her own life and activities, and the members of the Hunt they had found so far, or had clues to locate.

This was double un-good, to borrow phrasing from Orwell.

The very last item in the menu for this hidden portion of the Lightning Pathway website discussed new visions and revelations. It was right under the page listing the rewards, both monetary and metaphysical/spiritual that loyal followers of Lux could expect to receive if they found these lightning children, and if their information led to the "freeing of the holy gifts from the Celestial Mother" from their "blindness and amnesia brought on by pollution and trauma upon entering our degraded world."

"You're not going to like it," Sherwood warned us, as I moved the mouse to click on the link to take us to this last page we hadn't explored.

"Yeah, and we liked some of the garbage we've looked at already?" Kurt grumbled.

I sincerely wished he had been joking, even if a little bit. Sarcasm wasn't really joking.

I clicked on the mouse, and the page loaded.

At first, I wondered if the webmaster for Lightning Pathway had made a mistake and mislabeled the links between pages. The top of the page was just pictures, one after another, some thumbnails, other large portraits, three-quarter shots, from waist to head, and full-body shots.

I laughed.

I couldn't help it.

In every picture, Lux was glowing. He posed with dramatic hand gestures, arms spread. His head tilted back as he gazed pensively up to the sky, or his head was bowed and his long hair fell in a curtain around his face. Sometimes the glow was just around his eyes, sometimes it came from his hands, sometimes he was just a man-shaped silhouette, outlined in golden light. In every picture, the glow made it hard to discern his features. He was a stereotyped, athletic, bare-chested, glowing demi-god.

Dang it, but he reminded me of the hero of a micro-short-run TV show, only a pilot movie and four episodes, made in the 80s. It was about an ancient astronaut who had been left in a time capsule-slash-sarcophagus in a Peruvian temple, to wait until the planet was at the right point for him to wake up and help us helpless Humans through a potential crisis period in our climb toward enlightenment.

I had to wonder if Lux got the idea for his glow of power from the TV show. The alien charged his batteries by gathering up sunlight, and when he used his power to levitate or blast people with energy beams from his hands or heal injuries or whatever, he glowed. Mum showed me a stack of fanzines she had gathered up, mostly from curiosity about how far this fandom could go. It really intrigued her how much passion and devotion could be stirred up by a four-episode-long TV show, for people to write literally hundreds of fan stories. And create cartoons. And have conventions. Until the antics of some extremist wacko fringie fans and the jerky immaturity of the actor himself scared people away. There was a dog food commercial at that time where the dogs glowed, so some disillusioned fans referred to the character, and actor, as Mr. Hi-Pro-Glow.

For a second or two, I really hoped that when I thought I recognized Frankie Leonides, I was thinking of that actor. Then I thought of some of the fanzine stories I had read. Several of them came way too close to what the Lightning Pathway was doing. Several featured aliens using a similar TV show to make contact with fellow stranded ancient astronauts, and "re-educate" the American population to save themselves.

That was why I had to laugh, seeing the golden light surrounding Lux, who did look a little bit like the ex-surfer-dude actor, with the high cheekbones and long blonde hair.

I scrolled a little faster through all those photos, caught between snickering, shivering, and feeling a little sick, until I got to the "wonderful, astounding news and proof that our Celestial Mother is rewarding us."

Lux had been given revelation about a second band of intrepid interdimensional travelers, sent to give aid to the floundering people of our planet.

These travelers arrived quietly, left as infants and toddlers with no fanfare, no storms, and no identification, to grow up in obscurity until need and danger awoke their powers. They were intended as support for the lightning children and had been forming a community for many generations now. When the time was right, the minions of the Celestial Mother would break through a barrier between dimensions to bring them and the lightning children and the loyal followers of the Lightning Pathway to their home and reward. He was grieved to relate that many among the second group of children had been given misguided information from false leadership and had turned from their true purpose and servanthood. They had devoted their energies to thickening that barrier between dimensions, to delay their return to their eternal and enlightened home. He had been charged by the Celestial Mother with identifying the town where they had been hiding and misusing their powers for many decades. When he found them, he would cleanse the blindness from their eyes and wipe the illusion from their minds and harvest their powers, gathering them under his enlightened control, and tear down the last barrier.

Underneath that "revelation," he listed details for his followers to use in their search to identify the town and the children. He urged them to cast aside inhibitions when it came to the "paltry, misguided, limiting laws of mere mortals," and essentially hack computers, break into national security sites and ransack public records and closed files, to identify these children and awaken them to their true destiny. The details included descriptions of how the children were found, various abilities they might or might not possess, telltale signs that they hid their powers, and worst of all, included a gallery of pencil sketches of some of the lost children, given to him in visions.

Ethan cursed, echoed by Stanzer. At least, I thought they were cursing, because they were clearly speaking different languages.

The pencil sketches weren't that good, which was a relief. But not much, because I recognized Stephanie Miller, back when I was a little kid and she was dating Ben Miller. And there was a pencil sketch of Rodney, before he was taken away by the Rivals. And a sketch of Col. Hayward when he was young, probably in high school.

And a sketch of Kurt, Felicity and me, in middle school and high school, wandering through the quarries, back when we were playing with the idea that we were aliens. Specifically, when we had made that one frightening attempt to "phone home" on Halloween. In the sketch, we were wearing our Army surplus camouflage costumes.

Who had seen us and identified us and why had they taken this long to reveal our identities and our activities?

"Those are really bad sketches," Jane said, her calm voice breaking through the pounding of my pulse. "If you didn't recognize the surroundings, would you recognize those people? Would you recognize them if you weren't looking for them? I mean, you expect to see people you know, right? So you put the pieces together to identify them. But someone from the outside, how are they going to know? Especially since those are all old pictures, twenty and thirty years or more in the past."

Thank You, God, for Jane, so full of common sense. She was so good for us all.

Finally, we struck paydirt: a rogues gallery of pictures of the inner-inner circle of Lightning Pathway workers. LaRiche was at the top of the list or pyramid or whatever it could be called. His job description merely said he was Lux's right-hand man, defender, and troubleshooter. I shuddered a little seeing his formal photo put him, and everyone else, in all-black.

London said Sherwood was investigating LaRiche and Lux's histories. We were a little disturbed to see all the lawyers listed among the inner-inner circle. Several of them specialized in family law, specifically child custody.

"How easy is it for them to search adoptions and petitions for guardianship?" Angela asked.

A collective, subliminal groan seemed to rattle the room. The Hunt were mostly minors, and Angela had applied to be their guardian. Plus there was all that unpleasantness from LaRiche trying to intimidate Pendry's foster parents into handing her over. If they hadn't died in that fire, would one of those lawyers have shown up on their doorstep with enough paperwork to prove Pendry belonged to a loyal follower of Lux?

The damage had been done. We were going through proper channels. Various friends at Neighborlee Children's Home and town officials and social workers were on our side. We had no idea what signal flares had been sent up by our actions, and how far away they could be seen and detected by people who weren't friendly. The problem was what kind of power LaRiche and the Lightning Pathway lawyers had on their side. There was a very real possibility that if they came storming into Neighborlee with court orders to grab Pendry, they might pick up clues that other members of the Hunt were with us. We would have to use our extra-special, un-ordinary arsenal of semi-pseudo-superhero powers to keep them safe and free. The heck with handling everything legally.

Finally, we came to the end of the secret pages. We had done and learned all we could for now. Short of taking a field trip to the headquarters of Lightning Pathway and confronting Lux, there wasn't much more we could do. We had learned the hard way, dealing with the doppelgangers and the Von Helados, we were safest staying inside the borders of Neighborlee. The challenge ahead of us was gathering enough information and identifying our potential enemies so we could react properly when the attack came.

~~~~~

I met Daniel for a business lunch at Sheridan headquarters in Independence on Friday. I had a few tense moments when I left the borders of Neighborlee. The trouble with the doppelgangers wasn't that far behind us. Someone could be waiting to attack the first guardian or member of the Hunt who stepped out through the shield. But nothing happened. Maybe the enemy was still gathering strength. Or maybe they were still too far away to catch movement. Or maybe they were running around like headless chickens, trying to find out what happened to Emilio, and why he hadn't opened the door to give them access to our town.

To really ratchet up my tension, Daniel could have followed up on some of those weird looks he had been giving me lately, but he kept our lunch strictly business. Granted, it was friendly business, not slipping into Evil Overlord mode. Having his secretary join us to take notes sort of guaranteed nothing personal going on. Francine was a good friend, but I really needed her to leave us alone, so we could discuss the newest information London had dumped in my email that morning. Mostly the slow progress of investigating LaRiche and Lux and Lightning Pathway. There was one interesting news piece, about a woman who had gone nuts and attacked the headquarters of Lightning Pathway in New Mexico, determined to rescue her husband from them. Too bad neither of us was in the mood to laugh about the freakishness of it. None of the alerts tied to all the electronic documents filed to get custody and identification papers and an official identity for Pendry had gone off, so no unfriendly forces had discovered her presence in Neighborlee. Good for all of us.

Finally, Francine headed to her desk, leaving us alone in the conference room to ostensibly discuss activities for our Star Trek club. Always a good excuse to send people away, sometimes running in fear for
~~~~~

their sanity.

"When someone is too good to be true, or in this case their past is too clean, that's a warning sign," Daniel said, once we had gone over London's report. When I pointed out the news piece about the woman with the bazooka, he responded that there was nothing said about whether her claims were valid. She could be the certified wacko, not them.

"So you think Lux is dirty?" I asked, wondering where he was heading with this tendency to doubt what we all feared.

"He could be a dupe, just a figurehead. Your dream could mean that LaRiche is the puppet master, and he was the one moving Lux's hand to stab Pastor Rocky."

"Yeah, there's that."

My phone blipped rapidly, trilling up and down the scale in a ringtone London made up to signal she or Sherwood was trying to contact me. Daniel cocked an eyebrow at my phone, sitting on the end of the table between us. Updates were the whole reason for having my phone out and the sound turned on during a business meeting lunch.

"You're going to love this and hate this," London announced as soon as I opened up my phone.

Daniel got up and moved around the corner of the table, so he could see London, and I wouldn't have to twist my arm so both of us were in the lens.

"First of all, Ambrose Lux didn't exist ten years ago," she said. "We dug up a couple of police reports and some hospital records about a man matching his description being found washed up among wreckage after a storm … " She paused for dramatic effect. "Within the Bermuda Triangle."

"So he claims he has his mission from his New Age god thanks to surviving a wreck?" Daniel asked.

"He's never said that. He doesn't talk about the wreck or the storm because he was basically braindead or the next best thing, his body just wouldn't shut down for a good three months. He was just vegetating in a hospital, until he woke up one day. Rebooted. All his hard drives erased. No identity. No memories. No one claiming him. No one looking for him. He had to build his own identity from scratch. Which is a good description of what happened to anyone and anything that came close to discovering his identity." She paused again for dramatic effect.

"You were able to uncover all the things that were hidden?" Daniel guessed.

"The self-proclaimed humble Lux has avoided the spotlight from day one of his new identity, which is actually his *third* since washing up on that island beach. The identity the helpful social services people gave him. Then the one he took on when he helped to foil a major robbery and hostage situation, aided by his alleged celestial powers, and had to go into

Witness Protection. His most recent one came when he gained enlightenment and discovered that we are not the identities put on us by other people, starting with our parents, but the identities we give ourselves." She shuddered, looking like she had eaten something nasty. Did AI's eat? "I would really like to find the people who write that kind of self-congratulating garbage and shove them through a partially open doorway into another dimension. Times like this make me wish the electronic world of *Tron* really did exist, so Sherwood could involuntarily upload them and give them a taste of electronic reality, you know?"

"You've been watching way too many movies from the 70s and 80s," I offered.

That got a chuckle from her.

"Anyway, LaRiche has been there from somewhere around day three, looking out for his guru, acting as his mouthpiece, handling all the nasty, dirty, day-to-day living details for him."

"That fits a lot of scenarios and stereotypes and movies," Daniel said. His chin hit my shoulder a half-dozen times when he talked. I was so very tempted to shrug, giving him a really obvious nudge and hint to step back, or at least stand up a little straighter. He had ordered barbecue for our lunch, heavy on the garlic. While I loved eating garlic, it wasn't so great getting it secondhand on someone else's breath, rushing past my ear.

"LaRiche makes sure Lux keeps his hands clean and he can't be held accountable for things that are done without his approval or permission or knowledge," I said, theorizing aloud. "But we can tie what LaRiche did, trying to get his hands on Pendry, to Lux's teaching on the lightning children. Any warning signs of them getting close to the Hunt or Neighborlee?"

"Well …" London said, "this is the part you're going to love and hate. There's a lot of court action and claims and counterclaims and motions to annul and other legalese I don't want to pollute my brain with, but the bottom line is that Lightning Pathway is trying to evict the entire Grandstone clan and take over all their property in Neighborlee."

Chapter Eight

"Wow, that explains ..." I caught my breath and turned enough to meet Daniel's gaze, and he stepped back enough we weren't nose-to-nose.

"Yeah." He nodded.

That matched a few short discussions we had had over the past few months, since the doppelganger trouble, about how quiet the Grandstones were. Peaceful neighbors. Keeping to themselves. I made a mental note to check with Mr. Carr, of Carr, Cooper and Crenshaw, to see what kind of employee and lawyer Reggie had been the last few months.

"That explains why they aren't tormenting any of us," he continued. "They're too busy dealing with someone treating them the way they treat everyone else."

"All these attempts to get formal welcomes and invitations into Neighborlee make me wonder about some of the rules. If they own property, does that mean they don't need an invitation?" London said.

"Ouch. That's a tricky one. We probably need to check with Angela and her otherworldly connections and sources," he mused. "Why do I have the awful feeling we're going to be helping the Grandstones stay in town?"

"Please," I tried to joke. "I just ate lunch." The three of us exchanged worried, slightly nauseated grimaces. "Okay, details? When did it start? How did it start?"

"Still investigating that. There's a lot of reading to do, even for electric brains like ours," London said. "The short story is that through a lot of trickery that would make them jealous if they weren't the victims this time, the senior Grandstones got themselves involved in a really complicated, tricky deal that turned around and bit them a couple dozen times. They *thought* they were going to get their hands on a lot of hocus pocus, crystals and otherworldly cargo and ancient manuscripts and people with supernatural powers."

"But?" Daniel prompted, when she paused for a totally unnecessary breath.

"But they ended up losing their shirts and the family farm."

"What's not to love?" he murmured. He pulled out a chair so he could sit down next to me. "Other than the big problem that becomes visible once the confetti of the celebration clears away. This could be proof the Pathway group identified Neighborlee as the home of the lightning children."

"Until the Grandstones move out, they can't move in," I countered. "What about the Grandstone side of the story? Are they fighting the eviction? If they were packing up to leave, people would have noticed. They should be raising a ruckus, hiring a couple dozen legal firms to defend them, at the very least. Or even hiring twenty-four-seven security or an entire mercenary hit squad."

"Like I said before, polluting my brain with legalese," London said. "I did catch some really heavy email traffic, negotiating with auction houses, and companies to ship fragile and valuable cargo. Maybe they're getting ready to remove lots of highly sensitive and incriminating possessions before Lightning Pathway follows through on its nastier threats to evict them. If the courts come in and clear out their property for them, a lot of skeletons could be exposed to the light of day."

What were the chances this was some long-range revenge plan? Maybe Lux, whoever he really was, had been burned by a Grandstone scheme years ago. Maybe someone he knew and loved had been seduced by a Grandstone, or ripped off, or maybe someone he knew had been enslaved and had escaped, and told horror stories of Grandstone or even Rival nastiness, and this was just simple paybacks. Maybe the plan wasn't to take the property at all, but to harass the Grandstones and tie up their money and generally drive them crazy. Finally making the Grandstones feel as powerless as they had worked to make everyone else in Neighborlee feel for generations.

Yeah, it sounded nice, but kind of far-fetched. Until Lightning Pathway made their next move, we would have no idea what was really going on.

"I thought you said we would hate this," I said, while my brain was still spinning.

Daniel laughed quietly.

"Haven't gotten to that part yet." London's face went somber. "We caught some pretty heavily shielded communications ... the Grandstones are negotiating to pay off their huge debt by selling out Neighborlee. Some communications refer to Lux's writings about the celestial children. They've offered a list of people they claim they've kept under surveillance for years, who might have the qualities Lux wants. They're trying to finagle themselves into a position of power in his celestial kingdom, and implying he owes them for helping in his search."

"Yeah, that sounds like the Grandstones we know and loathe." I sighed.

"Do you have access to that list, so we know who to warn?" Daniel said.

"I've been digging through Grandstone computers and cloud accounts, but nothing has come up. Hopefully they're just bluffing, stalling for time. Or it's all stored in hard copy they can't get to. Maybe the Grandstones are trying to retrieve that information and keep Lightning Pathway's people from following them to the source. LaRiche hasn't responded. Lux never does, no matter how many emails are addressed directly to him, insisting they talk to the real power on the throne. We're keeping watch for any cloud activity, any attempts to access a Rivals website or cloud account we haven't found yet. If they try to access or send it, we'll snag it and make sure it never gets to its destination." She shook her head and looked as somber as I had ever seen her in all the years since she transformed from a digital copy of Doni Longfellow into a separate personality.

"One interesting development." Her face switched off the screen of my phone, and a photo that looked like Frankie Leonides appeared in her place. He was a mess, on his knees, dripping wet, either from a downpour or sweat. My vote was sweat, as in terror, because he was looking up at a glowering LaRiche. His eyes were big and his mouth was twisted like he might burst out in tears any second.

"This was caught by a security camera about two years ago," London said, after giving us a good ten-count to study the image. "Right after this was recorded, there was a fire in the warehouse where this camera monitored the loading dock area. The power was cut, and the camera ended up in a bin of equipment that was shoved aside and forgotten. This is noteworthy because all the security cameras in the area had odd blank spots. Not static, like a power surge or a glitch in the programming, but just blank spots. Everything erased, including static and the usual residue that a really good technical wizard can cut through to retrieve the supposedly erased images.

"Sherwood theorizes this image was saved because the camera was removed from the system before someone went in and erased the images of LaRiche and Frankie Leonides. Recently, someone got hold of the camera and the other junked equipment and checked for any surviving data when they were dismantling it for parts. They uploaded the memory, in the hopes that maybe the camera caught whoever or whatever started the fire."

"For all anyone knows, LaRiche did," Daniel said.

"Frankie, if that is Frankie, certainly doesn't look capable of doing anything," I added. "I feel sorry for the guy."

"The thing is, this confirms what Athena theorized, based on the sketches Bethany made. There are facial features, the underlying bone structure, that smear of birthmark on his jawline --" London highlighted the dark patch, like a warped boomerang, with a yellow circle on the screen, "-- that match with the few details we've been able to harvest from the images of Ambrose Lux."

"That doesn't look like a man who's in charge of a super-rich, powerful cult," Daniel said. "He looks like a worn out, terrified old man who's ready to collapse."

"And did," I added. "I agree, LaRiche is the puppet master. Frankie doesn't look capable of even playing the puppet anymore."

"We still don't know if Pastor Rocky's old friend is still alive. Or if he was even alive before the bus crash."

"I want to know what it has to do with your dream of Frankie stabbing Pastor Rocky," London said.

"Is there more than just this one frame of image?" I asked.

In answer, rain spilled down in front of the lens. The image moved in reverse, so LaRiche stepped backward around a sobbing, shaking Frankie, then backed out of the image. Frankie backed up onto his feet and ran backward, out of the image. For a few seconds there was just falling rain, then Frankie stumbled into the frame and everything moved forward, to get back to the image London originally showed us. It was the clearest image of them all. The video continued past that point.

LaRiche turned and looked around and shouted to someone who was standing outside the frame. A greenish, purple-edged streak shot out of the rainy darkness, straight at the camera lens. I jerked backward. The image died.

"Okay, that was freaky," Daniel muttered.

"And that's all we have," London said.

"Well, at least they know what started the fire. Knocking out the camera was overkill," I said. "Not that we can tell the investigators."

"I think we need to stop right here and share it with the whole group," Daniel said.

Since this involved Pastor Rocky, we decided to convene the meeting at the church. London got to work sending messages to everyone, asking them to meet us at the church, and to contact people who didn't have email or smartphones or regularly checked any kind of devices. Like Angela. Of course, Ethan was the middleman between her and the modern world, so contacting him would get the message to her.

I had the fun task of calling the church and letting Pastor Rocky know we were coming, with big news. When I called, Vivian answered the direct line to Pastor Rocky.

"Oh, good, Lanie. Pastor asked me to call you. He and Father Marty jumped in his truck and are heading to Nashville."

"What? Why? What happened?"

That got Daniel's attention. He closed down the call he was making and got up to cross the room to where I was sitting. I put my phone on speaker.

"He wouldn't say, except it was an emergency, and I was to give you all the boxes he put on the conference table in his office. And to ask you to have London monitor a place called Sanctuary Rescue Mission, on the north side of Nashville. He looked like he had had a shock, and it was changing to anger. You know how he is when he's jumping to defend someone."

"Yeah, I know." I shivered a little, remembering.

When I was thirteen, the youth group went to a Downtown Cleveland rescue mission to do some service work; cooking, laundry, painting dormitory rooms, things like that. An addict decided he didn't like the looks of one of the boys and went after him with a knife he shouldn't have had. Pastor Rocky didn't try to talk the guy down that day. He body-slammed him and knocked him across the room, shouting for all us kids to get out. He needed a few stitches, but the addict came out of it in a lot worse condition. Pastor Rocky rarely lost his temper, but when he did, the devil would be smart to be shaking in his snakeskin boots.

"You might want to ask your dad," Vivian offered. "Pastor called and asked him to fill in on Sunday and lead his class on Wednesday night. If he was going to give his reasons for heading out of town so fast, I think he'd tell Charlie if no one else."

I thanked her and hung up. Daniel grabbed the handles of my wheelchair and turned me toward the door before I could scroll through my address book for Pop's number. I waited until we were in Daniel's truck to make the next call and put it on speaker from the start. Only later did I think about my Jeep left behind at the office. Someone was going to have to come back and get it for me.

"What's wrong?" Pop asked me, when I nearly ran over his, "Hi, hon," to ask if he knew why Pastor Rocky had left town.

"There's just some weirdness and new information on that drummer from Pastor Rocky's band, and when we tried to call him to warn him, we found out he left town so fast and … Pop, is everything okay? Did he say what's going on when he asked you to fill in?"

Pop laughed. Of course.

"It's okay, hon. He's fine. He ran off kind of scattered because it's not often you get an answer to prayer so fast." His next words were muffled, and I could easily imagine him covering the phone to tell Mum what was up. "Funny you should mention … no, maybe not funny. You said the drummer?"

"Yeah, Frankie Leonides."

"What about him?" Daniel asked. At least he never looked at me, but focused on getting down Rockside Road in the knotted traffic getting on and off I-77.

"He showed up at a rescue mission in Nashville run by some friends of Rocky's, dragging two other guys from the band. Leo and Achmed.

They got tied up in some weird cult that's been flying under the radar. Frankie got them out, but they're in withdrawal and just a real mess."

"Did he say what the cult was?"

"No. Not sure if Frankie told them."

"So they're going to this rescue mission? Sanctuary?"

"That's it. They couldn't get tickets on a flight to Nashville until tomorrow, and they decided it'd be faster to drive. He promised as soon as he got a chance to catch his breath, he'd email all the information. He also said something about some boxes and a message he left for you. Any idea what's up?"

"We're heading to the church right now. Could you meet us there, you and Mum?"

"Good idea." There was a brushing sound, probably covering the receiver again, and muffled, I could hear Mum's voice. "What's going on, honey? Any ideas?"

"Well, we've got some conflicting information or evidence or whatever."

"We've got good reason to think this Frankie is part of a cult, basically," Daniel said. "Pictures of him, taken with someone who tried to get custody of one of Stanzer's kids."

"Ah. That can't be good. You think Rocky is heading down into a trap?"

"Why would they want to get their hands on Pastor Rocky?" I asked.

More muffled sounds. Mum asking something. What Pop said couldn't have sat too well with her. When he spoke again, his voice had a slight echo, and I guessed he had finally put his phone on speaker so Mum could hear what was going on.

"What did you kids find out about this Frankie?"

I filled them in, and that got us through the tangle of roads that led us around the airport and nearly home to Neighborlee. By that time, I had texts popping up on my phone, acknowledging the call to the meeting, and indicating who could come and who was tied up, either at work or on the road and unable to drop everything and join us. Athena and Wallace were already there and waiting in the church parking lot. Mum and Pop got in the van as we were talking on the phone, and were nearly there. Jane and Kurt and Felicity were at Hoax, dealing with a snag in deprogramming Emilio and freeing him from the connections with whoever was controlling him. Ford and Charlotte and Jinx were down in Columbus at an auction. Doni and Cosmo, Pete and Meggie were at Cedar Point. As if he could hear me going down the roll call list, Ethan called to say he and Angela were on their way. I had to bite my tongue to keep from apologizing, because today was their scheduled day to take a trip to their private garden.

Vivian saw us coming and hit the buzzer for the automatic door so we didn't have to ring and ask to be allowed inside. Sadly, we had to employ security practices even in Neighborlee. Granted, most of them were to keep Grandstone sympathizers from trying to sneak in and do some vandalism, rather than the usual trouble that other churches in other towns had to deal with. Even though the Grandstones hadn't made an attempt in more than ten years to claim our church was their property, some of their minions didn't catch on real fast, or read whatever memos were sent around listing the current targets.

"Oh, and Pastor wanted me to tell you that Stephen Grandstone has started in again, calling once a day, here and on his home phone, about the reunion tour of his rock band." Vivian sniffed, the only sign of irritation I had ever heard or seen on her in all the years I had known her. "I'm really surprised the big bully hasn't started camping out here with a dozen lawyers. He's started sounding frantic."

"Frantic how?" Daniel asked.

"Different people have different kinds of frantic," she said with a shrug. "Since I never deal with the man, how can I interpret him? But Pastor thought you should know, with all the strangeness going on."

There wasn't a lot waiting for us on the table when we got to Pastor Rocky's office, just two bankers' boxes and a good four inches of printouts. With the large number of people coming for the meeting, we decided to move to a classroom at the other end of the building. We could spread out more and have some security, so no one overheard the impending weirdness we would be discussing. As people joined us in the room, we got to work looking at what Pastor Rocky had left for us.

Two files sat on top, in a separate accordion folder from the other members of the band. The printouts for Achmed and Leo were twice as thick as anyone else. Part of that, we soon realized as we spread out the folders and checked the personal histories, was that the men with the thinnest folders had died within a few years of the band dispersing.

And yet they had showed up for that reunion concert and looked like they had during their days with the band.

The only folder thinner than the ones for the dead men was the one for Frankie Leonides. Part of that could be explained by the theory that he had vanished, lost his memory, or at least pretended to, and transformed himself into Ambrose Lux. But that generated another question: Why would he revert to his former identity? What could he gain from being Frankie Leonides again? And why would Lux, if he had once been Frankie, have that confrontation in the rain with LaRiche, where it certainly looked like he was terrified of his right-hand man?

Pastor Rocky and Father Marty had been doing a lot of calling and reconnecting with people and asking questions and gathering information. It was amazing what they had found out. Sometimes, people connections were more efficient than the fastest AI's.

After maybe twenty minutes of glossing over the folders and setting up a chart on a big rolling dry erase board, everybody dug in and really started reading, taking notes, asking if anybody else had read anything relating to something that stood out for them. We found out a few things that were very interesting. The members of the band in the reunion photos who looked like they hadn't aged since the band dispersed had all supposedly died within ten years of the final concert. The musicians who looked older, but certainly not as old and worn out as they should, all had come into large sums of money just before the reunion tour. The only ones in the reunion photos who looked their true ages were Achmed and Leo, and they hadn't come into any money.

So what did that mean?

There was a separate file for the backers of the reunion concert, with all sorts of money details, and lots of sticky notes attached in different places stating the information in the printouts was false. Yet a huge gob of money had appeared seemingly from nowhere to pull together the former members of Magna Magma, living and dead, rejuvenated and worn out.

Where did the money come from if the source of it was apparently nonexistent?

"This is interesting." Ethan gestured for the rest of us to come over to three folding chairs he had set up a few steps away from the table where all the paperwork had been spread out. He had three folders on those chairs, flipped open to the very back of the files. One report was nearly identical for each man.

Achmed, Leo, and Frankie had appeared for publicity photos, but they didn't take interviews. They didn't go out to party with the rest of the band. All three men vanished immediately after each concert. Indications were that they hadn't been on the bus when it crashed and burned. So maybe the stories of survivors were partly true. Members of Magna Magma were alive, despite the crash that was reported to kill everyone, but they were alive because they hadn't been on the bus.

"So what do they have in common that they weren't replaced by doppelgangers, they were prevented from speaking to the public, and didn't get big cash deposits in their bank accounts?" Pop said after looking through the three folders.

"Maybe a bigger question," Daniel said, "is why they replaced Pastor Rocky and Marty with doppelgangers. They were asked to participate, but they weren't offered huge sums of money. If Achmed, Leo, and Frankie weren't doppelgangers, and they weren't paid huge sums of money, if they were kept away from the public, maybe they were forced to perform, and extreme measures were taken to keep them from shattering the illusion. So why weren't Pastor Rocky and Father Marty coerced? What protected them?"

"God and Neighborlee," Angela murmured.

"We need to talk with him," Pop said. "Heck with waiting for him to take a rest stop." He stepped over to the table and pulled out his phone and dialed. Then he put it on speaker, so we could hear it ringing. I fully expected to get a voicemail, directing us to leave a message.

"Nag, nag, nag," Pastor Rocky said, and laughed, instead of the expected "hello."

That had to be a good sign, right?

"We've had some developments," Pop said. "Didn't want you walking into a dangerous situation."

"Okay ... So what developments are you talking about?"

Pop nodded to me, which I assumed meant I was supposed to take over. Oh, great. Thanks.

"I guess the most important question," I said, speaking slowly to give myself time to phrase it as best I could, "is the name of this cult that your friends are hiding from or escaping or whatever."

"The Lightning Pathway."

Several of us moaned, or in Wallace's case muttered something guttural. I had the feeling he had been studying Klingon with Pete and a couple of the other guys in our Trek club. It was appropriate to the moment.

"Did you say Frankie got the other two out? How? How did they get in?"

"Lanie ... what do you know?" Pastor Rocky said. "I'm hoping the wireless signal is bad, because I'm hearing a lot of doubt in your voice."

"Sorry, Pastor," Daniel said, and I was grateful he was taking over. "Basically, we've been following up on some of Lanie's dreams, and getting sketches, and they implicate your friend, the drummer. He seems to resemble the leader of the Lightning Pathway. So it's kind of weird that Frankie would be helping someone escape if he's the leader."

"Uh huh. So ... why do I have the feeling you're worried about me?"

"You're incredibly perceptive. Despite all the damage you did to yourself while you were a musician," Pop added.

That got a chuckle from Pastor Rocky.

"Well, the short version of the story is that I have a couple friends who run a rescue mission down here. A few days ago, these three guys came stumbling in, terrified out of their skulls and suffering some pretty bad withdrawal symptoms. At least, Leo and Achmed were suffering. Frankie was taking care of them, keeping them going, but he had raw wounds on his wrists and ankles and marks that looked like electronic burns. The doctor at the mission has seen this before and is pretty sure he's been restrained and tortured with a taser, at the very least. Some of the burns could be cigarettes. Frankie's not talking, and he nearly broke and ran when he was walking around, taking a break from looking after the other two, and saw a picture of me with the guys who run the place. There's kind of a rogues' gallery by the office, with pictures of important events, dedication ceremonies, things like that. They had to talk to him a long time to get him to confess he knew me. Then the other two saw the picture and they started talking about the band and someone who looked like me but couldn't be me, and my friends put things together. So, they called me. The important detail here is that Frankie didn't want them to get me involved. Does that sound like a trap to you?"

"No, not really," Daniel said.

"If Frankie were the leader of a cult, it's the most backward cult I ever heard of. He's been starved and beaten up and restrained. Usually, the leader is living like a king while everyone else is starved and abused." Pastor Rocky sighed. "Bottom line is that our old friends need our help. Marty and I have to at least take a closer look and figure out what's going on with them and see what we can do. If we can do anything."

A very important question didn't occur to me until after we had agreed to report in regularly to each other, said goodbye, and hung up. We sat in silence for a few moments, just looking at each other, then Mum and Angela got to work closing up folders and organizing things a little bit. The commonsense thing to do was move all the paperwork to Mum and Pop's place, where there was plenty of room to spread it out again and add information as it came in. Plus, they had two dry erase boards, usually used for organizing books, and lots of tables and folders and color-coded files.

I had a distinct sense of dissatisfaction. There was something wrong, but I couldn't put my finger on it. Other than the fact that if this person who claimed to be Frankie was really Frankie, then he wasn't Ambrose Lux. And then there was the whole coincidence of Frankie bringing the other two men to the one rescue mission where the men running it were old friends of Pastor Rocky. What were the chances? My gut said Pastor Rocky was the reason, the connection, but why?

Calculating statistics and odds wasn't one of my superpowers, but common sense said this couldn't be a coincidence. Despite Frankie acting so scared at seeing the picture, my gut said he did know Pastor Rocky's link to the mission. How did he, or whoever he was working for, or whoever was working for him, find and choose *this* rescue mission?

That was when the question slapped me across the face. I stopped short, so abruptly the folders lying on my lap nearly slid off. Pop saw me and grabbed hold of my shoulders, like he thought I would fall out of my chair. He demanded to know what I was thinking. I guess my expression was kind of frightening.

"Why Nashville, when Lightning Pathway is in New Mexico?" I said, managing to make my voice somewhat steady. "It's got to be a setup. But why? What do they want?"

"You think Pastor is walking into a trap?" Wallace said.

"Could be more proof they're after Rocky." Pop thumped the closest table with his fist.

"London?" Athena looked a little pale as she raised her phone to speak into it, without tapping anything to open it. "Can you access any security cameras at the rescue mission? Do they have security cameras? Can we see what's going on down there?"

"Good idea," Mum whispered, and wrapped her arm around Athena's shoulders.

"Bigger question," Daniel said, as he helped shovel everything into the boxes. "If things aren't good, can they stop the truck before Pastor Rocky gets there?"

"We'll try," Sherwood said, his voice coming out of the phone tucked in Daniel's pocket.

It must have vibrated, because Daniel kind of flinched and hopped sideways. We all managed grins, but no laughter, as we waited for London's response.

"On your tablets," she said, just a few seconds short of my feeling nervous enough to ask again, to make sure she heard Athena the first time. "This is very interesting. I don't know if it answers your questions or just adds more."

We had enough tablets among us to have only three people on each, which gave everyone a good view without having to twist their necks. London explained as different bits of video came on the screen. She had accessed the security system at the rescue mission, and went back to around the time Frankie, Leo and Achmed showed up. Each video had time and date stamps in the lower left corner. Several times she just showed frames, so we could study the images. We watched the three men arrive at the mission and talk to the greeters at the door, then get passed from one worker to another, getting fed and then examined by doctors. Leo and Achmed were immediately taken to the detox ward in the infirmary, according to the label on the recording. Frankie visibly declined once he was separated from the other two men, shaking and nervous and pale. He grew more distracted as the minutes ticked by, fast forwarded on the playback, as he answered questions and filled out forms.

When he rejoined the other two men, the change was just as rapid. I thought he was going to melt into a puddle, his relief was so obvious. He settled in a chair to keep watch over them, and apparently had to be badgered to step away and take a shower and shave and put on the clean clothes provided him. Fortunately, London sped up the progression of events, so we didn't have to sit and wait through real-time. The changes and improvements in all three men were encouraging.

Late night or very early morning of the first day after the trio arrived, our screens divided to show two views. We watched Frankie, still sitting vigil over the other two men's hospital beds, while shadowy movements approached the back door/loading dock area of the rescue mission. They took their time creeping up through the shadows. According to the clock on the video, it took more than half an hour. I didn't like creepy, shadowy figures with patience. It smacked of fanatical dedication.

About halfway through the wait for the creepers to show their faces, Frankie got fidgety. Just little twitches. Looking up as if he heard something. Flinching, looking around to the door, as if he thought someone was going to come through it. Then around the twenty-five-minute mark, he got up and paced, and kept going to the door to look out and down the hall.

At thirty-nine minutes, the creepers stepped into the dim light in the loading dock area. There were four of them. All dressed like Blues Brothers. Including the gangster-style hats and sunglasses. Seriously? Sunglasses at 3am? More BoBs.

At the same moment they stepped out of the shadows, it was like a switch flipped inside Frankie. He stumbled back to the beds and shook Achmed and Leo awake and tried to get them to their feet. Some alarm must have gone off, because a staffer in green hospital scrubs came in from another room and tried to stop him. Frankie was shaking his head and talking and fighting to get his friends out of the room. Something he said must have convinced the staffer, because he helped Frankie get the two men down the hall. The camera switched off and another view took its place. This one was labeled "panic room," and showed a thick door that swung open to allow the four men into the room. There were cots and blankets and what looked like shelves of supplies. The staffer and Frankie got Achmed and Leo settled, then the staffer left, pulling the door closed behind him. Frankie paced a few times, then leaned back against the only open stretch of wall, slid down so he crouched there on the floor, wrapped his arms around his legs and hid his face in his knees.

Chapter Nine

About the time the four men entered the panic room, the creeping BoBs outside froze. Their expressions were already hard to read with those dark glasses, but it seemed to me their faces went entirely blank. They turned around and walked away. No effort to creep, just calmly walked away.

"Okay, that was weird," Daniel said.

"Maybe I watch too much science fiction," Wallace said, "but that sure looked to me like a classic case of a telepathic link getting snapped, or an electronic signal dying, and the robots going back to their docking stations."

"That would imply that whoever was controlling them ..." Athena shook her head. "The signal or whatever was making them try to get into the building broke or died when those men stepped into that room."

"London," Pop said, "you don't happen to have any schematics for that panic room, do you?"

"The files with the adaptations for the room include soundproofing and blocking of electronic signals and thermal sinks. Essentially, anyone inside the room would be invisible to most heat or sound-seeking technology," London replied.

"Which implies the people at Sanctuary do provide sanctuary, to the extreme." He nodded and turned to look at the rest of us. "Okay, so it sure looked like Rocky's friend felt when those four got close, and they gave up when they lost the signal. So a two-way link?"

"Frankie needs to be searched for some high-tech gear, something that warned him. Maybe the same thing that was helping those four freaks find him in the first place," Ethan said.

"There is more," London said.

She showed us clips of Frankie interacting with different rescue mission workers during the following day. He reminded me of those sad dogs and cats in the commercials for an animal rescue organization, so woebegone and grateful for any little bit of kindness. If he had a tail, I would have expected to see it dragging a little bit and wagging every time someone talked to him. He stayed with Achmed and Leo all day and drooped visibly when the staff made him leave them the next evening. The camera followed him as he went to a bunk room and curled up, looking absolutely miserable among all those strangers. The time lapse sped through the hours, almost funny with the herky-jerky way Frankie tossed and turned.

Finally, he settled down and lay still. I started to feel a little relieved for him, because I knew what it was like to have a really restless night.

After about ten minutes, according to the time display on the screen, he sat up, stiff and straight, no more slouching. I got a shiver across my scalp before I saw his face. His expression. It was cold. The really freaky thing? Despite the grainy quality of the video record, due to the dim night light, Frankie's face sharpened, no more sagging. He raked his fingers through his shaggy hair, smoothing it back, and got up out of the bunk with an easy movement that implied power and confidence. The pitiful, battered, stray puppy Frankie was gone.

"Oh, that's not good," Daniel muttered.

"Can somebody go look for a pod in the basement?" Wallace said. He *ooph*ed, and I suspected Athena had elbowed him. When I glanced over, they were grinning at each other, and he leaned in and kissed her.

I turned back to watch Frankie stride with power and purpose out of that room. The cameras changed to watch him moving down the halls, and in the stronger light his features were clearer. Tighter. Colder. Anger sparked in those eyes. His shoulders didn't hunch like a puppy expecting to be hit, but were pulled back with what I could only call arrogance and yeah, anger. He reached the rescue mission's office and tried to go in, but the door was locked. He yanked on the doorknob and put a lot of effort into trying to turn it. I fully expected him to step back and either kick the door open or zap it with a lightning bolt from his clenched fist. That was just the impression he gave. He stomped down the hall, testing every door until he reached the security door leading to the lobby. When he reached to grasp the doorknob, he stiffened and his head snapped back and forth. He looked like he was being electrocuted or having a seizure. Then he just went boneless and collapsed in a pile on the floor. According to the rapidly ticking clock in the corner of the screen, he lay there for almost half an hour before someone came down the hall and saw him.

When they shook him awake, he was puppy-like, pitiful Frankie again and he kept shaking his head in response to whatever the staffers said. He stumbled and needed support getting back down the hall to the infirmary, where he was put in a bed in the same room in the detox ward with Achmed and Leo. His eyes, the one time he looked in the direction of the camera, were haunted.

"Somebody needs to warn Pastor," Daniel said.

Everybody seemed to turn at the same time to look at me. Why me? Hadn't he nominated Pop to take care of the church while he was away?

The knock on the classroom door startled all of us. Vivian tugged the door open and leaned in.

"Sorry, but that man is here, and he recognized your van and wants to talk to you, Charlie."

Just the way her mouth kind of pursed up, like she tasted something bad, when she said "that man" made me guess Stephen Grandstone was there. Amazing -- he had stepped inside our church, but the ceiling didn't fall in and he didn't burst into flames.

Pop started down the hall to the church office, with Mum right beside him. I was considering following them, if only to be a witness to whatever insane threat or demand the Grandstones were going to level on our church now. They had been far too quiet, and I couldn't find it in myself to feel sorry for them with the impending eviction looming over their heads even if it came from the Lightning Pathway.

My phone rang, with a number I hadn't used in years, but knew by heart: Neighborlee Children's Home.

It was Mrs. Silvestri. She wanted me to gather up "your team of troubleshooters," because NCH needed our help.

Stephen Grandstone had walked into the administrative office two days ago with a promissory note that was long overdue. He was ready to evict all the residents and teachers. His current stable of lawyers had all the documentation to hamstring anyone who stood against him.

Standard practice, for the Grandstones.

Yes, they had been too quiet far too long.

What wasn't standard procedure this time?

The promissory note was legitimate. Meaning he was entirely within his legal rights to confiscate the property that had become entirely Grandstone property by default.

It turns out that while one Mrs. Calpurnia Baumgartner was administrator of the children's home -- the same Mrs. Baumgartner who had advised Pastor Rocky to give in and let the Grandstones plan his life and career -- she had taken out an enormous loan in the name of the orphanage from the Grandstones. The promissory note had to be paid back in ten years. She promptly buried the paperwork, and deposited all that money in her personal account.

Mrs. Alcott, the current administrator, had called Mrs. Silvestri for help when she couldn't find Mrs. Baumgartner. The woman had vanished from the face of the Earth, and therefore wasn't available to answer questions, starting with what happened to the money and the paperwork. They had ransacked all the files, digging deep into the archive vaults, until they found a copy of the promissory note. The search had taken them two days.

Everything was legal, except of course that Mrs. Baumgartner had never asked permission from the board of directors for the children's home, and she had pocketed the money instead of putting it into the children's home bank account. The term of the promissory note had expired, and the wording made it clear that it would accrue interest at the current rate, adjusting with inflation and banking conditions until the holder of the note chose to collect what was due him. If the payout date of the note had passed with no effort on the part of the borrower to extend the deadline or start to pay off the money owed, then the holder of the note could demand everything be due by whatever date he so chose.

I repeat: everything was legal.

Hard to believe that a Grandstone was involved in something so straightforward and ... yes, I'm repeating myself ... legal.

While I was talking with Mrs. S, everyone gathered around, listening, getting more somber with every phrase they overheard. Athena later told me my expression was pretty grim. I promised Mrs. S we would get to work on solving the problem and ended the call, and then I had to take a few really deep breaths to calm myself before I shrieked something that should never be expressed within the walls of a church.

"London, I need you to find Mrs. Baumgartner, who used to be administrator for the children's home before Mrs. Silvestri." Then I took a few more deep breaths, before I looked around at everyone. "Grandstones have a totally legal promissory note from NCH and they're ready to cash it in and evict everybody tomorrow. It's decades overdue, which just makes it harder for us to fight."

"The timing is suspicious. Why do I have the feeling Stephen Grandstone's insistence on talking to Pastor Rocky is behind this note suddenly coming to light now, instead of decades ago when it defaulted?" Angela mused. Her voice was soft, but the fury in her eyes was strong enough to strike him dead, if he had been in the room.

He was in the church, though. Probably going into his snake oil salesman pitch to my folks right that moment.

I mentally yanked the door open, hard enough it banged against the wall. Before it swung closed again from the rebound, I was through the door, mentally pushing my wheelchair hard enough the wheels sang and my temples throbbed. The others had to run to catch up with me, tearing down the long hallway to the church office. Navigating the corner where the hallway ended, intersecting with the long hallway leading to the sanctuary and the church office, I nearly lost control and slammed into the wall. I managed to slow in time, although I think I went up on one wheel while making the turn.

Pop and Mum were standing with their backs to the church office door, while Stephan Grandstone paced in front of the door to the parking lot. I almost didn't recognize him, because he wasn't wearing his usual smirk or his self-righteous scowl that threatened doom and destruction on anyone who didn't give him what he wanted. Pop stood with his hands in his back pockets, looking almost relaxed. All three turned to look at me as I whizzed down the last ten yards or so of carpet to the doorway.

"Pop, this scumbuzzard is gonna foreclose on the children's home. What do you want from Pastor Rocky? You're holding NCH hostage to get what you want, aren't you?" I shouted, as I skidded to a stop a few yards away from them.

Grandstone's eyes lit up and some color returned to his pale, tight-drawn features.

"Lovely idea." He smirked. I wanted to leave tire tracks across his face. "It's a deal then. Simons gets the band back together for one final blowout concert by the end of the month --"

"How, when they're all dead?" Daniel barked.

"That's not what I hear." There was something odd in his smirk, the way it twitched. Almost like he knew something that made him afraid.

"Yeah, well nobody cares what you hear or what you think," Wallace grumbled.

Grandstone leveled a killer glare at him, but he just stuck his tongue out, and for good measure stuck his thumbs in his ears and waggled his fingers, as if they were antlers. Athena sputtered and elbowed him hard enough to make him bend double.

"Ah, yes, the wonderful promise of the next generation of defenders of this town." Grandstone's mouth twitched into his normal sneer, all fear or uneasiness gone. "As I was saying, one final concert right here in town in four weeks, or the orphans are out in the cold."

"It's August," Mum said.

"You know what I mean!" he roared. His gaze swept past me, at the others who had joined us, as he turned and stomped to the door. If he was wearing a cape, he would have swung it like Simon Legree, and twirled his stringy moustache for good measure.

"It's not a deal," Pop called after him. "We haven't agreed to anything. Rocky isn't even here to speak for himself."

Grandstone gave Pop the bird. In church!

I wanted so much for the panic bar to stick, so he'd hit the glass of the door with his face. The pneumatic hinge gave out a long, high-pitched squeal that seemed to make him move faster as he stomped across the nearly empty parking lot to his overpriced foreign car.

"Uh ... what just happened?" Athena said.

I was suddenly cold, as I replayed the last five minutes and realized what I had done with my fury.

"Pop, did I just mess up everything?"

"I don't really know, hon." Pop scrubbed at his face with his palms and Mum wrapped an arm around his shoulders.

"I gave him ammunition, didn't I?"

"What did he want?" Angela said.

"He wants ... " Pop made a strangling sound. "He wants the band back together. One more reunion concert of Magna Magma. Here in Neighborlee. That's what he's been badgering Pastor Rocky about for months."

"So foreclosing on NCH didn't have anything to do with bugging Pastor Rocky until I tied them both together for him." I felt sick enough, I was glad I was sitting down. Mum moved over to stand by me, and reached out to grip my shoulder, like now she might be feeling dizzy.

"Why would he want them brought onto Neighborlee's soil?" Angela mused.

"Here's a crazy idea," Ethan said, after we had stood there in the hall, looking at each other until the silence seemed to ring. "What if this drummer really is Lux, the leader of the cult? Not a lookalike, but the real man, but he's sort of split, two different people? It'd be kind of embarrassing if their divine leader is running around the country, thinking he's the drummer for a rock'n'roll band, and forgets all the things he's been telling his brainwashed followers."

"So they want to destroy Magna Magma and stop the problem from popping up?" Pop said. He slowly nodded, eyes narrowed in thought. "I've heard far crazier theories that proved true."

"Still doesn't explain why he's suddenly going after NCH," I said.

Pastor Rocky came up with an explanation, after we called him and left a message, and he called us back about twenty minutes later, at the next rest stop. He reminded us that the Lightning Pathway was going to take the Grandstones' property in Neighborlee. Maybe the Grandstones wanted to either talk the Lightning Pathway into a trade, or they were going to use the money from the sale of the orphanage property to pay their debt.

There were still too many unanswered questions, and a lot of blanks we needed to fill in.

For now, Pastor Rocky and Father Marty had been warned about Frankie's seeming split personality, as well as the weird connection between him and the BoBs. They both promised to tread carefully when they got to the rescue mission and saw the true condition of the three men. One of the most important questions was how or why Frankie had gone all the way to Nashville to seek help, when there had to be rescue missions in New Mexico where he could have gone for help. Pastor Rocky had a big To Do list to deal with, when he finally reached Sanctuary.

He and the friends running the mission needed backup. Especially if the BoBs came back, or Frankie stayed in his Lux mode long enough to get to the phone and make contact with his minions. Ethan and Stanzer decided to head down there and join them. Again, the next available flight to Nashville was a longer wait than if they drove, so they climbed into Ethan's car and headed down I-71.

Stanzer's departure essentially left Dawn in charge of the underage members of the Hunt. Angela was their legal guardian, but it was understood that Dawn was the leader. That didn't mean we were going to leave her to deal with things all by herself. The most important task resting on her shoulders was to monitor the website she and Stanzer had created, to try to make contact with members of the Hunt. This spring, the website had brought Cinden, Dayl, Ben, Serena and Obie to Neighborlee, and as a side bonus had led to the destruction of Wolcott, a traitor who had broken his vows to the Hunt and grew up to become a murdering despot.

Naturally, since we were all on high alert until we got a report from Pastor Rocky and Ethan and Stanzer, the next morning the reversal program on the Hunt's website had activated. Cosmo and Sherwood had had a little too much nasty fun creating shields and misdirects to keep people from locating the physical anchor spot for the website. Then they took it ten steps further and created a program to tag whoever dug deep enough into the hidden pages to prove they knew about the Hunt. Either they were members of the Hunt, or traitors. The reversal program activated tracers on all the devices linked to that person's account. Subliminal messages, both auditory and visual, gave instructions for how to find Stanzer. The tags, when the proper code was punched in, activated the GPS in their phones or tablets, to guide them to northeast Ohio.

Less than two hours later, the tag linked to the GPS program let us know someone was on their way, coming from the Dayton area. As far as Sherwood could tell, the people didn't know they were tagged. A tracer signal only he and London could access was following every step they took, every turn they made. Not only that, but Sherwood knew the music and audiobooks they were listening to in their car, and when they stopped for gas and pit stops. Every time they used their phone to take pictures and make notes, that information was being harvested as well.

"What, no pictures of the perps themselves?" I said, feeling a little snarky and a little old and left behind, because this was edging into Q's area of expertise. The new, young, snarky Q who considered Bond an old man.

"Sorry," Sherwood said, coming through Dawn's computer.

I was meeting with her and Angela and Ford in Stanzer's office. Dawn wanted us to know what was developing, and for all her technical wizardry as Athena's protégé, she felt better discussing the situation face-to-face.

"I've been focusing on other controls in the programming. I'm not able to turn around the camera just yet to catch whoever is using the phone. Sorry," he added.

"Hey, you've done miracles. I'm not complaining," I hurried to tell him.

The meeting didn't last long. We knew the make and model of the car and had an estimate of when the visitors would cross the border into Neighborlee. Sherwood sent the information to Gordon and other members of our support team.

One big problem made us worried that whoever had gotten that far into the website wasn't friendly. They hadn't followed instructions and filled out the contact form, not very well hidden on the website. Why were they coming to an unidentified place without making contact, getting clarification on vague instructions?

Were they enemies, thinking they were being clever and sneaking up on us?

Those enemies were going to get an unpleasant surprise, because the GPS would stop working before they crossed the border into Neighborlee.

Yeah, but that knowledge wasn't much comfort, with everything else weird going on lately.

"The instructions and the contact form are only clear for those who remember the written language," Dawn said, when I asked and pointed out the problem.

In that regard, I wasn't the old fogey that I felt like. Angela and Ford didn't think of it because they had far less experience with computers than I did.

"Whoever found the site might have been young enough not to know their letters, when the Hounds brought them to Earth. So they can't read most of the site. Our alphabet looks like runes, so we disguise our messages as artistic borders on the pages. The instructions to the Hunt are out in plain sight, yet hidden from those who don't know they're looking at an alphabet." She shrugged and looked even more unhappy. "They might have been a young child who had just started schooling when they left home, and can't read or write our native language very well. Plus, if they've lived on Earth long enough to be old enough to drive, what they did learn of our written language could be very dim and even mixed up in their memories. Wolcott and the chance of other traitors, and now creeps like the Lightning Pathway, are why we divided up the information. The Hounds enable them to hear and be conscious of some of the instructions, but not all. There's only so much we can do, so much information we can make available before we fall into the trap of traitors like Wolcott."

"Which just makes the other option more likely," Ford said. He sounded decidedly grumpy to bring it up. "Lux and LaRiche and their people know enough about the Hunt, they might have some of you under their influence. They're betraying you without realizing what they've done. Some of their musclemen could be on their way to meet up with you and attack. They didn't obey instructions and make contact because they want to sneak up on you."

"Then we need to be ready to show them just how wrong their thinking is," Angela said. "Neighborlee is your home, and Neighborlee takes care of its own."

We made one huge mistake ourselves: we forgot about the Hounds of Hamin.

Just after 1 that afternoon, Daniel and I were at the Sheridan house, filling in his parents and grandparents on what was happening, what we suspected, and what we were doing to defend ourselves, when Sherwood appeared on my tablet. He reported that the car he was tracking had gotten off of I-71 and the GPS had taken it on a detour. Instead of crossing the border into Neighborlee, it was now heading down a Cutterville city services access road, heading into the Metroparks. It would stop in fifteen minutes, in the old quarries, away from regular traffic. We needed to be ready to deal with whoever ended up there before they realized they had been stranded.

"They just used the contact form," Sherwood reported before I could do more than reach for my phone to call Angela and then Dawn. "Dawn is away from her desk and won't get it."

"Did you read it?" Arthur asked.

"That's interfering with ..." Sherwood grinned. "Good joke. I almost said that's interfering with the mail, but it's not really US mail, is it? They wrote in what I have to assume is a phonetic equivalent of the Hunt's native language. That supports Dawn's theory that they might have been too young to learn to read and write before they left their homeworld."

"Do you know where Dawn is?" I asked.

"She's out shopping, on foot. I tried to call her, but I guess she can't hear the phone in her purse. GPS says she's close to your house. Maybe she's --" He stopped and looked like he was listening to something or someone. "She just turned. I think she's heading for Divine's."

"Let's head her off." Daniel held out his hand to help me stand up.

"Something strange. The car has stopped about two hundred yards short of where the GPS is programmed to stop them." Sherwood shook his head. "I'm getting anomalous energy readings, like something is interfering with my programming."

"We'll figure it out." I reached for my tablet. Sherwood nodded and the screen blanked.

The Sheridan house was nice, but not terribly wheelchair accessible. Standard practice was to leave my wheelchair at the door and walk with the help of several spiffy canes Arthur obtained for my use. With all the strain we had been going through the last few days, my legs were undergoing a lot of tingling and numb spells, giving me more reason than ever to want some nasty retribution on Kerri and her minions. That battle we had last winter had set me back too far in my recovery.

Still, there were a few benefits to being wobbly. Daniel had a tendency for chivalry, and it was kind of nice to walk down the hall to the front door and my waiting wheelchair with his arm around me. Plus, being this close to him, I couldn't see when he got that weird expression, like he was happy and waiting for something to go utterly and horribly wrong. Yeah, some benefits all around.

He didn't have that expression on his face by the time I was settling into the passenger seat of his truck. Unfortunately, I made the mistake of looking back to wave to his parents, who had walked out with us. They were smiling and looking a little too pleased, considering the situation report we had been discussing before Sherwood interrupted. *Please, oh please, don't let them be getting stupid ideas like the ones I keep getting when he looks at me too long with that particular weird expression ...*

We caught up with Dawn two streets before turning down the dead-end street to Divine's. She sidestepped onto the lawn of the house she was passing as we pulled up next to her. Then she really looked at us, rolled her eyes and stumbled a little as she stepped back onto the sidewalk. It was good to know she was alert.

"Get in. Sherwood said the visitors sent you an email," I said, and opened the door, so she could slide into the cab behind me.

"What did they want?" she asked, punctuated with a grunt as she reached up to catch the door and pull it shut behind her.

"He didn't say. Respecting your privacy," Daniel said.

I met Dawn's eyes in the rearview mirror and had to laugh despite the seriousness of the moment. Her expression was evenly divided between "Huh?" and "Has he blown a fuse?"

"He looked," I said, "but he thought it was phonetic, trying to approximate your home language."

That got a nod and her frown smoothed out. She didn't waste any time asking questions and pulled out her phone. "I really have to get a thinner purse, or turn up the ringer to chop-and-liquefy. He tried six times to call me." She sighed and I heard her tapping away. Silence until we pulled up in front of Divine's. Then she let out a "huh," followed by a sigh.

"Good news or bad?" Daniel said.

"It's taking me a while. Hold on. It's long ..."

Chapter Ten

We waited a minute or two, and when I studied Dawn in the rearview mirror, she was frowning at her phone and moving her lips, probably sounding out the words. More support for the phonetic theory. We got out of the truck and Daniel helped me into my wheelchair. I was about to suggest that we go in and she could join us when she was ready, when Dawn put her phone away. She climbed out of the truck, and we walked slowly through the gate and up to the door of Divine's.

"It took a couple reads to figure out what they're saying, but … yeah, I was right. Clan Cari, secondborn, Andris … and Dabra, secondborn of sub-clan Shole. Both were five, six years old when they were given to the Hounds. He was here four years before she showed up, almost in his backyard. The Hounds brought her to him and they've been together ever since." She caught her breath. "They're married, and they have four children. They've been on the run from Lightning Pathway since one of them saw a Hound rescue their youngest daughter from a child molester."

"Wow, that's pretty bad luck," Daniel muttered.

"But if one of them could see a Hound, he should be on our side. He could be a Lost Kid, for all we know. Or another member of the Hunt," I said. As soon as the words left my lips, I wished I hadn't said them. That wasn't something Dawn needed to think about, with this heavy news that had just landed on her.

"Whoever he is, they think he's followed them here," Dawn said. "A Hound stopped them in the park, won't let them come any closer. They want to know what to do. They were afraid the website was a trap. They've been on the run, basically, since Lux and his goons tried to get them to join up about two years ago."

"Ouch," Daniel muttered.

"Why did the Hound stop them?" Angela said, startling all three of us. She was standing in the shade of her front porch. I swear, she wasn't there when we pulled up, and I didn't hear the front door open.

"They don't know. They're hoping we're for real, and the Hound doesn't want them to lead the Pathway creep to us." Dawn gestured with her phone. "The longer I wait to answer, the more doubts they're going to have."

"I have an idea," I said. "Kind of a version of Shock and Awe. And if Jane can get away from the shop, we can get there a lot faster than driving.

Respond, and tell them you're coming and you're bringing friends, and we should be able to deal with the creeps right away."

Dawn frowned for a few seconds, then she got to work. I glanced at Daniel as I pulled out my phone to call Jane at the spa. He was grinning, so he had a good guess what I intended. All I had to say to Jane was that we needed the Ghost's help to sneak up on some people and possibly rescue more members of the Hunt, and she was on her way over to us.

She arrived before Dawn finished a short message that took some effort to figure out how to approximate her homeworld language with the English alphabet.

"We need to get Sherwood working on installing your alphabet on your computer and phone so you can do that a lot faster," Daniel offered, once Dawn had hit the 'send' key.

She managed a nod and a tense smile. Then I explained my plan. It wasn't that I was suddenly a brilliant tactician. This was a somewhat nasty trick I had been wanting to pull for a while now, and hoped it would be just a trick, a joke, and not something we would have to use in earnest in a tense or even dangerous situation. Like right now.

Angela laughed and insisted on coming with us. Then she told Dawn to call Stanzer and let him and Ethan know what we were doing. Soon we were flying, inside a globe of the Ghost field, to the park to find the car with Andris and Dabra and their children.

We got there in something like five minutes, and got an answer to a question I don't think any of us had wanted to ask: why hadn't the Lightning Pathway goons confronted the fugitives when they caught up with them on the park road with no witnesses?

It was a stereotypical kind of face-off: a family in a blue minivan facing a black sedan with tinted windows. Four Hounds walked around the sedan that looked like it had been stolen from a Connery-era Bond movie. Why did bad guys always have to drive black cars? Every time one of them tried to open a door, a Hound shoved the door closed, hard enough we could hear the slam through the faint shimmering chime of the Ghost field, hovering a good twenty feet up in the air. We waited a couple minutes to assess the situation, and for Dawn to answer a phone call. Nice of Jane to adjust the Ghost field so we could get cell phone coverage.

"That was Gordon," Dawn said. "Stayn called him, and he's bringing backup."

"That works nicely," Angela said with a nod. "But I don't think we should delay any longer. I have to think Andris and his family are getting a little nervous."

Jane expanded the Ghost field as we descended, so by the time we touched down on the blacktop road leading through the park, the bubble was wide enough to enclose the minivan and leave room for us to stand around it. The little family inside stared at us. It must have been a little strange, even for members of the Hunt, to have people suddenly appear around them out of nowhere.

The minivan was now invisible. I heard the BoBs yelling in the black sedan. They got out of their car. The Hounds didn't stop them now, but retreated to settle around the minivan, partially in and out of the Ghost field. It didn't seem to bother them at all.

Dawn stepped up to the driver's side door and did some complicated gesture with both her arms. She explained later it was a ritual greeting and assurance of peace. Then she said something in what had to be their homeworld language, sort of bubbling and full of liquid consonants. Andris and Dabra and their children slumped a little in their seats and their faces lit up with relief. Dawn stepped back to let Andris open his door. I was standing along the front of the car on the passenger side, and the day had officially gotten a little too long for me. Well, it was kind of awkward to bring my wheelchair in the Ghost field, after all. I leaned on the front quarter panel as Dabra got out. She did that hand gesture and made a little bow to me and started talking in that language. I stopped her with a hand up in the air.

"Sorry, Dawn is the only member of the Hunt. We're just friends," I hurried to say.

Dabra gave me a relieved look. I found out later that she preferred speaking English. She and Andris had only started teaching their children their homeworld language maybe three years ago, and were ashamed to admit they had forgotten a lot of it. Well, duh, they were pretty young when they left home. They should have been proud they remembered as much as they did.

Dawn hurried to explain about the Ghost field, and that we were invisible to the enemy now. Then we all turned to look at the BoBs, who were stomping and staggering around the perimeter of the Ghost field. They kept bending over and reaching forward, trying to find the car. It was easy to see where the Ghost field ended, because every time one of them touched it, he sort of slid slideways, pushed aside or repelled. It reminded me of the scene from *Restaurant at the End of the Universe*, where Ford Prefect was going ga-ga over the frictionless coating on a spaceship, so it was nearly impossible to touch, their hands just slid right off it.

"So do we just wait here until they give up and go away?" Andris asked, once he and his family had been introduced to all of us.

"Something tells me they aren't the type to give up and go away." Daniel sounded almost amused, which was really not all that encouraging. "Look at them. They're true believers."

I took a really good look at the six BoBs, and I understood what he was saying.

Black suits, kind of frumpy, not fitting quite right. Black hats. Black, dime store style sunglasses. Black Oxford shoes. No fancy tech gear. Only three had pistols. Kind of snub nose revolvers, maybe. I didn't get a really good look at them. I had to go back to my original assessment of their car -- refugees from a Connery Bond movie.

"Wannabes," I murmured. "Men in Black, but with no alien tech gear to back them up. Or maybe they're Blues Brothers fans, kind of like how people dress up for *Rocky Horror Picture Show*."

"Reprieve," Daniel said, gesturing down the road coming from town.

Movement resolved into two vehicles coming around the bend in the road, past the thick clumps of bushes and overhanging branches. Gordon in the Neighborlee PD SUV, followed by another police cruiser.

The six BoBs were so busy trying to find the van, and being repelled by the Ghost field, they didn't notice the oncoming vehicles right away. When they did, they let out yelps and curses and dashed back to their car.

The Hounds sort of blipped out and blipped back in to surround the car again, and shoved the doors closed. Now the BoBs couldn't get the car doors open to climb in. I really, really hoped they had left the keys in the ignition and the Hounds had locked the doors.

One of them could see the Hounds. He backed away slowly, hands held up, as if that was enough to stop them from attacking.

They didn't, of course.

"We need to talk with that one, agreed?" Daniel pointed at him as he backed away from his teammates. One Hound was clearly herding him.

The other BoBs were still banging and pulling on the doors of their car, trying to get in. One even tried to get into the trunk, but a Hound sat on the lid and gave him a big doggy grin, teeth shining and eyes glowing. The guy was lucky he couldn't see what was looking down at him, or he probably would have fainted or maybe blown a few dozen circuits or wet his pants. Probably all three at the same time. Fun to think about, but not fun to have happen close by.

"Agreed." Jane frowned in concentration and twitched one hand at the BoB. He jerked and went up in the air, sort of tumbling around like the gravity went out on him. Which it probably did.

The other five didn't notice. They were too busy scrambling and tripping over each other, escaping Gordon and the other cop, who had gotten out of their cars and were taking their good old time approaching them. Granted, with guns out.

The BoBs tried to run, but the Hounds kept blipping in and out and stopping them. Unseen by them, but we could see and yeah, it was kind of hard not bursting out laughing. The Hounds either tripped the runners, or just stood there and the BoBs slammed into them and bounced off and fell to the ground, then a second later scrambled to their feet and tried to run. Usually, the panicking dummies tried to keep running the same direction, which led to the same results. I think they were honestly relieved to have Gordon and the other cop grab them and haul them into their two patrol cars and shove them into the back seats.

One Hound walked up to Gordon and bowed its head. Gordon reached out very gingerly and stroked down that long, blue-black furry neck. He kept looking from one side to another, the way people do when they don't want to look but they have to look.

Oh, heck ... Gordon could see the Hounds now. Just when had he crossed the line? When had his life-long exposure to the energy and magic of Neighborlee finally changed him? Or maybe it would be more accurate to say that his distant Lost Kid heritage had finally been activated?

Gordon had the sense not to make drastic moves and confuse the other cop with petting something that wasn't there. He dropped his hand back to his side, rubbing his fingers and looking a little dazed for a few seconds. I made a mental note to ask what it felt like, touching a Hound. I sure hadn't had the guts to try. Yes, the Hounds had touched me the few times they saved my bacon, but I hadn't been brave enough to touch one in return. Gordon said something to his partner, who immediately drove away with three prisoners. He had two in his car, but he was obviously waiting for us to show up and explain things.

"Guys, Gordon can see the Hounds," I said, just in case some of them didn't pick up on that.

"I would be surprised if he couldn't, after all this time and all this exposure to different levels of power," Angela said. "He does have some Lost Kid blood in him, after all."

"Think it's safe to come out of hiding?" Jane said. "Maybe blow some circuits in the two sitting in the car, make it easier to get answers from them?" She grinned at us.

Andris and Dabra and their children gave us those uneasy smiles, like they wanted to have fun with this, but they still had a lot of questions.

"That might help," Angela said after a moment of thought, "but think about Gordon. He still needs to take things slowly. He doesn't know about this, after all." She gestured at the field surrounding us, making us invisible and inaudible to those outside.

A Hound stepped into the Ghost field and nudged Dawn. She seemed to understand what it wanted. She shrugged and caught hold of the ruff of fur around the Hound's neck, and let it lead her out of the field. Fortunately, Gordon had his back to us, so he didn't react when she stepped out and became visible.

She basically told Gordon her interpretation of what we had decided and done. They agreed he would take the last two BoBs to the police station, come up with an explanation Chief Tanner could work with to justify holding them, and come back to talk with us.

Then the cruiser came back, a little faster than was justified on these back access roads. The other officer slammed on the brakes and jumped out of the car. He was waving and gesturing at the car, and we could just see the three prisoners, slumped over.

And of course, we had to wait until Gordon and the other cop conferred. Dawn waited until he had his back to us again, before coming back, without the Hound this time. Jane let her through the field.

"The three all started screaming and having seizures as soon as Jameson crossed the border into town," she said. "Gordon wants to take all of them to the hospital to get checked out and have the police in Cutterville take custody of them, since they were captured in the Cutterville portion of the park."

"That is very wise," Angela said slowly. Her gaze seemed to be on something else the rest of us couldn't see. "As soon as they crossed the border? As in, they have been influenced enough by the enemy they cannot enter Neighborlee?"

"Oh ... heck," I said, and really did wish I had wasted time to learn some conversational Klingon with Pete and other members of our club. Nothing I could think of to say would come close to how I was feeling right about then.

"Okay, the creeps in black who were spying on Pastor Rocky didn't have any trouble coming into Neighborlee, but now these guys do? Are we dealing with two different enemies again?" Jane said.

"What she said," I blurted. "You think Kerri has come back?"

"They could only get in at those bogus 'welcome' signs, before the shield got boosted. Or it could be like what happened with that P.I., Jones," Dawn said. "He was able to come through the shield at first, but when he got influenced by Kerri, he got bounced. Just like these guys."

"So -- what?" Daniel said. "Kerri's people are taking over the Lightning Pathway people?"

"Just what we need," Jane muttered. "Next they'll be making an alliance with Big Ugly."

"Not if we act swiftly. First, we need answers. Let's hope we get many answers from that one." Angela nodded at the BoB who was still struggling and going head over heels inside his prison globe of energy. It was a good thing we couldn't hear him, even if we could see him, because his face was red and his mouth was going and I was surprised he hadn't used up all the oxygen inside the bubble. Maybe that would be a good idea? Knock him unconscious, just long enough to shut him up and scare him into behaving?

Finally, the two patrol cars and their prisoners left. Jane released us from the globe of the Ghost field, while keeping the BoB prisoner. We took a little time to talk with Andris and Dabra and their children, making better introductions, figuring out what to do, explaining the situation in Neighborlee, and making some fast arrangements. Angela assured us Divine's would have more than enough furniture, linens, and dishes to fill one of the empty apartments in Stanzer's building. Daniel and I were put in charge of a grocery store run, to fill their refrigerator and cupboards and provide cleaning supplies. We were still figuring things out when Gordon called me.

"Okay, I am definitely, officially freaking out," Gordon said. "Did I see those big dogs that nobody else seemed to see? Did I really touch it, or did I just blow a few circuits?"

"Those are the Hounds of Hamin. Interdimensional guardian beasts for Dawn and Stanzer and the refugees they're trying to contact and bring to town for safety. What you didn't see were all of us hiding in plain sight, with some new refugees that the Blues Brothers were following. Be careful, when you get those weirdos into interrogation or whatever you call it. They could be panicky enough to get themselves locked up in a padded cell, which might save us all a lot of trouble." Now it was my turn to sigh. "Or they could calm down enough to think clearly and threaten charges of religious discrimination or hate crime abuse or prejudice or whatever. They belong to a really weird cult thing called the Lightning Pathway, and they basically know enough about otherworldly visitors to put them into their prophetic writings, so they think they're justified hunting down and capturing people like ... well, the family they chased into the park today."

I nearly choked, realizing just in time I was about to say, "people like us." Gordon was getting enough brain-blowing or frying or whatever today. He didn't need that, added on top of everything else.

"Okay ... I'll do my best. Is it good or bad that nobody else seemed to see them?"

"Gordon, you are soaking up magic and it's giving you the ability to see into a whole new dimension."

"Like I said, is that good or bad?" He chuckled and cut the connection before I could respond.

"How shall we deal with this one?" Andris said, when I moved back over to rejoin the group.

The sixth BoB had calmed down enough to just float inside the Ghost field. No more struggling and screaming or trying to break his way out. He just tumbled and watched us.

"Jane, I think the Hounds are more than adequate to deal with him, if he tries anything," Angela said.

A second later, the Ghost field flared bright, and vanished. The BoB dropped about four feet to the ground. He tried to land on his feet, but stumbled and went to one knee, and stayed there, catching his breath and glaring at us. Until his gaze focused on Angela.

"You. This is your doing." Something about his voice held a growl and an echoing effect. It reminded me of the Visitors in the two *V* mini-series. The special effect got dropped when it became a TV series. Probably too expensive to keep up.

Angela said nothing, but stepped up to the front of the group facing him and clasped her hands in front of herself. I had a vision of her dressed in Middle Ages clothes, the grand lady of the castle, with a breastplate and a sword in her hand, and her hair blowing in a stiff breeze as a storm rolled in overhead. The guy should have had the intelligence to be terrified and lose some of the attitude. Should have.

"Hand over the demi-gods to be put to proper use, and welcome us into the shelter," he continued, as he struggled to his feet. He looked a little irked to find his legs weren't cooperating fully.

"Why?" Daniel stepped past Angela, putting himself between her and the BoB.

Right then, his knight in shining armor tendencies were coming through. I really hoped he wouldn't need to put his immunity talent to good use protecting her. If Ethan were here, I wondered how he would be dealing with this idiot who dared to give Angela orders. Right now would be a good time for his armor to manifest like the sword had, to terrify the creep into some politeness, at the very least.

Or maybe this BoB had gone too far, and he didn't have the intelligence to be properly afraid anymore.

"Welcome us," the BoB growled, "or suffer the consequences when we knock down your gates and drink up your power and reduce it to ash and dirty rainwater."

The guy had a way with words and imagery -- not!

"You are never welcome," Angela said. Winter winds blew at the back of her quiet, calm voice. There was no hint of the humor that usually tinted her voice, even when dealing with the nastiest lunatic and entitlement-attitude twit. "You and your kind will never be welcome. May you always wander in darkness and silence and cold."

"Welcome us!" he shouted, rearing back so he sort of leaped to his feet and put about two feet of empty space between feet and ground.

Before his feet touched down again, the Hounds leaped. Two knocked him flat. One sat on his chest, the other sat on his legs. The man seized, arching his back. I was in just the right place to see sparks in his eyes. Poison green with touches of red. He bit his tongue hard, so blood trickled from the corner of his mouth after he collapsed.

Daniel put him in the black sedan, to take him to the hospital to join his fellow BoBs. The Hounds impressed on Dawn that this one had pretty much been erased. He wouldn't be able to tell his bosses anything. If they ever found him. Angela planned to have a long talk with Gordon, and then go with him to meet with Chief Tanner, to tangle the paperwork so the Lightning Pathway wouldn't find their minions for a long time.

The Hounds took the BoBs' car once Daniel drove back to the park to retrieve his truck. I didn't ask what they did with it. If they didn't destroy it utterly, like taking it through to another dimension, I hoped they took it so far away its discovery would lead the Lightning Pathway on a really wild and totally useless goose chase.

Dawn and I took the van with the children, to drive them to Stanzer's building to meet the rest of the Hunt. Dabra and Andris flew back in the Ghost field with Jane and Angela, to have a conference and settle some things, and gather up furnishings for the apartment. Dawn and I had the job of starting the indoctrination on the drive to the apartment. Then Daniel picked me up in his truck and we did a massive amount of grocery shopping in a very short amount of time.

The children felt the soft, brief tingle-zing in the air when we drove across the border into Neighborlee. They had seen the Hounds, and their parents had been teaching them about the homeworld, so we didn't need the "Hey, don't freak out, but magic is real" talk. They had also seen enough with the Hounds and the BoBs, we didn't need to waste time assuring them they were safe in Neighborlee. At least, safe until we got to work on all that necessary paperwork to create new identities for them, and get the kids registered for school, which would be starting in a few weeks. All that fun, tedious, normal Human living stuff. Thank goodness we had the Sheridans and their people working with us now. We didn't have to drop a huge load of career-threatening favors on Col. Hayward's shoulders.

Once the family was settled, we gathered at Divine's to discuss what had happened and what we had learned. Ford joined us, Athena and Wallace, Angela, Arthur Sheridan, Jane and Kurt. The situation was getting more confusing and grim. What exactly did Lightning Pathway want? Were the BoBs part of Lightning Pathway still, or had they been taken over by Kerri's group of rebel Fae?

Bottom line: someone wanted to be *welcomed* to Neighborlee. Someone who looked on the surface like an ordinary human, but maybe they weren't, had never been? This was different from the doppelgangers, but the clothes were close enough to that close call last summer, when we brought Mum and Pop home and forward through time from the Bermuda Triangle. When Kerri and her black-suited cohorts were trying to get their hands on the beads that Pete's mother had found.

Was Kerri involved?

"Gordon said all the prisoners had a second fit or seizure or whatever," Daniel said. "I'm figuring it was the same time the Hound squashed their boss. They have to be all tied together."

"Are you thinking about the sleepwalkers last winter?" I asked.

"Someone in control?" He sighed. "Yep."

"What bugs me is the whole asking to be welcomed into Neighborlee," Ford said. "Why do they need that? I know the shield was keeping the doppelgangers out, but you faced real people, ordinary humans today."

"Or at least they used to be," Arthur said, "until they got involved with Lightning. Wouldn't they have lost control of their shapes or their masks when they were knocked out, if they were doppelgangers?"

Jane reported that she had called Hoax, to see if anyone had any ideas and to have a team come out to do what needed to be done to examine the BoBs. We really wouldn't know anything until this new problem had been removed from the hands of the authorities and thoroughly examined with methods that belonged in a Marvel movie. The sooner they were out of the hands of authorities who would ask a lot of problematic questions, the better. We were all depending on Gordon to come up with a good enough cover story to not just keep them locked up, but stop them contacting their bosses.

We were lucky that Neighborlee didn't have a hospital, so they hadn't been sideways invited through the shield by being taken there for medical care. There was still a danger if the BoBs regained consciousness and tricked someone into formally welcoming them to Neighborlee. I knew at least twenty people at my church alone who worked at the hospital.

Plus, there were the commands in scripture not to welcome opposing spirits into homes or the fellowship of believers. We had spent several Wednesday night youth group sessions discussing the deep spiritual implications of this when I was in high school.

Angela readily admitted there were parallels when it came to spirit beings, and rules and guidelines in other worlds and dimensions. And when those beings visited Earth, they had to abide by those rules. Which was why some so-called charms, both physical and spoken, actually worked, when common sense said they wouldn't. Because what was being faced wasn't from this world and had to abide by otherworldly rules.

But the BoBs, as far as we could tell, weren't otherworldly visitors. Were they?

"They could be so strongly under the influence of those visitors, invaders," Angela said, "they are essentially operating on a metaphysical power of attorney. By proxy. What affects their masters affects them."

"But it all brings us back to the biggest problem," Ford said. "Someone wants to be welcomed into Neighborlee. Why? What do they want to win?"

"These people are using modern-day disguises," Arthur said. "New Age cults with their fancy words and light shows, to cover up some very old magic and old rules they are relying on."

"It's the ancient struggle since before I came into my guardianship," Angela said. "This could all be a distraction, going after the Hunt. It could be a new tactic, to get servants with otherworldly powers to tear down our protections. It could be a new enemy who has decided we are just the sort of tasty treat they need to add to their strength and their domain. But someone wants into Neighborlee, and we will not admit them. No matter what it takes."

We wrote up notes and Jane sent her follow-up report to Hoax. There was only so much we could discuss and speculate on and theorize before we were covering the same ground and wasting time.

Gordon called with a preliminary report on the six prisoners just as we were finishing up. The five underlings were awake and babbling and claiming they didn't know what was going on. Then a short time later they insisted on making phone calls, supposedly to whoever hired them to follow Andris and his family. One problem: the number was disconnected. It would take court orders and all sorts of paperwork to find out when the number had been disconnected. What were the chances that the phone number had been shut down just since the BoBs had their seizures? That implied that someone not only sensed the seizures when they happened but had the power and authority to give such an order and make it happen that quickly.

The sixth BoB was awake but unresponsive. The doctors were preparing to run all sorts of tests on him, but they already suspected brain damage. When the Hounds erased someone, they really erased.

Basically, the BoBs had been disavowed, or maybe more accurately they had been discarded after messing up their capture assignment.

We weren't getting any answers any time soon. And we were still waiting to see what Ethan and Stanzer came up with when they had spent time with Frankie, Achmed and Leo.

~~~~~

Pastor Rocky called after dinner to report on the situation. His friends running the rescue mission were also medical doctors and had privileges at several local hospitals for a limited number of hours each month to use some pretty high-tech equipment. They ran full physicals on the trio, putting them at the top of the list after Frankie's seizures and his change in personality and the attempts of the BoBs to break in. They diagnosed Leo and Achmed with general malnutrition and a wide variety of physical damage resulting from months in stressful conditions. They couldn't remember what had happened. They had no memories of the reunion tour concerts, or even getting contacted by the other members of Magna
~~~~~

Magma. The same for Frankie. He didn't know what they had been going through when he found them. He couldn't remember how he ended up in the main compound of the Lightning Pathway, but he thought maybe he had had a flashback from a bad acid trip maybe thirty years ago. Apparently, that acid flashback had wiped most of his life since then from his memory. He had an impression that he had gone into rehab and gotten clean and sober, and hoped he had stayed that way. He was sure he had gotten completely out of the music biz, because everyone he knew in the industry was a bad influence, meaning they were more likely to get him hooked on drugs and drinking again than they were to help him stay dry.

That partly explained why he had seemed to vanish off the face of the planet. Some of the memories he could dredge up gave the impression he had done migrant farm work and took jobs that paid under the table and went from one homeless shelter to another.

How had he found Achmed and Leo at the Lightning Pathway compound?

His memories began with an explosion of some kind. He remembered fire and sirens, and waking up in a hospital room of some kind. When he went looking for something for a killer headache, there was no one around, and he somehow got outside. He was barefoot and his clothes were torn and burned, and there was yelling and screaming and sirens and a fire in the distance. All the activity was around the fire, so he went the opposite way, looking for clothes. He found his way into another building that seemed like a hospital, but all the lights were off. Apparently, there was a power outage in the compound. He found clothes, and found Achmed and Leo, drugged and tied to hospital beds. He was so happy to see his old friends, and so sure that he was going to get blamed for the chaos on the other side of the compound, he grabbed everything he could, dumped his two unconscious friends into a wheeled hamper and got out of there. He got past the walls and went into some woods, where he found a barn that was falling apart, and hid there until the other two men could regain consciousness. That took three days, and during that time he ventured out at night to find supplies. Newspapers in dispenser boxes and eavesdropping on radio reports and looking in windows to see TV news filled in enough pieces, he learned he was in New Mexico, the place he escaped from belonged to a group called the Lightning Pathway, and someone had attacked their compound.

Chapter Eleven

That was more than a month ago, which coincided with the report London had found of the woman who took a bazooka to the gates of the Lightning Pathway compound, trying to free her husband. She vanished after explosions rocked the compound, but London found security camera images of her. She matched images of a woman seen to be very affectionate with Frankie at several after-concert parties at the start of the reunion tour. There were no official records of Frankie or Lux marrying anyone, but we all found it entirely believable that he had partied hard and crazy with a woman, who, under the influence of drugs, believed they were married. And still under the influence of drugs, had been crazy enough to attack the compound.

The only question was how she had trailed Frankie to the compound, after the entire band had been reported killed.

Frankie waking up to himself in the Lightning Pathway compound raised more questions. Was Ambrose Lux a doppelganger who had stolen Frankie's appearance and life for nefarious purposes? Maybe Frankie was just an unlucky body double, grabbed, drugged, and programmed to take the heat when disillusioned followers attacked? Or was LaRiche the actual boss, making Frankie just an unlucky figurehead?

I was getting really sick of all the doppelgangers and mistaken identities and lies and messed up memories and suppositions. Who could we trust? Did anyone have any answers? What kind of stories would Achmed and Leo give when they were detoxed and coherent?

Pastor Rocky got blood and tissue samples from his friends to hand over to Col. Hayward for testing. The men running the mission knew their limits. They were concerned enough for Leo, Achmed, and Frankie to want as much help as they could get. And honestly, they were afraid to turn over the blood, urine, and saliva samples to local health authorities once the name of Lightning Pathway came up. The self-proclaimed "ministry" already had a growing reputation among the down-and-outers, moving northward from their headquarters in New Mexico. People who had escaped the influence of Lightning Pathway were regularly silenced, but the stories they told about the tactics used on them still spread, despite the powerful connections LaRiche used to polish the public image. If only a fraction of the stories were true, the Lightning Pathway had people everywhere. So when Pastor Rocky offered to get the samples to more secure hands, his friends running the rescue mission leaped at the opportunity.

They agreed to personally deliver the samples, rather than trusting to a commercial delivery service. That meant waiting a few days to drive back to Neighborlee. For security, and the increasingly creepy situation, the wait was worth it. We hoped.

Finally, we got to ask the hard questions. Starting with why Frankie went all the way from New Mexico to Nashville to that specific rescue mission. How did those three men, two of whom were still having a hard time staying upright for more than an hour at a time, get all that distance without being caught? Clearly Lighting Pathway was on their trail. How else would the BoBs have showed up at the rescue mission right after Frankie, Achmed and Leo attained sanctuary?

Frankie was difficult to interrogate. He was exhausted to the point of being incoherent a large portion of the time, because he got so little sleep. He woke with nightmares a dozen times in the day or night. Achmed and Leo were slowly coming out of the worst of the withdrawal, but their recovery progress was hard to predict. Pastor Rocky talked with Frankie as much as possible. His general impression was that his old friend had been living in a haze for years and had no idea how much time had passed. He claimed he couldn't remember the reunion tour, much less getting together with anyone from Magna Magma.

Why did I find that story so hard to accept? Pastor Rocky wanted to believe, but admitted he had some major guilt-trip baggage influencing his perceptions and decisions.

Arthur offered to put the three men in treatment at a Sheridan facility. Achmed and Leo could finish drying out and detoxifying, and Frankie could have full-time supervision and testing. The facility was near Aurora, so a safe distance from Neighborlee. I think that made us all feel a little better about the very real risk that bringing the three of them to our home territory would guide the Lightning Pathway to our doorstep.

Reluctantly, we passed along to Pastor Rocky the news about Stephen Grandstone's visit to the church, and the demand for the concert in exchange for releasing Neighborlee Children's Home from the promissory note.

"That man is like a rabid dog with a bone," Pastor Rocky muttered. "Why is it so important to him to meet Frankie face-to-face? That's what he wanted, more than a concert. He said he was willing to let bygones be bygones if I'd do him that favor. Frankie was his hero, and he'd give anything for a chance to just shake his hand."

"Bygones?" Ford said. "That sounds like a Grandstone, constantly insisting that he's innocent and everyone else is the villain, attacking him for no good reason. Sure, for an autograph, he's going to be generous and forget all the crimes you never actually committed against him? How gracious." He punctuated that with a snort.

"When did this conversation happen?" Athena said. She was busy tapping away at her computer, and I had the impression, without seeing the screen, that she was working hard with London. "Back when the reunion concert was still wishful thinking? Or maybe right after you got that first call, inviting you to join in?"

"You know ... the timing did seem a little too close, now that I think about it," Pastor Rocky said, after a short thoughtful pause.

"Back before the Lightning Pathway put the squeeze on the Grandstones and decided to evict them?" Wallace said. He and Athena shared a significant glance.

"Okay, you two," Ford said, "what are you thinking, or theorizing or whatever?"

"It's a possibility in one of the scenarios Sherwood and I have been assembling," London said. Athena turned her computer around so we could all see London on the screen. "What if Lux and Frankie *are* the same person?"

"Then fleeing from Lightning Pathway would be an act, fake, a trick," Daniel said.

"I just had an awful idea," I said. The theory that leaped to the front of my mind made me physically queasy. "Pastor Rocky, how did he know you were a member of Magna Magma?"

Silence rang through the room.

"How do the Grandstones know half the things they know?" Pastor Rocky finally said. He let out a loud, shuddering kind of sigh. "You know, I think I'm finally getting too old for all this. I should have asked that question the first time he came after me. I was just shocked enough and scrambling for balance, when he confronted me with knowing I used to be Drake Abbott, and August Miller before that. I should have denied knowing what Magna Magma was, in the first place."

"You told him the truth, and he didn't believe that," Ford pointed out. "You said you weren't in contact with anyone. Why would he believe you if you said you weren't Drake Abbott and August Miller?"

"Grandstones are such liars, they can't conceive of anyone else telling the truth," Stanzer said, his voice somewhat muffled, meaning he wasn't sitting close to Pastor Rocky's phone.

"True."

"The more important question might be how long he has known your other identities," Angela said. "How long has he been sitting on that knowledge, saving it until it was useful? London, did you ever find that list of names of people the Grandstones were going to turn over to Lightning Pathway, in exchange for erasing their debt?"

"There was a partial list, on Rosco Grandstone's computer, in an email where Stephen said they were all useless names, none of those people were living in Neighborlee anymore," London said. "Odd. Augustus Miller, a boy found on Old Mill Road, in August, is on that list."

"So he knew." Arthur snorted. "Notice he lied to his own brother?"

"Just when we could really use some division in the ranks," Ford muttered.

"All the names have some biographical information," London continued. "Many have notations that they are either dead or proven useless, or they escaped the control and monitoring of the Grandstones."

"That's the answer," Pastor Rocky said. "He's holding me like an ace card. To save his own neck, if not the entire family. Maybe he was hoping to use my singing voice. Or the plan all along has been to turn me over to Lightning Pathway."

"Ain't no way," Wallace said. "No way we're letting you leave town. I mean, you've got our wedding to perform, right?"

Some of us managed to laugh at that. Athena leaned over and kissed him soundly, kind of noisily, but I noticed Ford didn't mind at all.

"I'm sorry."

The quiet admission from Pastor Rocky stopped all of us.

"Don't be ridiculous," Angela said. "None of this is your fault. You couldn't know how your past would make you a target for these creatures."

"I should have put it all together sooner. Erik was talking about how maybe now they'd get me to sing. The promoter, Richardson, kept insisting I had to sing, and there was a new song made just for me. Grandstone talked about how I needed to get over myself and sing." Pastor Rocky groaned. "He even made veiled threats about how I owed his whole family big time for slapping his father in the face, rejecting the help he wanted to give me. And I never put it together." He made a choking sound that might have been an attempt to laugh. "The only person not pushing me to sing was Frankie."

"That doesn't make sense, if Frankie is Lux," Kurt said.

"No, it doesn't, does it?" Angela rubbed her temples, and that was a bad sign, because she never admitted to headaches or weariness. "There are so many pieces to this puzzle, clues we haven't found yet. And I fear that some of the clues we have picked up ... don't belong to this puzzle."

"Maybe the Grandstones and Lightning Pathway started one puzzle," Ford said, with a shrug, "and it wasn't all there, so they started another one? And maybe a third one? They keep changing puzzles when one gets too hard?"

"Or maybe there are more people trying to work on different puzzles on the same table?" I said. Yeah, that sounded a lot more intelligent in my head than when it came out of my mouth.

"Hey," Wallace said, sitting up, "that might be part of it. They're not changing their plan, but it's getting changed as more people get involved? Like that Kerri chick and her Men in Black, and this Helado woman who was giving you and Ethan grief a few months ago. Maybe they're involved, wanting in on whatever the Lightning Pathway's action is?"

"Oh, my dear Wallace ..." Angela nodded. "That might be it. Or at least part of it. Dare we hope these different forces are working against each other? And the Grandstones are grasping at straws, attacking the orphanage now because their ploy to turn Pastor over to Lightning hasn't worked out ... because Lightning Pathway went after him themselves ... but they lost control of their ace in the game?" She frowned slightly, but it was a thinking frown, not one that warned of worry and maybe pain.

"So maybe they're working against each other?" Ford said. A slow smile grew on his face, and it wasn't a nice smile. "How do we use that?"

"That is the question." She paused, her gaze losing focus as if turning inward. Her mouth twisted in a tight, crooked smile, and she nodded. "We make them think they're getting what they want, but it will turn out to be a trap."

"Meaning?" Ford said.

"Pastor Rocky?"

"Still here," he said. He sounded just as tired as I felt and most of the others sitting around the speakerphone looked.

"Could you prime the pump, so to speak? Talk about the reunion tour, make them think you regret missing it, and you wish you could have one more concert with them all."

"Don't know if that will work. Achmed and Leo don't seem to remember much of any of the concerts, and Frankie doesn't even want to talk about it."

"Well ... start them talking about the good old days, and how much you miss performing with them. Get them to start singing. I don't know, put on a little concert for the residents of the mission. Get them back into music and make it easy for someone to suggest you do one more concert." Her eyes narrowed and her mouth flattened, still smiling, somewhat grimly. "I'll wager someone will convince the rest of you that a concert on your home territory is a brilliant idea."

"Ah. Right." Another long silence, while I pictured him struggling for words, probably for the first time since he became a minister. "When that happens, where do we go to perform?"

"We'll start pulling strings up here. You bait the trap," Ford said, "leave it up to us to build it."

~~~~~

One little problem with getting the band back together: Magna
~~~~~

Magma played old-style rock'n'roll, but everybody in the rescue mission seemed to be Country & Western fans. The lines where the two crossed over were pretty short. Pastor Rocky reported that once Achmed and Leo sat down at the piano and picked up a saxophone, and Freddie reluctantly joined in, keeping the beat with a kiddie drum set, the only song any of them knew that was even close to County & Western was the theme song for *Rawhide*. So they played *Rawhide* over and over, multiple variations, changing keys and riffing on new lyrics, a dozen times in an hour.

No one seemed to mind. Several of the residents offered to teach them some "real music," but no one took it as an insult or even criticism. As Achmed and Leo healed, they were in good enough moods to be willing to learn something new.

This went on for two days.

Then the Grandstones and the Illinois Nazis attacked.

Yes, they were linked.

Sherwood caught movement in the mission's outside security cameras. When he clarified and magnified the images, he found Reggie and Freddie Grandstone, in stocking caps and fake moustaches. They approached mission residents when they went outside to take smoking breaks, trying to bribe them to help get them inside. The only people who paid them any attention were suffering from hallucinations, so they believed any faces they didn't recognize weren't there.

Some backward searching through security cameras all around the rescue mission helped Sherwood track the Grandstone brothers to their car. It was a rental. Once our AI's had that information, they got into the rental agency system and accessed the car's GPS and computer system. They discovered the Grandstones had followed Stanzer and Ethan all the way from Neighborlee.

Well, that was embarrassing.

London still had some scores to settle with both Grandstone brothers, for the harassment they had been putting Doni and Athena through, so she decided now was the time. She froze their credit cards and their cell phones. Sherwood got into their car's computer system to shut it down, and then altered their driver's licenses, adding all sorts of fake speeding and parking tickets. When they had the inevitable Grandstone hissy-fit and attracted police attention, they would get hauled in until their highly paid lawyers got them out of trouble.

London didn't check their emails until after things got weird. By the time she and Sherwood got to work on paybacks, the Grandstone brothers had done their damage. They called in the Illinois Nazis and sicced them on Frankie, Achmed and Leo.

Maybe they weren't official members of the Nazi party, but their cars had Illinois license plates and they all had swastika tattoos. One of them even had a buzz haircut -- and she was a girl.

All of them were girls. They were members of a wacko extremist Magna Magma fan group, and had decided they were reincarnated lovers of the band members from previous lives, and the world would implode if they didn't reunite with their time-lost honeybuns.

We thought the woman firing on the gates of the Lightning Pathway compound to rescue her husband was bad? These girls were ten times worse. Loud, nasty, wearing the strangest outfits, dripping with makeup, their hair dyed strange and multiple colors, looking like a mixture of Catholic schoolgirl-hooker-steam punk-Goth.

These girls barreled their way into the front lobby of Sanctuary Rescue Mission, yelling and waving flowers and guns and bottles of liquor and vials of all sorts of drugs. In the chaos, the shouting and shrieking and debris being tossed everywhere, two BoBs got through the security door, and crept down the halls.

Pastor Rocky got to them first.

They pulled guns on him.

He pulled the power of the Holy Spirit.

Pastor Rocky was my hero, going way beyond his bravery and calm when a speed freak broke in during a service when I was in high school.

The security video didn't have audio feed, so we couldn't hear what was said in the playback, but it was pretty obvious to me. The BoBs pulled their guns in near-perfect synchronization. They spoke, probably demanding to know where their targets were hiding. Pastor Rocky smiled at them, raised his hands to rest against their foreheads in blessing, and bowed his head to pray. He closed his eyes, and didn't see the poisonous green flash when his hands touched their foreheads.

The BoBs went down like they had been chopped off at the knees with that horizontal slicing disk from *Indiana Jones and the Last Crusade*.

Then they both turned to ash.

Can we say freaky and cool, at the same time?

Pastor Rocky went to his knees, which was understandable because of that flash. At least it wasn't from the guns firing. He sort of hunched over, gasping for breath, and opened his eyes. He later told us he didn't remember a single thing from the moment he saw those two in their black suits, black hats and dark glasses, except he immediately launched into a prayer of blessing for them.

If that was the way God "blessed" people who were out to hurt others … okay, this might be blasphemy, but *Go, God*!

The security video and the layer of gritty ash maybe two inches deep in the hallway and coating Pastor Rocky were all the evidence anyone needed that something Neighborlee freaky was going on.

Stanzer and Ethan were helping to deal with the girl Nazis, and felt that jolt of energy flash through the mission at the moment of disintegration. They broke and ran, ready to do battle. They found Pastor Rocky and got him to the panic room, where Frankie had hauled Achmed and Leo just a few minutes before.

That was it. That was all they needed to see. It was time to get the refugee trio out of there before something worse broke the doors down.

Kurt and Ford drove down to meet them and provide more security on the drive up. Arthur rallied his people to put together a safe house to deposit the three and handle the remainder of their recovery. No one had to say anything about the most important part of the deal: none of them would be allowed over the border into Neighborlee.

Right after Kurt and Ford headed south, our cameras posted in the overgrown lot across the street from the gates of the Grandstone estate showed Stephen Grandstone leaving in a hurry. He wasn't driving one of his big, fancy, look-at-me-I'm-rich cars. That was suspicious behavior.

When London contacted us, I was at the newspaper office, Jane was sitting on the edge of my desk, and Daniel was slouched in the chair against the wall. We were having a low-key conversation that was taking forever, since we had to stop whenever one of my coworkers was within hearing range. Granted, a newspaper office wasn't a good place to discuss strategy to deal with invaders from another dimension of reality working with extremist cults who dressed their members in Salvation Army reject black suits and dark glasses. Because, you know, reporters are nosey to begin with.

The message popped up on my phone first, with Jane and Daniel's phones blipping a few seconds later. Daniel was getting to his feet at the same time Jane slid off the desk. She held out her hand to me.

"Care to go for a joy ride?"

"I'll cover for you," Daniel said, and headed for Conrad's office.

Jane and I waited just long enough to make sure no one was watching, then she engaged the Ghost field. We went invisible, then shot up through the ceiling, and the offices overhead, and the storage room attic, then were out in open air. One nice thing about Neighborlee is that the buildings don't go very high. Stanzer's building is one of the tallest, at six stories. So we didn't have to rise all that high in the air before we could zip across town, heading for the Grandstone estate, looking for the very un-Grandstone-like nondescript car. Stephen wasn't rescuing Reggie and Freddie, because Sherwood was monitoring all the family phones and their father, Rosco, hadn't gotten a call yet. In fact, all the Grandstone phones were unusually quiet. So if Stephen hadn't gotten a call, where was he going and why did he need to fade into the background?

We started having second thoughts when he pulled onto the on-ramp, heading south on I-71. We followed, but once we passed the exit for

Rt. 303, we both started having second thoughts.

"Okay, if he keeps going once we pass Market Street and Akron ..." Jane shrugged and pulled out her phone. "I can have someone fill in for me and cover the spa. How about you?"

I pulled out my phone and checked my do-list for the rest of the day. Three more articles were sitting in my queue for copy editing. I could do that on my tablet. Fortunately, I had grabbed my backpack when we flew away. All my assigned stories were already turned in for the next edition, and I had three weeks' worth of Terry columns turned in. Not that I was thinking about being away from the office and my computer that long. It wasn't like we were going to another dimension ... but maybe another state?

"How's the wireless signal in here?" I asked, once Jane finished talking with her assistant at the spa. She wrinkled up her nose at me and thought for a few moments.

"I can reduce the intensity of the shield around us, to increase the strength of the wireless signal, but not for very long. Might let in some wind, and it messes with my concentration and focus."

"How sticky is this thing?" I gestured down at Grandstone's car.

Jane only took about ten seconds to figure out what I was suggesting. She laughed and made the bubble speed up, until we were on top of his car. I guessed from the crooked twist to her mouth, she was thinking of something nasty, most likely landing hard and making the car bounce and maybe scaring him a little. She didn't, though. We didn't want to cause an accident. For one thing, we wanted to know what he was up to, and for another, there were innocent people on this highway.

Once Jane got the Ghost field bubble attached to the trunk of Grandstone's car, that took a lot of strain off her. We settled down to work via our smartphone and tablet, me on copy editing and her on making up an order for the spa. We kept track of the highway signs, and when 71 merged with 76 around Akron, we had to come to a decision: stick with him to the bitter end, or head home and hope this last-minute errand had nothing to do with Pastor Rocky and the threat to Neighborlee Children's Home and Magna Magma.

Jane got a brainstorm while we were debating how much longer we should stay stuck to the back of his car. Her next call was to London. Could she access Grandstone's phone and determine if he was using his GPS function, and if so, figure out where he was headed?

This necessitated some very careful adjusting of the Ghost field so we could drop through the roof of the car and land in the back seat, without it enclosing Grandstone. We didn't want him to know he had uninvited passengers, after all. We nearly smothered ourselves, holding back laughter, when we realized we could have been a lot more comfortable and riding in the back seat for the last twenty miles. Jane adjusted the Ghost field, thinning it so London could reach through her phone and tap into Grandstone's phone and GPS.

He was headed for Cincinnati.

Oh, just great.

London did a search of the address. She took so long coming back to report to us, we both got worried. Talking wasn't a temptation, sitting just a few feet away from one of Neighborlee's wannabe robber barons. So we just sat there, quietly waiting. He didn't play music or have the news on, or an audiobook. He just drove in silence, scowling at the highway ahead of him, his knuckles white with the intensity of his grip.

Finally, London came back. The address was a former factory complex that was being partially torn down, and partially converted into a new facility for ...

Wait for it ...

Lightning Pathway Ministries.

"What are our chances he's going down there to have it out with someone?" Jane muttered. She scowled down at her phone. "This is too big for us to go in there without backup. These guys creep me out to begin with, forget about all their talk about celestial powers, which might just be true. London, could you ask everybody available to meet at Divine's? We're heading back."

She didn't wait for London to respond, but pulled us up and out of the car. We both gave a good hard kick to the roof once we cleared it. The car jolted a little underneath us, veering maybe two feet toward the divider line. Not enough to cause a crash, but enough to prove we had startled the creepazoid. We both sputtered and muffled laughter as we got high enough that we didn't have to worry about semis with those big windbreak shields on the cabs. Then Jane put the pedal to the metal and went near-sonic. It was a good thing the Ghost field protected us from the wind, because I had a vision of our clothes getting pulled off by the air friction, otherwise. We were back in Neighborlee in fifteen minutes. Then it took another twenty minutes for the editorial area to clear out so we could settle back down at my desk and become visible again without freaking anyone out. I had to take my Jeep, or people would start asking questions. Daniel was waiting, looking rather grim.

London had done more than notify everyone who was able to drop what they were doing to have a meeting. She contacted Arthur Sheridan, Col. Hayward, and the headquarters of Hoax, as well as Ethan and Stanzer. By the time we got to Divine's, several of Hoax's field agents were already on their way to the address in Cincinnati. Katie, Jane's friend who moved fast enough to make Quicksilver look like a plodder in a marathon, was on her way, to keep watch on things. Everyone was especially interested in being in place before Grandstone showed up at the old factory, to see what kind of a welcome he got.

The Sheridan group had property down in Cincinnati, meaning a large workforce of descendants of Lost Kids. Specifically, Lost Kids who had needed to be rescued from the machinations of the Grandstones on behalf of the Rivals. There were scores to settle, two and three generations back. More important than having reliable fighters, if it came to that, we knew they had motivation to take risks, if necessary.

We didn't talk very long. What was there to say? We needed to figure out what kind of connection there was between Lightning Pathway and the Grandstones, besides the obvious one of someone giving the Grandstones a taste of their own medicine.

Jane could only carry so many people inside the Ghost field before the size of the bubble interfered with speed and wind resistance and drained her too quickly. We ended up with Jane, Daniel, Maurice, and me. Daniel to contact the Sheridan forces who would be gathering around the factory, and Maurice for his mostly restored magic. Me, for my telekinesis and ability to catch all the details and keep them straight, when I wrote up the report later.

We had no intention of going in and having a battle. We just wanted to be careful and present as small a target as possible when we snuck in. Jane could keep us invisible, and permeable enough that bullets wouldn't do us any harm, if shooting started.

Half an hour after we walked in the door of Divine's, Daniel supported me out the door so Jane could initiate the Ghost field. Because, you know, it just wasn't smart to try to penetrate the defensive net around Divine's, even if we were in a hurry.

"You might want to hold onto each other," Jane warned us as the Ghost field bubble started rising. "We won't exactly be going light speed, but that creep has more than an hour lead on us, and it's going to be kind of disorienting if you watch the scenery speeding past."

Maurice muttered something about being space-sick, and how rude Guber and the other Fae in town were being, all of them out of town to deal with some election in the Fae Realms. I found out later he would have asked them to help transport us, otherwise. While he had most of his magic back, he still had to be careful about how quickly he used up his energy. We were bringing him along for the big emergency rescue, so it wasn't smart to use up his energy on essentially being a transporter beam. Although, thinking about being space-sick made the convenience feel a little inconvenient. I would rather trust to Jane and going at hyper-speed. I had flown with her before, after all.

It turned out we didn't have to worry about being disoriented, although Daniel did keep his arm around me, and I didn't mind a bit.

Maurice conjured up a nice illusion inside the bubble and left a large section about four feet high and eight wide for Jane to see through, since she had to do the driving. The easiest way of getting down to Cincinnati was to just follow the highway, with occasional surges upward to avoid power lines and bridges.

London had created a link with Stephan Grandstone's GPS, so Jane's phone blipped at us when we passed him on the highway, just before he reached the I-270 bypass that circled Columbus. Yeah, we were going fast, covering the distance of two hours of driving in maybe forty-five minutes.

We got to Cincinnati, another hour-and-a-half of driving time, in just under half an hour. Jane brought us down in a parking lot surrounded by trees, in the back section of an industrial park complex maybe ten minutes of driving from the factory. The Sheridan people were waiting. Comforting in a scary kind of way, they had night vision goggles and Kevlar vests, high-tech earbuds like on TV series about government agent-type folks, but no guns.

Katie arrived less than a minute after we stepped out of the bubble, while Daniel was still supporting me, heading for a convenient car bumper to sit on. She had pictures. Gobs of them, snapped with a camera equipped for infra-red and night vision.

LaRiche, Ambrose Lux's right-hand man, or perhaps puppeteer, appeared in many of those pictures. It was amazing how many Katie got, and how clear they were, considering she had to keep moving fast enough to be less than a blur and a stirring of the air.

There were two distinct groups of people in their all-black outfits. Their style, the visible expense of their clothes, distinguished them. Men in Black wannabes, and Blues Brothers afficionados. They stood in two distinctly separate groups. LaRiche seemed to be in a snit toward both of them. Was that good for us or bad?

Chapter Twelve

Kerri was there, with the Men in Black version of the BoBs. She looked like she had aged twenty years since the run-in with her and the doppelgangers, back in the early spring. That had to be good for us, right?

A second Men in Black group walked in, near the end of the long string of pictures Katie snapped in her whirlwind tour of the lower level of the factory complex. There were only four of them. They all wore dark glasses, just like the previous two groups, and escorted Mrs. Von Helado. Katie's pictures showed Kerri backing away from Mrs. Von Helado, with very clear fear and loathing twisting her face. Mrs. VH looked at her, and I really expected to see laser beams coming out of her eyes and setting Kerri on fire. So, two enemy gangs, not one?

What were the chances of finding out what Kerri had done to get Mrs. VH icy furious with her, to warrant that look? If looks could kill, Kerri would have died and gone to dust about four years ago, just in anticipation of that encounter.

In the last photo, Mrs. VH looked right into the camera lens.

Wise of Katie to get out of there before alarms went off and someone tried to catch her.

"What are the chances they sensed you? Do you leave an energy trail of any kind that they could follow?" Daniel asked, once she had described the sensation of the temperature dropping in the meeting room.

Why did bad guys always insist on meeting in shadowy places, where the walls were hard to see and there was a sensation of water about to drip from the ceiling?

"Thought of that. We have a scrambler Ambercrombie keeps refining and updating. Kind of the equivalent of spilling dirt and leaves across your path in the forest." Katie shrugged and exchanged a grim smile with Jane. "At least, it's worked in the past when the Rivals have gotten too close. No telling how well it will work with these people, since we don't know anything about their strength or gifts or energy levels."

"Or if they're even human," Maurice said. "Kerri and her gang, at least, are rebel Fae, managing to slip through some of the restraints put on them. That old hag who went up against Angela and Ethan ... " He shook his head. "I'd have to get close to them to determine what they are, where they're from. My sensitivity isn't up to where it needs to be to really assess them. I'm focused too much on inspecting chocolate for carob poisoning.

Kind of like being a drug-sniffing dog. Messes up the schnozz."

Time was running out. We wanted to be in place before Grandstone got there. The only real certainty we had of being invisible, unheard, un-smelled, hopefully completely un-sensed, was to use the Ghost field. To avoid strain, and to make the bubble of Ghost field as small as possible, it was just the four of us: Jane, Daniel, Maurice, and me. The Sheridan people would surround the place and move in as close as they could manage without setting off alarms. We hoped. They had several people who were like Kurt, able to sense energy in use, and it would be up to them to keep the rest of the team out of sensing range. Katie hung back in the rendezvous area, to meet up with the Hoax team if they arrived in time to be of any help.

When we got to the factory, the raggedy Blues Brothers types were walking patrol. Thanks to my growing sensitivity, and the magnification effects of being inside the Ghost field, I saw sparkles of something that hopefully wasn't magic, but some kind of psionic power, flickering over all of them. Especially around their dark glasses. Maybe that was why they wore those dark glasses, to have enhanced sight, maybe augmented hearing? Maybe it was all sci-fi high-tech stuff in those glasses?

Following the path Katie had mapped out for us, we flew up and into the center of the building through an open courtyard arrangement, probably where trucks used to be loaded. It meant fewer walls to go through. I could imagine that going through metal wasn't fun, and brick wasn't much better, for Jane.

We dove down through the courtyard, all broken asphalt and gravel and lots of leaves and other debris gathered through the years. Traveling through all that concrete wasn't fun. I held my breath and hoped no one noticed. When we came out in the basement level, we were in tunnels. Following Katie's directions, we found the room where LaRiche was meeting with the two creepy teams. Mrs. Von Helado and her bodyguards were gone. I was relieved. Kerri was still there, and I admit, I did find some satisfaction in seeing how much she had aged. She just didn't look well. Served her right for coming against Neighborlee and threatening my little brother with a tricky contract.

LaRiche was arguing with some of Kerri's men, while she stood at the end of the table closest to us, looking through several books. He kept glancing over at her, pausing briefly in his arguments. I could only hope I wasn't imagining it, and he was nervous. Why? What was in those books?

"Books?" Jane whispered. "What kind of books would someone like her want?"

"Angela's books," Maurice said, and flashed us a nasty smile. The bubble of Ghost field moved us closer to Kerri.

"Think he's the one who stole them, or had them stolen?" I said.

We got as close as we could to Kerri without touching her. No telling what her reaction would be if she could feel the Ghost field, and none of us wanted to share space with her, anyway. I leaned as far forward as I could without actually touching the Ghost field. What if I fell through? Four books stolen from Divine's this spring were still missing, and there were three on the table. I tried to get as good a look at their covers as I could, alternately scrolling through the photos stored on my phone for the images taken from Guber's time-traveling video camera gizmo.

"Think it's worth the risk, trying to take them back?" Maurice whispered, when we all agreed those were either Angela's stolen books, or unreasonable facsimiles.

"I need the rest," Kerri announced, and slammed a book closed.

"I'm working on it," LaRiche shot back, without breaking the glare he focused on the lead BoB. "The energy keeping us out has changed again. It's like they know we're out here and they're prepared and watching."

"Don't fail me again."

"Get off my back and let me do my job."

"You aren't doing it. That's why we're here. To help you." She bared her teeth at him.

"Yeah?" He sneered. "I thought it was to cover your backside and shift the blame for your own failures. The old hag was about to eat both of us, you know."

"She has fears of her own." Kerri seemed smug for a moment, just an upward twitch of her lips before she resumed glaring at LaRiche. "We wasted too much energy and effort, investing in you and your plans. If you don't come through --"

"Get off my back!" His voice rang off the low ceiling and the metal support beams overhead. "The fool is our only tool left. He'll give us what we want. Before the deadline," he hurried to add.

"He had better. We've waited too long for this opportunity. The celestial tide is finally reaching low ebb, and we need to strike --" She paused and tipped her head back, as if she could look up and through the ceiling and the courtyard and dirt overhead. "He's here. Impress on him that he doesn't dare fail us this time."

"He won't. We have something he'd willingly sell his pitiful soul to obtain. Selling out his home and the few powers the land grants him is an easier choice."

A door that seemed to be nothing but darkness coalesced out of thin air on the far end of the room. Kerri scooped up the books and stalked to the door on her too-high heels. I wanted so much for them to break. I probably could have broken them with my mind, but using that kind of energy would give us away. The six Men in Black henchmen followed her, each stepping into the darkness and vanishing.

Stephen Grandstone came stomping down the stairs, escorted by LaRiche's minions in their old-style clothes. Why, I have to ask again, do bad guys feel obligated to always dress in black?

"Where is she?" he snarled as soon as he stepped into the room.

Funny, but his voice seemed to be shaking. I had never seen a Grandstone afraid and furious at the same time.

"What makes you think she's here?" LaRiche almost purred. Definitely, he was the one in charge. Now that Kerri was gone, of course.

Grandstone yanked his phone out of his coat pocket, tapped it, then thrust it screen forward at LaRiche.

"Ah, yes. Proof of life, I believe they call it."

Grandstone flinched. I was getting that nauseated, creepy feeling, and was pretty sure I didn't want to understand what was going on.

"Bring her," LaRiche said, without glancing away from Grandstone. He gestured at one of the chairs on the other side of the room.

Grandstone shook his head, and they just stood there, glaring at each other, until one of the BoBs left the room and came back maybe fifteen seconds later.

Leading Sylvia Grandstone.

I reached for Daniel and caught hold of his hand and held on tight. He stared, looking a little green where he wasn't pale. He swallowed hard a few times. Jane demanded an explanation, managing to stay in whispers.

"That's his daughter, Sylvia," I said, and couldn't go on. It was just too weird. Especially when Sylvia crossed the room with tiny, shuffling steps, her head just slightly tilted to the right, eyes kind of vacant and unblinking. At least she wasn't wearing the same clothes she had worn the night she died at Eden.

Or was that even creepier?

"Isn't she supposed to be dead?" Jane said after a few seconds of waiting for either of us to add more information.

"Yep," Daniel said, his voice little more than a breath.

"Holy *Walking Dead*, Batman," Maurice whispered

"Try *Corpse Bride*," I said. "She was chasing Daniel, trying to trick or blackmail or whatever him into marrying her."

During all this, which really didn't take even a minute, Stephen Grandstone spread his arms and waited, but Sylvia didn't come to him. She didn't return his smile. She barely seemed to notice anyone was in the room. Finally, he sighed and stepped up and hugged her.

That didn't last long. Maybe because she just stood there, no reaction. I had to wonder if she wasn't breathing, if maybe her heart wasn't beating, and her father could tell. For the first time in my life, I pitied a Grandstone.

"She'll be better soon?" he demanded, turning back to LaRiche.

"If you do your part. Which you haven't yet." LaRiche's voice was pleasant enough to make me flinch. I hated nice, civilized conversations that covered over viciousness and malice.

"I'm trying!"

"Not hard enough." He held up a hand, stopping Grandstone from retorting. In two fingers he held out a piece of paper. "I need to have the rest of these books. Get better minions, this time. The idiots you hired last time failed me miserably. Maybe your nephews will finally do something right for a change."

Grandstone didn't react, making me think he didn't know about Reggie and Freddie's most recent failure.

"Put your money -- oh, that's right, you don't have any money." That purr came back into his voice. "I was going to say put your money where your mouth is, but maybe you should put your blood where your mouth is. Despite the imagery, you know what I mean?"

"They can't get inside. None of our family has been able to get inside Divine's Emporium for three generations."

"And that is why you have failed me in the simplest tasks. All this trouble could have been avoided, you could have had your daughter back, fully restored and alive, if you had simply completed the first, simple task I gave you."

"I welcomed you to Neighborlee!" Grandstone didn't flinch as his voice rang off the ceiling. "My whole family welcomed you."

"Yes, and you proved how little authority you have in that town you believe is yours to rule. Meaning you have no authority. You aren't even welcome there, on the land you own. You are barely tolerated by the spirit and the heart of the town. Your welcome has no influence, no weight, no impact. And then that fool preacher dared to stand against us, all unknowing. He is tied to the defenses. He must welcome us, or we cannot enter. And if we cannot enter, who do you think the master will devour when he breaks free from his prison at long last?"

"Look, we've been trying to take control of that town for years, my entire family and the Guild. That's all we've been doing for --"

"And look what happened to those who commanded you and trusted you."

"The Guild didn't command us. We were partners."

"Keep believing that, if that comforts you. They fell sooner than you did, that is for certain." LaRiche glanced at Sylvia.

I looked at her, for the first time since the conversation started. Weird, but Sylvia seemed to be aware now. Her eyes seemed to have focus ... and she was watching LaRiche, not her father.

Okay, now I was officially freaked out.

"I need help," Grandstone finally said, after visibly struggling to get the words out.

"I thought you might." He gestured to a BoB, who stepped out of the room again.

The wait was longer. Grandstone turned to stare at Sylvia, and doggone it but he had tears in his eyes. How weird, to feel sorry for a Grandstone. Well, at least we had proof that despite all the nastiness of their family, he really did love his daughter. I wondered if Sylvia had any love for her parents. If she was able to feel anything right now. Did zombies have feelings? Was she a zombie? Maybe she was a doppelganger, created to give LaRiche leverage over Grandstone?

And yet there was still that unsolved mystery of what happened to Sylvia's body when it vanished from the morgue, and who had taken it.

The BoB returned, leading Earnest B. Tass. How come none of us were surprised by that development?

Grandstone took a step back, his nose wrinkling as if he smelled something unpleasant. As soon as Tass saw him, he went pale and started to turn away, but the BoB caught him by his collar and stopped him.

"No! Don't make me go back there. I told you before, I can't get in," Tass whined.

"Use the holy oil my people made for you, to take control of their minds. Wait for the witch to come out of her home, then spray it on her, then command her to welcome you inside." LaRiche gestured at the paper Grandstone still held in his hand. "Procure the books. The descriptions are there. Then do whatever you want to the witch once you have them."

"This is too crazy," Jane whispered.

I flinched, because all this time I had been trying to convince myself this was a dream.

"He means Angela, doesn't he? Who does he think he is, calling her a witch?" Maurice said. He didn't even try to whisper now, and nobody seemed to hear us.

"There's an old belief that grants power over people and things if you learn their real names, their true names, soul names, whatever," I said, thinking aloud, and trying to distract my brain a little, because I was scrambling too hard for answers and explanations. "They like to slap labels on everything and everyone, to try to have power over them. Put them in boxes. Limit them."

Grandstone and Tass left, and then things got really freaky. LaRiche waited until the sound of their footsteps faded to nothing, and the BoBs left the room. It was just him and Sylvia. He held out his hands ... and she smiled and walked up to him and held out her hands. I got that oogie chilled feeling when LaRiche took hold of her hands and smiled down into her eyes, and she smiled back. Not a big smile, but it was clearly a smile. Sylvia was somehow alive, even though I know she died two New Year's Eves ago.

Or something else was riding around in her body and looking out through her eyes.

"Soon, my darling," he said, purring again. "When we have the knowledge and power, and we fix you ... nothing will stand in my way. That old hag thinks she can order me around and scold me like a puppy that messed on the floor? Once I have those books and I rip the power out of her hands ... then we'll see. Then we'll rule, won't we?"

Then he leaned down and kissed Sylvia's cold, dead lips.

I couldn't make myself feel sorry for him. The guy deserved all the grossness that landed on him.

"Sir!" A BoB darted into the room, waving a long rifle that looked like it belonged in *Starship Troopers* or some other futuristic movie. "We have intruders on the perimeter."

"Deal with it!" LaRiche snarled.

He reached into his coat and pulled out a long chain of black beads, with several round disks hanging on it. Those certainly looked like the weird coins we had dealt with last winter, when all that trouble with the doppelgangers and other invasion plans hit Neighborlee.

The coins in his hand sparkled, kind of a muted, sick greenish-reddish shade. Black light rippled all along the chain of black beads.

Sylvia staggered and slumped backward and her color went bad. Sort of greenish. I had a moment of choking on the mental image of her going very greenish, like rotting flesh, and sort of dissolving all over the floor. She dropped crookedly into a chair, eyes closing, just as LaRiche turned and looked right at us.

"Get out!" Maurice yelped.

Jane didn't even snap back at him. The bubble of Ghost field shot straight up, fast enough I fell back, slammed into the bottom curve. Daniel fell sideways, landing half on top of me. He wrapped his arms around me and struggled against the force of gravity holding us down, as we shot up through the ceiling and the courtyard and out of the building.

I was blinking hard, trying to adjust to full sunlight, when Jane sent the bubble into a dive. Light flashed below us or ahead of us -- I was having a hard time keeping up and down and sideways straight for a few seconds. We wove in and out among support pillars in one big, half-dismantled, two-story-tall room. Daniel got us both sitting upright, and he kept holding onto me with one arm, while digging in his pocket with the other hand.

"Get ready to grab him," Jane said.

I struggled to sit up on my own as Daniel let go. Maurice helped him stand up again. Ahead of us, one of the Sheridan people was dodging and ducking and shooting, and three black-clad figures were chasing and shooting and weirdly, making no effort to take cover. Maybe they thought they were impervious to bullets?

Maybe they were dead, just like Sylvia, so it didn't matter if they got shot?

My oogies limit had just overloaded.

We zipped in between the shooters and their target. I flinched as the bullets hit the Ghost field. Jane bared her teeth, her expression fierce with the force of her concentration. The Ghost field slipped over and around the Sheridan man, swallowing him.

Fire slammed into my shoulder and flung me forward, knocking me breathless, hitting Daniel and almost knocking him off his feet as he and Maurice hauled the man up inside the bubble.

"Sorry! I'm sorry! The timing --" Jane bared her teeth. "Hold on. Going up!"

"Anybody else you can see in trouble?" Daniel said. He helped the rescued man sit up and get his balance in the bottom curve of the bubble. Then he looked at me and went white.

"What's wrong?" I reached for him and choked on the need to scream. Fire ripped down up arm and across my shoulders.

"Man, something freaky," Maurice muttered, bending down and leaning over me to look at my shoulder.

"They shot me?" I squeaked.

"Yeah, but that's no bullet. It's still in you -- and it's trying to grow roots." He grabbed hold of my arm. "You probably won't like this --"

Now I screamed, and everything went all black and green and red sparkles, but whatever he did, it worked. When I could see and breathe again, Maurice was holding up both hands, frowning at something about the size of a ping pong ball, hovering in between his hands, kicking and turning somersaults and shooting off poisonous green and yellow and black sparks inside a tiny Ghost field.

Daniel was busy on his phone, checking that all his people got out. Jane was zipping around, following any flashes of light from gunfire, taking us in and out and around, phasing through walls and steel girders and up through ceilings and down through floors. If I didn't have that receding wave of fire seeping out of my shoulder, I probably would have gotten airsick from all the up and down and tilting.

"What is that thing?" the Sheridan man said. He looked about as green as I felt right then.

"Don't know. Nothing I've heard about in the Fae Realms." Maurice brought the kicking, spinning thing closer, and it shot off more sparks, like it was trying to hit his face. "I've got the feeling its cussing me out, but I don't know the language."

"If it's aware, we probably should get rid of it," Daniel said. "Don't want to take it back to our rendezvous spot, or risk it following us home."

"If it's gotten a taste of Lanie, it might still be able to."

"Oh, thanks." I shuddered, fighting down a surge of nausea, and hoped that was all emotional reaction and not some sign that nasty little ping pong ball had injected me with venom or something worse. Like maybe parasites, to grow more of its kind in my blood?

Oh, great. I was making things even worse with my imagination. Maybe I was delirious?

Daniel checked his man over, making sure he didn't have any nasty surprises sticking to him. Despite the fire and the pain and the force of the blow, that ugly little thing hadn't actually broken the skin. Still, it felt like it had dug lava roots into my arm. I was going to have one killer bruise.

All the other Sheridan people had gotten out without being spotted, as far as we knew. If we were lucky, the BoBs were the kind who shot first and asked questions later, and didn't have the brains to think of strategy, like following the invaders to see where they came from and identify them. Daniel told his people on the ground to meet up with others who had some sensing gifts, and make sure they were safe before meeting at the rendezvous spot. We had to deal with the ping pong ball before it turned into a bomb or cloned itself or led its bigger, nastier brothers to us.

"I'm sorry," Jane said, as we flew out of the industrial park area and followed the web of highways, headed roughly south, judging by the angle of the sun. "I had to thin the field enough to take him in without scorching him. Just for a couple seconds. Long enough for that thing to get through the shielding."

"Hey, guys?" The Sheridan man was sitting facing me, legs spread, looking down through the field. "I think we're being followed." He pointed.

Jane turned us right. A car a few dozen feet behind us slid right into the next lane, earning a few horns and squealing brakes. It was a dark car. From the height and angle of the sun and the shadows of the buildings, I couldn't tell what color it was, but chances were good it would turn out to be black. What was with these guys in their old-style suits and nearly vintage cars?

"It's like they stepped through a time-warp with all their clothes and equipment," Daniel mused, as he settled down next to me and helped me turn so I wouldn't get a crick in my neck from watching the car. Which kept following us.

Jane made turns at every intersection and side street we came to, and that car followed. Even when, as evidenced by cars slamming on brakes and blaring horns and near-misses, the driver turned the wrong way down a one-way street.

We ended up at the river, in an area of mostly concrete and mud, where the highway crossed the river, with different on- and off-ramps and bridges. By this time, Maurice was sweating a little from the effort to control the nasty ping pong ball, which looked redder and shot off more black sparks than anything else. Maybe the sparks were its language? So maybe it really was cussing us out?

"I've got an idea," Jane said. "It's kind of risky, but if we don't know what we're dealing with ... well, sorry, but I don't feel any guilt killing that thing. Who knows what it's made to do, when you use it instead of bullets?"

"I like how you think." Maurice bared his teeth. Then a big drop of sweat got into his eye and he winced. "I'm ready to try it. Kind of getting cramps in my hands, y'know?"

Jane set us down in the shelter of some concrete support pillars, in the shadow of an overpass. I didn't think we had lost the car tailing us, but we had at least delayed him. Or them. I really hoped we only had one pursuer. She dispersed the Ghost field and we got blasted with hot August air and the fumes of thousands of cars passing by and through Cincinnati, and the smell of the Ohio River after a dry summer. From the rough ground around us, more dried mud than cement, or maybe dried mud covering the cement, this was an area that usually saw a lot of flooding of the river. But not this year.

Daniel supported me over to a cement highway divider that had been broken into several pieces. The overpass we were hiding under was about fifty feet up in the air, and I had a sick mental picture of a car, or several, hitting that sloping concrete divider hard enough to knock it over the side. I settled on the rough seat, grateful I didn't have to settle on the ground. And then grateful that Daniel stayed there with his arm around me. Why couldn't he be like this all the time, considerate and acting without thinking, instead of having more and longer lapses when he gave me those weird looks like he was happy and then scared a second later, and waiting for me to bite his head off?

Jane and Maurice finally figured out what they were going to do. He stepped back and spread his hands, and now I could see the light dancing between his palms and fingertips, keeping the ping pong ball imprisoned. Maurice watched Jane. She took a deep breath and nodded. The light died from his hands with a nearly audible pop.

Chapter Thirteen

A car's engine revved and something banged and brakes squealed and there was the rattling of gravel under wheels. I turned, nearly right off the cement divider, and saw that black, old-style sedan come sliding down a path from the highway above where it shouldn't have been able to get through. How did I know? There was a chain link fence. Or rather, the remains of a chain link fence, snapping back and forth from the impact that broke it.

From the corner of my eye, I saw a flash of reddish light as the ping pong ball monster fought against the Ghost field Jane wrapped around it.

The black sedan slid closer and the BoB leaped out of it, nearly knocked flat as the front wheel caught on something and it swung around. He leaped over a pile of debris left by the river who knew how long ago, and pulled out a chunky looking pistol and fired.

Daniel stepped in front of me. I nearly shoved him out of the way, with a half-conscious plan to try to grab the incoming ping pong ball with my brain and squeeze it like Jane was doing with the first one.

Behind us, something screamed, rising higher in pitch and out of audible range in just a few heartbeats.

Daniel stumbled backward. I reached to catch him. The ping pong ball turned red and burst into flames and then green-black smoke, before vanishing.

The BoB gaped and sort of went limp for a moment, his shooting arm dropping to his side.

A gun went off behind me and I swear, the bullet that passed between Daniel and me flew close enough to scorch my ear. The BoB stumbled backward, arms splayed, with a gusher of red from high in his chest. He shouted something that I swear was, "But I'm invincible!"

Then he went up in flames and green-black smoke

I grabbed for Daniel because my legs had turned to rubber and I was sliding off the divider. He latched onto me and we held each other upright. The Sheridan man, whose name I finally learned a short time later was Winslow, staggered up to us, demanding to know if we were all right.

"You big dummy!" I said, when I could finally catch my breath. I punched Daniel in the shoulder. "What did you do that for?"

"Invincibility," he said, then winced and rubbed his shoulder.

"Yeah, well, nice idea," Maurice said as he and Jane came over to join us, "but considering these things are totally out of anybody's experience and knowledge? Not smart depending on things you know against things you don't know. You know?"

Then he winked and we all kind of laughed. Not very long or very loud. We were all kind of tired and punchy. And need it be said? We got out of there as quickly as we could. I thanked Winslow several times for shooting the BoB, even though I was still kind of freaked out by how it reacted to the gunshot. What was with these guys?

We had a very hurried meeting with the rest of the team. Hoax hadn't shown up yet. Katie said she would wait and take them to the factory to see what they could do and find out. We dropped off Winslow and the four of us headed for home as soon as we could. While yes, we would phone ahead to warn everybody, we wanted to be there to make sure Tass and his mission failed miserably.

Jane flew us back north, insisting she had enough energy to do the supersonic thing again. We had to beat Grandstone back to Neighborlee, and keep Tass from doing whatever nasty tricks he did with his not-so-holy oil. We would deal with undead Sylvia and LaRiche later.

We knew Grandstone's car and license plate, so we notified Gordon to keep an eye out. The odds were pretty even that Grandstone would just take the straight, shortest route from the highway to Neighborlee. I got the task of calling Angela to warn her, just in case Tass didn't get bounced like a mosquito hitting a bug zapper when he tried to enter Divine's. She sounded amused when I stumbled through repeating the conversation, and her being called a witch.

"Lanie, dear, I've been called far worse things in my many years of service in this war. I've lost count of the number of otherwise fine, moral people who were convinced that I was an emissary from Hell. Even after I had stood between them and the powers of true darkness and destruction. Some of them were honest and ethical and prayed for understanding and insight, and we eventually became friends. Others refused to admit they had been wrong, and stood against me, to their destruction and my sorrow." She chuckled. "I find it amusing when ignorant, uneducated, sloppy buffoons dare to throw such labels on me, when they have no idea the true meaning of those words."

"Angela … it's not right." Yeah, I was an editor and a former schoolteacher, and that was all I could come up with? Only part of my limited vocabulary and thinking ability could be blamed on the really rough day I had had.

"No, but consider that the true Master warned such things would happen. If such evil could be perpetrated when the branches were green, imagine the evil they would work when the branches had dried."

It took me a few moments to realize she was quoting from the Bible, leading up to the crucifixion. I know Angela meant it as comforting, but I couldn't take it that way. I was really tired, and sick of so many things being unfair. When were we ever going to catch a break? Yes, we had been winning this battle to defend our small duty posting, for generations before I was born or dropped on Neighborlee, but that was no justification for the struggle to keep going forever and ever, was it?

Before I could resume whining, Angela promised me she would be careful, and she would call some of the guardians to keep watch on Divine's. Then she told me to try to take a nap, and laughed softly as she said goodbye.

I had to sputter a little. Yeah, right -- take a nap, flying about eighty feet up in the air, with nothing visible between me and the highway speeding by below at over 150 miles per hour? We couldn't block out the blur below us because Maurice was tired from the struggle to contain and then destroy the nasty ping pong ball. He couldn't spare the energy to create the illusion and block us from seeing. He was helping Jane keep us invisible.

Wouldn't that be a hoot, appearing on the 6pm news, the 7pm news, the national news, with snippets of video snapped by phone cameras as we zipped by?

Nope.

I curled up against the curve of the bubble and tried to find a comfortable position, closed my eyes, and did a lot of semi-coherent praying as we sped north, hoping to get there before disaster struck.

As it turned out, we worried for nothing. Or almost nothing. Maybe all those prayers worked. Or maybe it was the power of the prayer chain at church that had ensured victory long before I started praying.

Gordon wasn't there to witness the fireworks. He wagered that Stephen Grandstone would revert to his sneaky ways when bringing someone in to sabotage Divine's Emporium, and he would take a back road from the highway, cutting through the Metroparks, just as Andris and Dabra and their children had done. For once, Gordon was wrong when it came to predicting Grandstone actions. Jensen Lucas and his partner, Al Paulson, were waiting in the high school parking lot, watching the intersection where Sackley Road crossed the border into Neighborlee. They spotted Grandstone's car. Jensen was about to put the patrol car into gear to pull out into traffic and follow him when his car veered from the middle lane into the right lane. Fortunately, no one was in that lane. And then the car veered up over the curb and onto the tree lawn. Al leaped out of the car to run to see what had happened, while Jensen drove the patrol car out of the parking lot, turned onto the side street, and made a right turn onto Sackley.

Al got to the car just in time to see Grandstone haul Tass out of the car, writhing and gasping for breath, red-faced and sweating and spasming. He left the fat faker sprawled on his back, jumped back in his car, and took off.

And immediately plowed into the patrol car.

Fortunately, Jensen had the dash cam on, and caught everything. There was no way Grandstone could claim that he had been sideswiped and pushed onto the tree lawn, although that was exactly what he tried to do when he had his day in court. Al was wearing a new body camera, and he caught the struggle Grandstone had hauling Tass out of the car, and just how he left the man, clearly having a seizure, lying in the grass. And gave him a good kick in the ribs before he took off.

Gordon got to the scene before the EMTs. He searched Tass and confiscated his bag of tricks, including several vials of falsely labeled "healing oil," three lighters, several cans of Sterno and three cans of lighter fluid. The healing oil, which Tass was stupid enough to proudly proclaim he was going to use to cast the demons out of Angela, was a toxic mixture of hallucinogens and several designer drugs, along with neural toxins that reportedly white supremacists and other terrorist organizations had paid thousands of dollars for just an ounce.

Chief Tanner made sure several jail cells were kept between Grandstone and Tass, so they couldn't talk and line up their stories. Both of them ended up trying to throw the other one under the bus. It was a very happy ending, though delayed by weeks and months of litigation and investigation, to a truly strange, mind-bending, exhausting, painful day.

Throwing Stephen Grandstone into jail didn't help us with the threat to Neighborlee Children's Home and the demand that the remaining living members of Magna Magma perform a concert. Rosco Grandstone picked up where his brother left off, waving around documents and bringing in more lawyers.

London and Sherwood hadn't located Mrs. Baumgartner, or learned what happened to that money. Her bank accounts from that time were hard to track down. Just the fact that a woman running a small orphanage in the 60s had more than one bank account should have raised red flags. The check had indeed been made out to Neighborlee Children's Home, and until we could prove it had gone to Mrs. Baumgartner and not NCH, evidence weighed heavily in Grandstone favor. For the first time in decades of frivolous quasi-legal action.

On top of the slowly growing public effort to humiliate the children's home, Rosco was demanding that ticket sales go directly into his hands, even before the concert took place. The contract he sent over made reference to and amended "previous agreements," even though there was no agreement, just demands. We had to wonder if he didn't know anything about the deal his older brother had made to get Sylvia back. Considering the other signs of one Grandstone keeping secrets from the other, maybe he didn't know the family estate was about to be lost. Maybe he only saw this as a money-making venture, and a chance to finally give someone in Neighborlee a black eye.

Reggie and Freddie returned home in disgrace, escorted by Cincinnati cops, and handed over to Cuyahoga County authorities for processing. All that sabotage had finally tipped the scales against them. Not just the false claims and violations London had put on their records, but the actual actions and their attitudes and words, when they came up against cops who didn't know or care who Grandstones were.

Carr, Cooper and Crenshaw fired Reggie, at long last. He had gone too far. The entire town acknowledged the sacrifice the law firm had been making for years, allowing Reggie to work there and keep an eye on him, curtailing his most extreme actions. Freddie reportedly didn't wait for the architectural firm he worked for to fire him. He had a screaming, swearing fit when he walked in on some senior members of the firm discussing his uncle Stephen's predicament, and laughing about how the Grandstones never seemed to learn. When he refused to apologize, and demanded an apology from them, and they refused, he quit.

Typical Grandstone attitude, lashing out at others, cutting off their own noses to spite someone else's face. We were waiting for both Grandstone boys to have hissies when their respective former firms didn't apologize and grovel and beg them to come back to work.

The expected, typical Grandstone temper tantrums didn't occur. The Grandstone estate was suddenly too quiet. Kurt, Jane and I went on a recon mission four days after the whirlwind trip to Cincinnati, and descended down to the level of the walls around the compound that supposedly protected their privacy. All was dark and quiet. With the Ghost field, we went into their garages, and finally through the walls of their houses.

Everyone was gone, except Rosco. Grandfather Albert had been confined to a hospital bed since he had one of his famous temper tantrums and crashed his car into the old police station, necessitating a new police station. He had been removed from his reportedly palatial hospital suite. Freddie and Reggie were gone, violating court orders. So was their mother, Teresa, and their aunt Matilda, Sylvia's mother and Stephen's wife. Over the course of the next few days, various small moving companies showed up and hauled away loads of art and antiques and china and personal belongings.

The Neighborlee effect, the subliminal message of "go away, we don't like you," hadn't driven out the Grandstones, but apparently terror of the Lightning Pathway had accomplished that long-cherished hope.

What's the line about preferring the devil you know over the devil you don't?

~~~~~

The prayer team got together and held vigil in the sanctuary of our church for the entire long drive from Nashville up to Neighborlee, when Ethan, Stanzer, Pastor Rocky and Father Marty drove back with Achmed, Leo and Frankie.

We knew better than to bring those three men over the border into Neighborlee. Either they would have seizures, proving they were under the influence of our enemies, or bringing them inside the shield would open Neighborlee to the influence of these enemies who had apparently been trying for years to finagle a welcome.

The clock continued to tick in the countdown for the concert that would save the Neighborlee Children's Home. Rosco Grandstone insisted the concert had to take place in Neighborlee. We found a way around that, while letting him believe he was getting his way. We could put up with some gloating on his part as long as he failed in the end.

And the prayer team continued to pray, holding up the shield around our town.

An interesting little fact that Athena had learned in school, but no one had remembered until it came in handy, was that the Cuyahoga County Fairgrounds spread out over land that belonged to three different towns. Two of the archway entrances to the fairgrounds were on streets in Neighborlee. One of the four performance stages on fairgrounds property backed up to those entrances, and anyone who didn't study the map of the fairgrounds would assume that stage was in Neighborlee.

Meaning the performers would not actually be on Neighborlee property.

The back of the stage was two feet from the border. Anyone who took a running leap off the back of that stage would jump from Cutterville to Neighborlee. If they didn't bounce off the shield.

The plan was for Pastor Rocky to jump to safety if the situation during the "back from the dead" Magna Magma concert, as it was starting to be called on social media, got ugly. If our fears all came true, and the other musicians went zombie and attacked him, they would fry when they tried to follow him and slammed into the shield.

In theory, anyway.

The night after the caravan arrived from Nashville and the three refugee members of Magna Magma settled into their new quarters at the Sheridan facilities in Aurora, the dreams returned. For Ford, Felicity, Athena, Doni, and me. We all dreamed different things, but when we got together, achy and exhausted from tossing and turning all night, the dreams added up to the same thing. Big Ugly was restless. He was waking
~~~~~

up. And he was angry.

Athena, Wallace and Cosmo huddled with London and Sherwood, and put together a website in just a few days to promote and handle the tickets for the Magna Magma: Back From the Dead concert. They also brought in a group of hackers known as the Partycrashers, to help them defend the site against the wacko extremist Lavaheads and the usual troublemakers who liked to tear things down just so nobody else could enjoy them.

We scheduled the concert for the weekend after Labor Day. Rosco Grandstone had a snit about that, but even he couldn't force the fairgrounds to cancel the events that had been scheduled months ago to take place over Labor Day weekend. He seemed to find some satisfaction in reports that Magna Magma fans were caught trying to set up camping spots throughout the fairground, breaking into buildings and trying to create nests in cellars and attics, and avoid paying for tickets. Others took to trying to camp in the back yards and front yards of people living on Sackley Road and the streets with the other fairgrounds entrances, so they could be close when the gates opened.

During the drive up from Nashville and all the work to set up the concert, Frankie lived under tight surveillance. He never had any more of those spells where he went cold and regal, and Ambrose Lux looked through his eyes. At least, none that anyone noticed.

So, once the details were made and contracts signed and promotional materials went out and the advertising began -- and the ticket sales started pouring in from around the world, not just across the country -- Rosco Grandstone took the ticking clock off his Facebook page, and he went into magnanimous dictator mode. We could breathe a little easier. For a few minutes at a time. We had a lot of work to do, just keeping watch for LaRiche and his minions, Mrs. Von Helado and her minions, and Kerri and her minions to start closing in, preparing to attack. If they were trying to get Lux back, if they were preparing to finally enter Neighborlee when they took over the Grandstone property, or if they were going to grab Pastor Rocky and use his voice as a weapon to rule the world, who knew? All the guardians cared about was making sure none of those dread destinies took place.

Pastor Rocky spent a lot of time counseling with Achmed, Leo and Frankie. Pop and the board of trustees and the deacons took over his responsibilities, and the prayer team went in rotating shifts with at least ten people in the sanctuary any time of the day or night. This was war. The enemy had focused his nasty eyes on and aimed his claws at our pastor. We weren't putting up with it.

Ethan spent hours every day in his and Angela's garden, limbering up and practicing with his armor, lance, sword, and shield. We hoped he wouldn't need to use them, but just the fact his armor had appeared in the hidden garden kind of indicated that trouble was approaching.

Gordon and Chief Tanner both pulled as many official strings as they could, and non-official ones, but LaRiche and Sylvia had vanished. No evidence remained behind that they had ever been in that factory. Lightning Pathway still had its name on the deed, and there were all sorts of permits and registrations and plans filed to cover the renovations taking place on the property. But nothing that could be used as evidence that the leadership of the so-called ministry had ever stepped foot there, or anyone had been inside the building.

For all we knew, LaRiche and his goons and the corpse bride had stepped through a dimensional doorway or teleported, or they had the ability to generate their own Ghost field or some version of it, to travel invisibly. Which generated the next logical question: why hadn't they sensed us watching them?

Unless they had, and they were playing games with us? Tricking us into making mistakes and handing Frankie or Pastor Rocky or both men over to them?

That concert and the expected confrontation couldn't come fast enough. Yet in another sense it was coming way too quickly.

The only people who seemed at all relaxed about this whole mess were Pastor Rocky and Father Marty. If any good was going to come out of this, it would be that two old friends had had a chance to make peace and find new common ground.

Athena reported that tickets sold out within the first week. Our friends in the fairgrounds administration reported that Rosco Grandstone kept trying to trick their underlings into turning over the information about the concert event, so he could ensure everything was "above board and transparent." Considering he had nothing to do with the concert and no control over the arrangements, and certainly no access to the figures for what had been paid already, we suspected he was trying to exchange yet another revised contract for the one that had been signed. He had already tried to have himself put in charge, and to trick my Pop and the others running the show into signing a document saying *all* ticket sales went directly into the Grandstone bank account, rather than all profits *after* the fairground fees and expenses had been paid. London and Sherwood were having fun frustrating and scorching the hackers Rosco had hired to try to break into the website and shanghai the controls.

We had to wonder if he knew that the return of Sylvia, conscious and functioning, was part of the deal. We doubted that Rosco would put that sort of effort into rescuing someone else's child, since he hadn't done anything to rescue Reggie and Freddie, other than violate their parole agreement and send them out of town.

With all the hacking attempts thrown at the website and the work of monitoring the shield and the buildup of activity indicating Big Ugly was getting ready to strike, London and Sherwood didn't have time or energy for anything else. Wallace took charge of the pictures Daniel had snapped of the BoBs during that brief chase and snatch-and-rescue in the factory in Cincinnati, as well as the security camera photos of BoBs here in town and around the rescue mission. We needed to identify the minions of Lightning Pathway, to have as much ammunition as possible to use against them.

The breakthrough came from Wallace's irritation with the retro outfits the BoBs were wearing. Being the fashion plate of the group, he did a search for the design and maker of those uniform outfits -- pants, shoes, jackets, shirts, and hats. The effort to create a specific search program for those clothes took him less than half an hour, while he was taking a break from defending the concert website. He also added the faces posted on the Lightning Pathway website. Cosmo linked those images to the security cameras around town and for half a mile outside the border of Neighborlee, and set up a program to alert us if anyone resembling those images tried to enter.

Four days before the concert, the alarms went off at half a dozen points around the border. The cameras at banks and speed zones and loading docks of businesses showed vintage black sedans swerving and pulling over, sometimes turning around and narrowly evading crashes. All the drivers' faces were in the database.

So LaRiche's minions were trying to get into Neighborlee, and couldn't.

We should have been a little more frightened, but we were distracted by the breakthrough Wallace had made in identifying the BoBs and leaders of Lightning Pathway.

His program identified the BoBs and the designer of their clothes. They were all in the same big file for an unsolved mass disappearance.

Back in the mid-60s -- which explained the style of clothes -- a rising fashion designer named Morocco Jones essentially destroyed his career and his reputation after a two-month desert sojourn. He returned raving about an encounter with a hyper-dimensional being that promised incalculable riches and power. All he had to do was gather enough willing and sensitive souls into a group mind, to provide the power to break down the gate between that alternative dimension of reality and Earth, and allow the Cosmic Master to come through and take his rightful place as ruler of Earth's dimension.

Part of the plan included erasing individual identity by dressing everyone alike. Hence the outfits. Along with massive doses of mind-altering drugs. Jones and his right-hand assistant and fellow prophet,

Manfred Cortez, led their followers back into the desert for a consultation with the Cosmic Master. Most of them were never seen or heard from again. The few who came out of the desert had fried their brains on days of ingesting nothing but drugs and inhaling various hallucinogenic smoke compounds. They told of seeing the air split open before a massive spiral pulled everyone else down into it.

Everyone but Jones. He was found in a catatonic state, scorched by the desert sun, dehydrated and mumbling confusing bits that made no sense, such as, "I thought we'd have jet packs in the future." He died within two weeks of being retrieved from the desert.

Manfred Cortez was either LaRiche's twin, his lookalike son, or LaRiche himself.

Considering how many of the faces of the BoBs were in the file of Jones' followers ... the simplest theory was that they had been sucked into the future.

Or LaRiche was a doppelganger, maybe all the BoBs were doppelgangers, and the original followers of Jones had been eaten by the Cosmic Master, aka Big Ugly? If that had happened, we could only hope they had given him indigestion, like we hoped the Rivals had given him a few years ago.

The other theory was that they had failed to help the Cosmic Master tear down the dimensional gate to Earth, and some kind of boomerang effect threw them forward to the future. What were the chances that if the Cosmic Master was Big Ugly, Cortez/LaRiche and his followers had enough energy now to break down that gate?

Or had that been the intent of that desert meeting all along? Send them forward to the future, where they would have the technology to pull off something calculated to break down the gate that kept Big Ugly from using Earth as a jumping off point to multiple dimensions?

Talk about making a deal with the devil, as Tass had accused Pastor Rocky of doing not too long ago...

Chapter Fourteen

So, with the days counting down to the concert at the fairgrounds, we were on high alert, watching for signs of the BoBs and Kerri and Mrs. Von Helado, and reverberations from underground as Big Ugly prepared for the nasties on our side of the dimensional doorway to open it. We were understandably distracted, and didn't realize something huge was missing, until just days before the concert.

Specifically, the Grandstones weren't throwing major legal hissy fits. Stephen was still sitting in jail, waiting for his day in court, and Rosco wasn't doing anything to get his brother out of jail. Wasn't harassing judges. Wasn't filing all sorts of claims of persecution and questionable methods, and attempting to get access to the videos of the whole ruckus with Earnest B. Tass in front of the high school. The Grandstones had done that regularly through the years: fight to get access to evidence and then try to destroy it or erase it or contaminate it or switch it out for something to prove their story and contradict the truth.

Instead, there was silence.

What was Rosco waiting for, and why wasn't Stephen having coronaries and seizures in his temper tantrums that his brother wasn't moving Hell on Earth to get him out, or at least into more comfortable surroundings?

Did it have something to do with zombie Sylvia after all? Or did the Grandstones have a major ace up their sleeves that we hadn't even guessed yet?

Then we ran out of time to theorize and research. The next phase of LaRiche's plan hit us square in the face. Metaphorically.

Wednesday was the first rehearsal on the fairgrounds stage of the five remaining members of Magna Magma. Pastor Rocky had just finished replacing two strings on his electric bass, and looked up after one test strum.

"Do you see that?" he asked me.

I tapped my tablet screen to put in a colored stripe on the page I had been reading, as a bookmark, and looked up at him. I followed the line of his arm, to see what he pointed at.

Three men in new-dark jeans and untucked white shirts sauntered away from a black, vintage sedan, aiming for the stage.

"Yeah." I took a deep breath to fight down the shiver that dug claws into my back and dove for my intestines. "Were you hoping I didn't?"

"Pretty much." He swallowed hard. "I was hoping I was having an acid flashback."

"Since when did you do acid?"

"You can always hope someone slipped some in your Mountain Dew when you weren't looking. A better choice than the trouble heading our way." He carefully put aside his bass and stood up.

"Who are they?"

"Dead men walking." He pressed his hands together, signaling emergency prayer, and headed out to meet the three new arrivals.

Okay, considering how young those men looked, their retro hair styles ... I had to guess these were not just the former members of Magna Magma who had died in the bus crash, but doppelgangers. The original doppelgangers, or new ones who took the places of the ones who had died in the bus crash? Did any doppelgangers die in the bus crash?

My head was starting to hurt, just spinning through the possibilities.

I tapped through my screen to get to the link to London and Sherwood. When he answered first, I picked up my tablet and hit the control to shift to camera mode. I didn't even have to tell him what was happening. Sherwood caught the identification and implications right away. Right as he said he was sending out the alert to the scattered members of the team, a shout came from the left. Father Marty came running from the RV we had borrowed from the Wallowitzes, friends from church, to use as a dressing room and hiding place during rehearsals. Behind him, Frankie, Achmed and Leo were running in the opposite direction.

"Kurt, we've got runners," I said, almost before I hit the speaker button on the walkie-talkie left with me for just such problems. Meaning the three of them freaking out and making a run for it, not the appearance of doppelgangers pretending that everything was fine, and nobody was supposed to suspect they were fakes and replacements.

I got a staticky response from Kurt and hoped that was confirmation that he was heading them off at the pass. I wheeled over to meet Father Marty while trying to keep an eye on Pastor Rocky. Then I thought of something.

"I've got a lot of static, how about you? Bad sign? By the way, we've got doppelgangers moving in. Not a coincidence?"

Kurt didn't respond right away. He was busy heading off the three panicky men, who to be charitable were still detoxing and recovering from whatever Lightning Pathway did to them. When he did respond, after getting them in his truck, the signal was clear again. He had dealt with the source of the problem: a BoB in a van that had probably been to Woodstock, with some kind of electrical coil that was jamming radio signals. Kurt dealt with the energy interference easily enough, thanks to his convenient ability to control machinery of any kind.

Frankie, Achmed, and Leo saw the BoB and ran to Kurt with open arms, so he didn't have to run them down and bully them into his truck. Then when they got back to the stage, I had to wonder how much their reasoning and cognitive skills had recovered. Why? They saw the three doppelgangers, who claimed to want to rehearse with them, and welcomed them with open arms. That was just so not right.

"What do we do?" I asked Pastor Rocky, when the six trooped over to the stage with the waiting sound equipment and large assortment of musical instruments we had managed to borrow and rent in less than a week.

"Let them rehearse," he said after a few seconds. Then he took a deep breath and seemed to be having a brief mental or maybe spiritual debate. "Marty ... you got your gear on you?"

"Never leave home without it." Father Marty nodded and managed a thin, determined kind of smile.

"I think it'd be wise to clear the air before we make any music."

"Gotcha." He winked at me as he scurried over to the RV.

"What are you up to?" I asked.

"What we should always do before going into spiritual warfare. Make sure our armor is in place." Pastor Rocky wasn't looking at me but watching the stage where the six men were picking up different instruments and giving them a test strum or blow or tap, and chattering away as if there was nothing wrong, they had been playing together for the last fifty years without a break.

"Ethan is on his way over," Sherwood reported, speaking through my tablet.

"Meaning?" He paused in bending over to pick up his Bible that had been lying open on the table.

Pastor Rocky's Bible made me itchy. Not because as the daughter of writers I got hives when I saw books that had been written in or were dogeared and waterlogged. But because every page I had ever glimpsed was full of notes written in the margins and a rainbow of highlighters, and little flag stickers and sheets with extended notes slipped in between every other page. I always felt kind of guilty over how much time Pastor Rocky spent with his Bible, even after all these years of ministry. You'd think a guy would have the book memorized by now, but I had seen him reading and making more notes just this morning while waiting for the sound check and all the electricians and engineers who had volunteered their time and skills -- all from our church -- to finish their work.

"He didn't say."

Father Marty came back to join us by then. He was a little flushed and looked more somber than he had been through all the weirdness so far. He wore a priest's stole around his shoulders and had a Bible and a prayer book tucked under one arm while he struggled to put his clerical collar on, and his jeans pockets bulged with several bottles. I swallowed down the question that wanted to blurt out of me: was he planning on having an exorcism? Or was all this gear more along the lines of last rites? Either way, serious stuff.

Any other time and place, any other town ... well, any other town, we probably wouldn't be in this situation. Pastor Rocky and Father Marty would probably still be good friends, even serving on opposite sides of the theological dividing line. I had a few seconds of doubt because I didn't put any stock in the ability of supposedly holy water and holy oil to do any good. However, this was Neighborlee, and we knew just how much power belief had over events and outcomes.

This was getting way serious, and yet there was this knot of peace in the center of me that seemed to be pulling things straight and calm. It was weird, but comfortingly weird. In this situation, weird was good.

"Ready?" Pastor Rocky said, looking to me, then to Father Marty. We both nodded and headed for the stage.

The six men on stage stopped and watched. When we got to the stairs on the right side of the front, I got out of my chair and held onto the railing as I walked slowly up the steps. Pastor Rocky folded up my chair and lifted it up onto the front of the stage. Father Marty came up the stairs after me and supported me as I walked the few steps to where my chair waited, unfolded it, and helped me sit. In that time, Pastor Rocky came up the stairs.

The back of the stage was open where the thick multiple layers of canvass had been pulled up to allow air flow. From the corner of my eye, I saw a figure climb up the steps there and stay in the shadows. I figured that was Ethan. I guessed all he was going to do was watch, make sure the three doppelgangers didn't do anything nasty.

"How about -- no, I'm not giving you the option," Pastor Rocky said, and chuckled. "We're going to bathe this rehearsal in prayer. I know we're going to need it, if we're going to give our loyal old fans the concert they're looking forward to." He held out his hands. "What do you say?"

The three doppelgangers just looked at him, blinking, mouths twitching a little like they couldn't think of what to say. Achmed and Leo both nodded. After all the good that had been done for them at the rescue mission, it made sense they'd be all for more prayer, having seen how well it had worked so far.

"Man," Frankie said, shaking his head and grinning. Then he took two steps back, away from Pastor Rocky. "Is that all you ever do? When'd you get so boring?" He chuckled, a ragged kind of sound, but he didn't sound nervous or afraid. Which was kind of weird.

"If you think prayer is boring," Father Marty said, "you're doing it wrong." He tugged on the bottom edges of his stole, straightening it.

"Yeah, that's fine for you guys, but me, what we need is to practice. Hard and long. Right guys?" He gestured at the three doppelgangers, who nodded.

"If God isn't in it, what good is it?" Pastor Rocky stepped up and caught hold of a hand each on two of the three doppelgangers, bowed his head, and started in on praying. "Father in Heaven, please protect us and guide us and drive away the forces of evil --"

The doppelgangers screamed in unison. Two tried to yank their hands free. The third leaped at Pastor Rocky.

Father Marty swung his Bible around and slapped the doppelganger across the face with it. He shrieked louder and seemed to expand. That's the only way to describe it. He went pale and then a heartbeat later hit the stage as a pile of pale gold pebbles and dust. The cloud from the impact rose up in the air. I closed my eyes against the dust and tucked my face into the crook of my elbow.

The two remaining doppelgangers kept screaming, getting louder. Pastor Rocky continued praying, asking for God's protection. They yanked their hands free and staggered, running, toward the back of the stage.

Ethan met them, swinging his sword. It burst into flames when it touched the closest doppelganger and went through him like a knife dipped in lighter fluid and set on fire, going through a gelatin mold. The kind full of all sorts of chopped vegetables. And yeah, just as messy when it liquified and slid off the edge of the table to splat on the floor.

Except the doppelganger turned to dust and pebbles and scattered across the stage. The second one skidded through the debris and fell to his knees, shrieking words I didn't understand, that sent a chill through me.

Ethan swung again with that sword and this one disintegrated too.

The seven of us just stood or sat there, and looked at the dust and pebbles that had been people a few minutes ago.

"Okay, that was freaky. You sure we're not having a flashback?" Father Marty said.

Frankie laughed, but the other two men staggered and clutched at each other and looked around like they expected something to swoop down at them and attack. They went pale and their eyes widened and sweat spilled down their foreheads and temples.

"Sing," Ethan growled, pointing that shining sword at Pastor Rocky.

For a second, I thought maybe he had lost it, then I remembered what he and Stanzer had both reported, when they returned from Nashville. Pastor Rocky had never sung, in all the years I had known him, but he had sung healing to the derelicts and wounded and lost. Not to all of them, but the ones whose spirits were ready to accept. Pastor Rocky's gift had never gone away, despite all the years of neglect through fear.

Don't ask me what the words were, or to try to reproduce the tune. I can't. Pastor Rocky picked away at his old acoustic guitar and let his healed heart flow through his voice. His eyes glowed and this incredible smell drifted across the stage. It was all the good things, the best things I had ever smelled in my life, constantly changing, bringing up flashes of memories. Campfire smoke and the scent of burning marshmallows. Vanilla candles and baking sugar cookies. The air after a torrential downpour. Snow on a brilliant, silent morning. Chocolate and peppermint. Baking bread. Freshly cut grass.

Sensations came with the smells. The feeling of my folks holding me and laughing together that first Christmas as a family. My favorite blanket, fresh out of the dryer, wrapped around me. The tide splashing across my bare toes. That feeling of completeness and giddy anticipation that I sometimes felt in that split second between dreaming and waking, when the dream felt more real than the physical world. And then faded.

The clatter of several instruments falling over jolted me out of the drifting, happy, drowsy feeling. I turned to see Achmed sliding to the stage on his knees, his eyes half-closed, no longer shaking, and a smile relaxing his face. Leo sprawled backwards, propped up on his elbows, shaking his head and blinking like he was waking up.

Father Marty was on his knees, arms spread, stretching to the skies, tears streaming down his face. The most glorious smile made him glow, just like Pastor Rocky's eyes.

Frankie hunched down on the chair where he had been sitting when the attack started, fingers white-knuckle gripping the seat, eyes wide and staring at some spot in mid-air, and looking like he was either going to be sick or burst into tears.

Pastor Rocky stopped singing, and for a moment I couldn't make my lungs draw in enough air. Everything turned heavy and thick around me, and I was glad I was sitting in my wheelchair, because I couldn't have stood up to save my life. Ethan took the last few steps over to me and gripped my shoulder. He gave me a crooked little smile that conveyed so clearly that he felt the same aching sense of loss that I did in that moment.

"Man ... I don't remember doing anything that made me feel like that," Achmed said, his voice cracking. "So this can't be a flashback. What'd you do to us?"

"That wasn't me," Pastor Rocky said. His voice had a background note that sent hints of that sweetness and completion through me and made me shiver with longing.

Maybe his gift wasn't so much singing as it was allowing his voice to peel back a tiny bit of the barrier between us and heaven?

"That was God's mercy. He uses me to heal. I'm grateful, because I certainly don't deserve to be used like that, after the way I misused my musical talent, back when we were a band."

"Man ..." Leo shook his head, a soft smile lighting his face. "If you ever sang with us, we could have cleaned up."

"We could have ruled the world," Frankie said, his voice scraping like it was filled with shattering rocks.

"It wouldn't have been caught on tapes. Waste of time," Father Marty said.

"So this is part of what you were talking about before?" Achmed settled back, scooting around until he sat on his bottom with his legs clasped to his chest and his chin on his knees. "No wonder you bailed on us and signed up, if you get to have that moving through you."

"You're such a loser," Frankie growled, his head bowing lower, his shoulders shaking. His fingers were so bloodless from the pressure, I thought he might dig them right through the metal seat of the chair.

"Marty ..." Pastor Rocky glanced at me and Ethan. "How about you take the guys back to the trailer and have a talk with them, clear up anything they don't understand?"

Leo chuckled and swore under his breath. "If we don't understand what you've been talking about all this time, then we're even more hopeless than any of us thought."

"Then does that mean you're ready to sign up?" Father Marty said. He pushed himself to his feet and wiped the last tears off his face. "Come on, guys." He glanced once at Frankie, gripping the seat of his chair and ignoring everyone. He mimed praying to Pastor Rocky.

I said a quick, simple prayer, because, duh, that was the smart thing to do. When we're in over our heads and we don't have the strength or the smarts to handle a really big job, it's just plain stupid to keep trying to do it all on our own. We have to ask for help. And ask from the top.

Ethan, Pastor Rocky and I were silent until the other three had gone into the trailer and I heard the door click shut.

"Frankie, are you in there, or did Ambrose Lux come back?" Pastor Rocky said.

I stiffened badly enough I probably could have flipped myself out of my chair. Ethan's hand stayed on my shoulder, and he raised the sword he had been holding at his side all this time.

"It's me." Frankie raised his eyes. In just those few moments since he bowed his head, his face had gone almost skeletal. Dark patches smeared his eyes. "But I don't know how long. Oh, man, you gotta help me. Drake ... they want us. They're coming for us. I can't remember, I don't know any of this most of the time, but that singing ... you gotta keep singing. It tears down the walls they keep wrapping around my brain, making me forget. I messed up big-time. Letting Lux in. Take over. Can't get rid of him."

"Yes, you can." Pastor Rocky tugged on the bench he was sitting on until he faced Frankie and caught hold of his shaking hands. "You just need to ask for help, that's all."

"That's what I'm doing! I'm beggin' you, man." He grimaced. "They're coming. All of them. Lux is laughing all the time, in the back of my head. Can't wait to take you over and use that golden voice. He took me because he couldn't get you, but now he's using me to get you and we gotta run and hide. I'm tellin' you, Drake, there's nowhere to hide, but we still gotta try."

He raised a shaking arm and pointed at the back of the stage that still waited for the canvas to be dropped and the barrier raised.

"It's right there. Safety. We gotta get through that wall. You can take me through, can't you? On the other side, they can't get to us. It's all light and it's warm and pretty. On the other side. But I can't get through. You gotta help me get through. Please!"

Frankie staggered up from the chair and stumbled a few steps toward the back of the stage. He flung himself off, startling yelps from me and Pastor Rocky.

A flash of light made us all flinch and close our eyes. There was a thud, and when I opened my eyes, Frankie was lying on his back on the stage. He rolled over on his side and curled up partially into a fetal ball.

"It won't let me through. You gotta help me, Drake," he said, his voice a rasp.

Pastor Rocky slowly shook his head, shaking, and locked gazes with Ethan. I was starting to have fond memories of that short time in the hospital when the doctors had me doped up and floating after my back was broken. This was reality harsher and more solid than anything I had ever encountered as a guardian. And considering all the weirdness we had seen and done over the years, that was saying a lot. I thought about the doppelganger that immolated itself on the shield earlier in the year, and flinched at the thought of Frankie being caught and just hanging there, burning to ash. Probably screaming and disturbing everyone in the houses on the street that backed up to this part of the fairgrounds. If they called the police, this wasn't something we could explain and cover over with a half-truthful story, like we could just twenty feet away inside the safety of Neighborlee.

"What do you want?" Ethan said, his voice soft, yet solid and sharp, like his sword. It glowed faintly, visible now in the backstage area with the canvas sheeting blocking the sunlight.

It made me think of Bilbo's sword, Sting, and how it glowed when orcs or goblins were around. Was that what was happening here? Was this why the sword had manifested? Why the sword and not the entire suit of armor?

"Sanctuary." Frankie chuckled, a broken, hiccupping sound. "Almost got sanctuary at Sanctuary." He sighed and seemed to deflate a little. "Please, Drake, let me in. Help me get away from them."

"All right, Frankie." Pastor Rocky covered his face with his hands for a moment and bowed so his head was almost even with his knees. He straightened and walked to the back of the stage, saying, "I welcome my friend Frankie Leonides to Neighborlee. Only Frankie Leonides. Only the man who truly wants healing and freedom. Only the man who is telling the truth and wants to become like a child again."

"Man ..." Frankie chuckled and rolled onto his back. "What kind of stuff are you on now? Can you get me some of that? You're crazier than I ever was."

"Lanie, when I say, hold him," Ethan said. He walked to the back of the stage and stood a moment, talking softly with Pastor Rocky, both of them with their backs to me and Frankie.

"What are they doing?" Frankie had gotten to his feet while my attention was off him.

That felt like a big mistake. I had already figured out that when Ethan said "hold him," he didn't mean give him a big hug of Christian fellowship. He meant grab Frankie with my mind and put him in the best imitation of a tractor beam I could manage. No matter how many mental circuits I blew out.

"Conferring on how to open the door for you," I said. It was the truth, just not the whole truth. "So ... how long has the sleezoid been in the driver's seat? Since you washed up out of the Bermuda Triangle, or maybe when LaRiche took over?"

"I don't know what you mean." He managed a thin smile but couldn't hide that momentary angry flash in his eyes.

Yeah, I had finally caught on to what Pastor Rocky and Ethan both feared: Lux was in the driver's seat, just pretending to be suffering Frankie. He had suffered during the singing that healed Achmed and Leo. Probably the attack by the doppelgangers had been meant to bring Lux back into control and shove Frankie out of the driver's seat. Maybe permanently. And as a bonus, incapacitate Pastor Rocky, maybe get him helpless so he could be taken over by another nasty being like Lux.

"Those creeps at Lightning Pathway did a good job, wiping your footprints, making it seem like you just vanished. Not good enough, though."

Ethan nodded to something Pastor Rocky said. He raised his sword, and I nearly swallowed my tongue when Pastor Rocky put both hands on either side of the blade, holding it flat between his palms. That was a good way to slit his wrists, if not cut his hands off. I imagined that blade was sharper and stronger than anything ever known on Earth. Like the sword of the Spirit, separating soul from flesh, bone from marrow.

"We've got some people on our side who know the Internet better than anyone, because they're inside. They can be everywhere at once if they have to. They found stuff LaRiche and his creeps haven't been able to wipe yet. Of course, the fact they managed any of it is pretty amazing, considering they're all refugees from the 60s."

"Is that so?" Lux's voice had a rasp like sand blowing across steel. He took a few steps closer to me. I hoped I had the strength to give him a really strong, hard wallop with my telekinesis, if I needed to. Like if he went for my throat.

Never underestimate a poor little crippled girl. My legs don't work, but that just means my brain is twice as fast and nasty, when I need to be.

"Yeah. Too bad they couldn't find and wipe away the pictures and the really freaky story about Morocco Jones and the big desert trek to speak to the Cosmic Master. Finding all that info kind of made everything else unravel."

Yes, I was babbling, and it was kind of stupid to reveal we knew all this dangerous information, if that really was Lux looking out of Frankie's eyes again. The risk was necessary, while Ethan and Pastor Rocky prepared for whatever they needed to do. I just hoped they figured it out fast, because I was running out of things to say to distract Lux.

"I'd like to meet these friends of yours." He took two more steps closer.

Um, nope, that was not the direction I wanted him to go.

Then Pastor Rocky stepped back, and Ethan jumped down to the ground behind the stage. Pastor turned around and his face got stern as his gaze landed on us.

"Frankie."

Lux didn't turn but pulled himself up taller, his shoulders hunching and widening. It reminded me of some elastic super-villain working himself up for the big pounce on a hapless little goody-goody twit who didn't know when to shut up.

Yeah. Me.

"Frankie!" Pastor Rocky spread his hands, palms up, the same way he did when he was leading really important, intense prayers in emergency situations. Okay, prayer was good right about now.

"What?" Lux turned around and he sort of shrank and faded a little, and he was all pathetic Frankie Leonides again.

"Are you ready to step over the line and ask for shelter and healing?"

"Always. Been ready and waiting all my life." He hurried the dozen or so feet to where Pastor Rocky waited.

"Who am I speaking with?" He guided Frankie to stand with his back to Ethan, his heels on the edge of the stage, facing me. "Frankie or the invader calling itself Ambrose Lux?"

"What?" Frankie/Lux shook his head and managed a confused, "this is a big joke, right?" kind of smile.

"By the power of the Spirit and truth, I command you to speak the truth," Pastor Rocky said. Then he opened his mouth and sang.

This was different from the singing that had healed and calmed Achmed and Leo. I shivered from the power in it, the sense of something huge and overwhelming and beyond my comprehension. It rose up out of Pastor Rocky and overshadowed the stage, the fairgrounds, spreading to cover Cutterville and Neighborlee, maybe all of Cuyahoga County. The entire state of Ohio, if he kept on singing.

Frankie screamed.

"Lanie!" Ethan shouted.

I grabbed hold of Frankie with my mind, just as he turned and brought a knife from inside his shirt. I nearly let go from the shock, seeing that nightmare again in my memory -- Frankie stabbing Pastor Rocky with the drumsticks that turned into knives.

"Who are you? Who is in control?" Ethan said, and his voice had an echoing vastness that threatened my control.

The commonsense part of me shuddered and demanded that I get out of there. I could just leap out of my wheelchair and fly all the way home. I did not want to be here, not under the weight of all that power and authority and purity. I was a mess and if any of that immensity touched me, it would burn away all the junk from my mind and heart and soul, and there wouldn't be much left.

Frankie snarled something that didn't sound like any language I had ever heard. Not even Klingon or the tongue of Mordor.

"Let Frankie speak. And only Frankie. You have no power to speak," Ethan snapped, and reached up from behind where Frankie's body hovered, one foot in the air, to touch him with that gleaming sword.

A massive black spark burst out of Frankie with a deafening snap-crack sound that made all the hair stand up all over my body.

"Please." Frankie -- this really was Frankie this time -- burst into tears. "Get this thing out of me. It's eating me up. Am I crazy? Somebody, stop it. Drake, please, man -- help me?"

"Do you want to be free?" Ethan said.

"Yes."

"Do you want to be healed?"

"Yes!"

"Do you understand everything that Rocky has been telling you and trying to teach you, and do you submit to the one true authority --"

"Yes! Come on, man! Help me! It's squeezing the life --"

"Then come!" Ethan's voice made the stage shake under me. "Frankie Leonides and only Frankie Leonides is entirely welcome to find sanctuary in Neighborlee. Fall and trust." He took a deep breath. The awesome sternness left his face. Ethan looked exhausted as he leaned a little to the side to look around Frankie. "Now, Lanie. Let go."

I let go of Frankie and gasped in relief, because I was getting a massive headache.

My gasp turned into a scream.

Frankie fell backwards, off the stage.

Right onto Ethan's sword.

Pastor Rocky's song stopped.

The lights died, all light sucked into that sword that went right through Frankie's chest.

And yet there was no blood. Like the sword wasn't metal, but all power.

Separating evil soul from flesh.

Blackness burst out of Frankie's body, a dense shadow in the shape of a man that spread out and grew wings and twisted and arched up in the air and bombed back down, aiming for Ethan. He leaped up and swung that sword as Frankie fell out of sight, behind the stage. Sword met shadow with a thunderclap. There was a smell like I imagine a skunk coated in week-old liquefied corpse wreathed in methane would make as it hit a pool of lava. Just for a second, before everything incinerated.

Before I could inhale from the shock -- it was over.

Pastor Rocky went to his knees as Ethan landed on the stage, just in the same knees-flexed pose of Iron Man.

"What the --" Father Marty snapped off a string of what had to be Latin cuss words, accompanied by the slam-crack of the trailer door opening, " -- just happened?"

Chapter Fifteen

The sonic boom wave hit me and knocked me backward, tipping my chair so I turned a backward somersault. Pastor Rocky burst out laughing. I burst out laughing.

It didn't last long, but man, it felt good to release a lot of crazy-making tension. About the time I needed to stop and catch my breath, Father Marty and Achmed and Leo had gotten to the stage. They fumbled around a little, helping me get upright and get my wheelchair back on its wheels. And about then, Ethan was helping Frankie to his feet. They were far enough away from the back of the stage, they were definitely over the border in Neighborlee. Ethan slung Frankie's arm around his shoulders and he turned and started walking away toward the small parking lot, still on Neighborlee soil, where I assumed he had parked his car.

"That, my friend," Pastor Rocky said, as he struggled to his feet, "was *not* an example of a good old-fashioned exorcism."

"Where's Frankie?" Achmed asked. He looked right at Ethan and Frankie, but clearly he didn't see them.

I checked later, and Pastor Rocky saw them, but Leo and Father Marty very clearly didn't. So what made them semi-invisible? Maybe all that power of Ethan's sword, burning through Frankie, burning away all the rot that Ambrose Lux had wrapped around and through him?

We told the truth, when security asked us what had happened, what caused that sudden loud explosion and that flash of light. We just didn't tell the whole truth. Frankie fell backward off the stage. While we were all focused on him, the noise and the light happened, so if something fell or circuits blew, we had no idea where. Frankie was so shook up by his fall, Ethan was taking him to a friend who was a doctor.

That was also the truth. Ethan took Frankie to Divine's. Angela's doctor friend came from the Fae Realms to make sure he was thoroughly cleansed and freed.

It was a given there wasn't going to be a rehearsal that afternoon. With only a few days left until the "Return from the Dead" concert, things weren't looking so good. I was all for canceling.

One problem, however. From what Frankie could remember after Lux was burned away, the big plan all along had been to surround Pastor Rocky by Lightning Pathway minions while he was performing and vulnerable and take him over. Like Frankie had been taken over by Lux through the vulnerability of his music. There was a power struggle between Von Helado and Kerri, and LaRiche was maneuvering to usurp all their power through Frankie and Pastor Rocky. The really scary part was that this was indeed tied into what Kurt and Portia and others who were sensitive to the power in the air and soil of Neighobrlee feared: Big Ugly was getting ready to make another attempt to break out of his prison. LaRiche had maneuvered everything to sacrifice Von Helado and Kerri and their minions, and take Big Ugly's power.

Which was kind of stupid. We had seen plenty of times what happened when the minions stood up against Big Ugly. Didn't anybody learn anything over the generations? If Big Ugly got out, he wasn't going to be shoved into another bottle or lamp and forced to play the part of the genii. He was going to be set free, able to go anywhere.

Nope, didn't want that to happen.

We had to find a way to tap the power, direct it elsewhere and put Big Ugly back to sleep. Otherwise the rumbling and stirring and restlessness would just keep growing. Undirected power made crazy things happen, as the legends of Neighborlee weirdness down through the decades proved.

Didn't want that to happen either.

We had already figured out what LaRiche wanted with those books he sent Tass to steal from Divine's. LaRiche thought he was going to bring Sylvia completely back to life. The problem for him, and us, if he had succeeded, was that Sylvia's soul and mind wouldn't have returned to her body. She had gone on to her reward. However, the combined power and the warped instructions of those books would have opened a doorway for something to come through from another realm and inhabit Sylvia's animated, preserved dead body, to give an illusion of resurrection.

LaRiche wouldn't have the passionate reunion with the Sylvia he loved. Whether the creature using her body would kill him or pretend to be Sylvia to use him for its own ends, the end result would be bad news for the rest of the Human race. Starting with the people of Neighborlee.

LaRiche, Lightning Pathway, the Von Helados, Kerri, all their minions, and Big Ugly all had to be dealt with. Experience had proved that there was no such thing as "once and for all." We would just have to be satisfied with knocking them on their backsides hard enough they couldn't bother us for a few years. A few decades would be preferable.

Time to call in the big guns.

There just wasn't time to get everyone together at one time for one big meeting. Angela and Ethan coordinated us, meeting with everyone as they had time. We had worked together long enough, we could trust each other to know what needed to be done and do exactly what our leaders told us to do when they told us to do it.

I was grateful not to have another meeting to go over things we already knew. Besides, Pastor Rocky and I were wiped out from that fun little battle with Lux. I nearly fell asleep driving home. I curled up on my couch before dinner, and didn't wake up until mid-morning the next day, with Daniel banging on my door, afraid something had happened to me.

Mum and Pop and some of the leaders of our church spent the rest of the afternoon and evening with Achmed and Leo and Father Marty, helping them understand what was going on and giving the two new believers a crash course in their new lives. Preparations for the concert kept going, after some minor repairs to the stage. Most of the lights and some sections of wiring had to be replaced. They had gotten burned out by what was now called an unexpected power surge caused by a faulty transformer half a mile down the road.

Now that we knew it was entirely safe to have everyone inside the borders of Neighborlee, the last two rehearsals were held in secret, in the sanctuary of our church. Much to the disappointment of the rabid Magna Magma fans who had slipped past the security people and climbed fences and evaded security cameras and were camping out everywhere, hoping for a personal encounter before the concert.

I got no peace at the office. Too many Lavaheads decided harassing the local newspapers might give them an inside scoop. All the local papers were getting calls, and then drop-in visits. These people didn't believe in gates and fences and barriers across doorways. They just walked into and through newspaper offices, like a great big scavenger hunt.

Oddly enough, the Grandstones acted totally out of their usual vindictive pattern and didn't reveal to anyone that guitarist Drake Abbott had changed his name to Peter Simons when he got his soul back and turned everything over to God. So no one went looking for Neighborlee Gospel Church or the apartment building where Pastor Rocky lived. Really, would any of them have believed if someone told them their idol had become a minister? They probably would have laughed, and then got mean when they realized it wasn't a joke.

London and Sherwood spent a lot of time following the data searches Lavaheads did, to track down the surviving members of the band. That included searching their pasts, trying to contact their families, get their phone and credit card numbers. Whenever our AI friends caught up with someone making headway, they scrambled the information and often inserted false information, sending them off on even more wild goose chases.

I think most of us were relieved when concert day came, just to have the waiting over.

The plan was simple and highly risky. As Angela put it, we were going to give our nemeses exactly what they wanted: passage through the shield protecting our town.

At the same time, we would impress on them most vigorously the age-old maxim: *be careful what you wish for*.

If we opened the door, we had the power to dictate where it led and where the invaders went.

The preparation involved everyone. The Hunt joined together to focus and call up the Hounds of Hamin, to ask them to stand guard around the fairgrounds. They needed to prevent the BoBs slipping in among the rabid fans, while tricking them into taking the opening left for them, without any suspicion on their part.

The prepared anchor for that very crucial doorway was right behind the stage, with a narrow line of ground between the stage and the border of Neighborlee. What was to keep one of the creeps from jumping the gun, snagging hold of Pastor Rocky, and using him to open the shield to let them all through?

When I voiced my worries, Angela just gave me that superior little smirk and admitted that was a risk, but would still work in our favor. Pastor Rocky was bait just as much as I had been when Toby, Jay and Steve had been hunting me. Fine, she had a point, but the safety of possibly the whole world, heck, the entire Human Realm, didn't rest on me coming out of the battle alive back then.

A few bright notes amid all the chaos. First, Pastor Rocky and Father Marty had hauled all their memorabilia out and put it up for sale. They had to sign a lot of it and joked about writer's cramp. The memorabilia sold faster than discount tickets before a home opener game. Even ridiculous, useless bits of things like napkins with ideas for lyrics scribbled on them. I did see one wide-eyed, dazed fan walking away from the booth, clutching a napkin and muttering about finding enough DNA to clone her own Drake Abbott.

Besides helping Pastor Rocky by clearing out storage space, all the money was going to Neighborlee Children's Home.

Even better was the reaction when Rosco Grandstone came sauntering through, playing the part of the benevolent despot who had arranged the concert. He could afford to be in a good mood, when he thought he was raking in money, clawed hand over greedy fist. He saw the crowds around the memorabilia booths and his eyes lit up at the sight of all that money being handed over, and all those credit cards being swiped and tapped for payments. He walked up to the college boys from our church who were handling the sales and demanded to see the list of receipts so far. The college boys each in turn said nope, sorry, they had orders not to give that data to anyone. Rosco drew himself up to his full height and let the college boys know in very grandiose, snotty tones that all proceeds for the concert were going to him directly, so don't take that tone and hand over the data.

At that point, Jake stepped out of the shadows where he was keeping an eye on things and waiting to take the next full-to-overflowing cash bag to the office for safekeeping. He let Rosco know that the agreement signed with the Grandstones, canceling the debt the orphanage owed their family, was for ticket sales. Period. Nothing was said in the contract about souvenir or refreshment sales, or rental of folding chairs, or autographed photos, or the sale of CDs or download codes for individual songs. The Gramophone, our local music store, knew just who to contact to obtain over three hundred copies of each of the five albums Magna Magma had made, along with a pirated greatest hits album that Marty had been wise enough to snag control over about five years ago. Within an hour of the gates opening to let the fans in, all the CDs had sold out.

None of that money was going into the Grandstones' pockets.

Of course, Rosco didn't realize that none of the money from ticket sales was going to go into his hands either. He never read the contract he signed, just like he never had any contact with his brother Stephen from the time Pastor Rocky and Father Marty agreed to hold the concert. There were two contracts sent to Carr, Cooper and Crenshaw regarding the cancellation of the debt. One stipulated that the debt would be cancelled if Stephen Grandstone had a private meeting with Frankie Leonides before the concert. It said nothing about turning over ticket sales. The second contract said, in very convoluted language, if the concert succeeded, then the debt to the Grandstones would be canceled and no money would be handed over to them.

Stephen expected to do something to awaken Ambrose Lux to take over Frankie permanently, and return him to his loyal followers. Probably with Pastor Rocky kidnapped or even brainwashed, to support the Lightning Pathway's agenda. His debt would be canceled and he probably expected Sylvia to be returned to full life and awareness.

Rosco expected the concert to fail. He was working around his brother, removing all the legal support, to keep Stephen in jail so he wouldn't be able to have that private meeting. He wanted the money, and to keep the Grandstone estate in the family's possession. Probably he expected to turn Pastor Rocky over to Lightning Pathway for a reward, and another reward for returning their spiritual leader to them. That was just the way Grandstones thought. And it was almost a relief to theorize that he was finally doing to his own brother what the Grandstones had been raised to do to other people. Knowing Rosco, and the lack of any concern for his sons, he probably planned to make a run for the gates with the ticket sales before the rabid fans realized the concert had been canceled and demanded their money back.

Rosco signed Stephen's contract, thanks to some fancy sleight-of-hand from Mr. Carr. Stephen knew about everything his loving brother had done to keep him in jail. We had arranged to have Stephen secretly removed from jail the day before the concert, and to give him his required meeting with Frankie. But Ambrose Lux would not be making his appearance. Well, his name wasn't listed in the contract, was it?

Along with the Grandstones maneuvering against each other, and betting against us, Lightning Pathway, Von Helado, Kerri and their various BoB minions were moving in, preparing to strike. Plus, we had Big Ugly, coiled in the interdimensional underground, waiting for the gate to rattle and loosen enough for him to burst through.

Lots of prayers went up from Neighborlee Gospel Church, and all the other churches in Neighborlee, as the clock ticked closer and closer to the hour when the concert would begin.

I wasn't there when Stephen Grandstone had his meeting in the borrowed RV with Frankie Leonides. Pastor Rocky was there, and about a thousand winkies, according to Maurice, who had the fun job of impressing on them what they needed to do. Sitting on the table in the RV was a big pitcher of what appeared to be lemonade, but was actually Angela's special heavy-duty neutralizer. Nobody was going to offer anyone anything to drink. Of course, we were betting on Stephen Grandstone staying true to form and striking first.

He did.

Pastor Rocky said he was a little too pleased to see him there, confirming our suspicion that it was a two-for-one deal: restore Ambrose Lux to his followers and help capture the man with the magic voice. Grandstone signed the place on the contract where it stated he was cancelling Neighborlee Children's Home's debt, and then he struck.

He pulled out one of those cursed coins on a chain I was getting a little tired of hearing about, and offered it to Frankie, as a gift from a devoted fan. Could they get a picture of the two of them together, with Frankie wearing it?

Before Frankie could finish reaching out his hand to take the gift, the winkies struck, swarming Grandstone. He dropped the chain and coin. Pastor Rocky picked it up, burning his fingers. Fortunately, not his chording fingers. He tossed the coin into the pitcher. It let out a *whoomph* and a cloud of greenish-black smoke, and the RV shook. Gordon and a team of court officials and Jake's security experts piled into the RV and hauled Grandstone out, to head back to jail. He was too stunned to resist. We could only speculate the coin had some kind of control over him and neutralizing the coin had knocked him off balance.

He probably never noticed the entrance of the enemy forces as he was being hauled away.

My first warning was when a shiver ran down my spine. The rowdy, rippling crowd sort of parted like the sea before Moses. Kerri and her black-clothed minions slithered down a visible aisle, aiming for the right side of the stage, as the audience looked at it. We had left the back of the stage unguarded by our people on Angela and Ethan's orders. That didn't mean I had to like it, or even agree with it. I just had to trust our leaders.

Daniel joined me in one of the shelters off the right side of the stage, where we had a good view of the backstage area. The other shelter held Magna Magma, preparing to step onto stage once Pastor Rocky and Frankie joined them.

"Your grandfather didn't happen to fill you in on what we're supposed to be doing, did he?" I asked him.

"Nope." He frowned, studying the enemy team moving along the side of the stage to the back, with no one stopping them.

"Did he say why we aren't being told why we're doing what we're doing? Or not doing?" I added.

"Something about if we know, we'll be thinking about it, and we've got too much to handle without the added strain of not thinking about what we hope will happen, in case the enemy manages to read our minds and figure out what we want them to do, so they won't do it."

"Wow ..." I could only shake my head. "Are you sure that's what your grandfather said?"

"That's the simplified version." Then Daniel glanced at me and managed a crooked grin.

"Arthur is one deep guy."

"Among other things." He grunted and checked his watch, then leaned out of the shelter to study the sky. "Wish it would get dark faster."

"Why?"

Now he turned to look directly at me, instead of giving me those sideways looks that still kept creeping me out. "Don't you know the monsters don't come out until dark?"

"That's Kurt's line, and it's supposed to be, 'the monsters don't come out until midnight.' And he was wrong, and he'll be wrong again."

Funny, but I felt better arguing with him, although it couldn't really be called arguing. Sniping. Releasing tension.

Daniel's head snapped up and he turned, as if he could see through the side of the shelter. At the same time, I got that slightly nauseated feeling spiraling down the back of my neck, into my stomach.

"You feel that?" he said.

When I nodded, he grabbed the handles of my wheelchair and pushed me out into the crowd.

Funny thing about wheelchairs and crowds. Either people deliberately step in front of oncoming wheelchairs with a look that dares the passengers and pushers to hit them, or people have this sixth sense that guides them to get out of the way before someone has to blow a horn or yell for them to move. Fortunately for us, the rabid Lavaheads had radar tonight, and they danced and hopped and spun out of our way, so that in less than five minutes we were darting behind the stage, going past the shelter where the musicians were hiding. It really wasn't that much good for defense, since it was a pre-fab building with plastic panels for walls, a sliding opaque window, and a door with just a pin through a metal bar for a lock. If the fans knew Magna Magma was in that little shed, they would have stampeded, and probably run over their idols in their exuberance.

When we got there, Mrs. Von Helado and her black-suited goons were just stepping out of a black cloud that merged with the thickening shadows backstage. LaRiche's BoBs were gathering around, appearing from the crowd, kind of like roaches slipping out of the cracks in cabinets and floor tile.

Later, I wondered what would have happened if I had gotten really bold and ordered them to leave, in the power of the Spirit and truth. The problem was that I doubted. I fought down the words building up pressure in my throat and on my tongue, and just sat there and glared at the invaders.

Besides, there was that order from Angela to let the enemy do what they wanted.

Mrs. Von Helado turned her head just a little, breaking from the glare she was focusing on LaRiche with enough intensity to set him on fire. Her gaze swept over me and I got cold. Really cold. Daniel reached down and gripped my shoulder -- the cold vanished.

Mrs. Von Helado flinched and blinked and looked around. As if suddenly, she couldn't see me.

"That's interesting," Daniel whispered. He kept gripping my shoulder and started to pull my chair backward with one hand. I told him to stop and gave a hard mental shove. Of course, I nearly ran his foot over. He didn't make a sound until we were away from the backstage area. We went to the band's shelter and Daniel tapped a sequence. Oh, yeah, real super-spy stealth stuff going on here -- "Shave and a Haircut."

The door opened wide enough for us to slide inside. No one was looking at us, all attention focused on the stage, fans jumping up and down, starting to sing along with the recorded song being played.

"Everybody is here," Daniel reported.

"Waiting backstage?" Pastor Rocky exchanged a long look with Ethan, then they both turned to Frankie, who looked a lot worse for wear. At least thirty pounds thinner, his hair thinner, the lines of his face sharper. But he looked peaceful, almost sleepy. "Ready, pal?"

"No." Frankie blinked and seemed to come awake, like he had been sleeping with his eyes open. "But I gotta, don't I?"

"We'll be there right next to you. We won't let them take you."

"Better not. If they kill me, I'm coming back to haunt you." Frankie tried to smile.

The other three were in the far corner of the little shelter, with Father Marty leading them in prayer. Yeah, we needed it.

A chime sounded. Time for Magna Magma to come out and give their rabid fans what they wanted. I caught hold of Pastor Rocky's hand and squeezed it hard. I shivered, seeing him fit perfectly into the images from my dream. The one where he died at the hands of Frankie. Except for his shorter hair, and the lack of beard ... well, maybe he didn't fit *perfectly*, but he was wearing the same clothes. I had deliberately been vague about what any of them were wearing, to try to avoid influencing the dream. Yeah, that never worked for the Ancient Greeks, when they tried to stop prophecy from happening, so why did I try by not doing anything?

The dream wouldn't come true, it couldn't come true. I kept repeating that silently to myself. The dream and its outcome had been canceled because Lux wasn't a passenger in Frankie's head anymore.

"Lanie." Ethan handed me a piece of paper. "Don't read this until they make their move. We're depending on you and Daniel to anchor Frankie."

I almost asked, "To what?" Then I figured that was why he gave me the paper, so I had instructions but wouldn't know them until the time was right. What if we didn't have enough light to read by, backstage?

Well, duh, I had a light on my phone. When the enemy made their move, whatever that was going to be, they wouldn't notice a light. But would I have time to read the note and react before all was lost?

Daniel kept his hand on my shoulder, and I used a little mental boost to push me along. We stayed far back from the stage, where we could keep an eye on the three groups who didn't seem to like each other. At least, from the way they kept glaring at each other, I had to assume it was an unfriendly partnership, or unwilling. They were too busy focusing on the stage, and from the movements of their heads, like the video of the cats watching a ping pong game, they were all focused on one person.

I really prayed they were focused on Frankie, and not Pastor Rocky. We were banking on the BoBs and their bosses wasting time trying to wake up Lux and get him to emerge and take control of Frankie again. How long until they realized Lux had been evicted, he wasn't asleep in the back seat? When they realized that, would they shift to Pastor Rocky? Switch to a Plan C? What were our chances they were going to give up and go away with their slimy tails between their legs?

Well, we could always hope.

LaRiche paced back and forth, glaring at the canvas covering the back of the stage, through the first two songs. Kerri seemed to find his growing discomfort amusing. At least, I thought I saw a smile on her face. It was difficult to tell in the stripes of light and shadow, where spotlights slipped through gaps in the canvas, and backyard lights penetrated the barriers of tall bushes and poplar trees and wooden fences, separating the fairgrounds from the back yards of the houses of Neighborlee. I wondered what it was like for the people living there. Did they get used to the noise and traffic, and people trying to cut through their yards to get into auto shows and fairs and other events without paying at the gates? There were always a few incidents every year during the Cuyahoga County Fair, when someone would park in a resident's driveway, blocking the resident, and there would be an argument over having to pay to use the driveway.

I worked myself into a headache, trying to watch LaRiche and zombie Sylvia, Von Helado, Kerri, and their small teams of BoBs, without them noticing me watching them. Trying to pray, so I wouldn't think too hard about my instructions written on that piece of paper. And all this time, Daniel stood behind my chair with a hand on my shoulder, and I had to believe his invulnerability gift was making us at least partially invisible to the enemy.

Either that, or they were ignoring us because they thought we could do nothing.

The fourth song of the night stunned me, because Pastor Rocky started to sing. That wasn't in the plan any of us knew about.

It probably was a keystone for Angela and Ethan's plan, though. I said an extra emphatic prayer that they really did know what they were doing.

"Now," Mrs. Von Helado snarled. "Prove you're not totally worthless."

LaRiche glared at her for a moment, but he said nothing and stomped up to the edge of the stage. He spread his arms and his BoBs gathered around him. A few touched his back and arms, and the others spread out from them, touching the backs and arms of the ones in front of them. Not too creepy -- until they gave off a rippling, bluish-purplish glow.

Chapter Sixteen

A yelp came through the sound system. A shadow leaped across the backdrop, caught in a spotlight, a huge man-shape that shrank to man-sized, until it hit the canvas. A man's body hung spread-eagle against the canvas wall, about five feet off the floor of the stage.

LaRiche was definitely making his move. Pastor Rocky was still singing, though his voice did waver for a few seconds when the body hit the canvas.

Smoke wreathed it. That had to be Frankie, as LaRiche tried to take control of him. Was he burning?

This was clearly the enemy making their move. I pulled out the piece of paper and turned on my phone light to read it.

When they grab Frankie, the paper read, *take him back and send him through between the green stakes. Then get out of there as fast as you can.*

That was all it said. What if they grabbed someone else? What if they grabbed Pastor Rocky?

"What green stakes?" Daniel said, when I handed him the paper to read.

I swept the beam of the light from my phone across the backstage area, and found two green croquet stakes, pounded in the ground about three feet back from the border of Neighborlee. They were about five feet apart. Okay that would be an easy enough target to hit. I hoped.

But still, what if they grabbed someone else?

Smoke billowed out from the shadow on the canvas, and Frankie popped through, the canvas where he touched it vanishing in a shower of char. He thudded to a landing on the last ten feet of the backstage area. LaRiche caught hold of his head and the BoBs got in each other's way, trying to grab hold of his arms and legs or just take a handful of shirt. Out front, the crowd roared, stunned when Frankie vanished.

Then they clapped. The Lavaheads probably thought it was a special effect, part of the show.

The BoBs hissed and winced and some let go, sparks dancing off their fingers. LaRiche snarled at them and they grabbed hold again, but tentatively. I could see that even from twenty, thirty feet away. What was going on?

"Wake up!" LaRiche snarled, and his hands glowed as he pressed them hard against the sides of Frankie's face. More sparks shot off and he started to withdraw, then cursed in that unfamiliar language that scorched the air and his fingers curved like claws, digging into Frankie's face.

Frankie howled and writhed and kicked his arms and legs free of the BoBs. LaRiche was trying to awaken Lux -- but he wasn't there anymore. How soon would he realize that? And what would he do to Frankie?

"Please, Lord, protect him," I whispered, then nearly slapped myself.

Well, duh, this was what I was there for. To protect Frankie. I mentally gathered up my telekinesis into a long, thick cord and snapped it out, grabbing hold of Frankie around his waist. I had a mental image that made me cringe, just for a second. What if I grabbed him by an arm, and the BoBs held on tight enough ... it broke off?

They weren't holding on at all. Forget about holding on tight enough to resist my pull. Frankie slid out of their hands, shooting off more sparks. I whipped him up in the air and over in an arch. He yelped and his legs and arms flailed and he was probably terrified, but I had to do what Angela told me to do.

The BoBs and LaRiche and zombie Sylvia, Mrs. Von Helado and Kerri and their better-dressed, black-suited minions all clumped together, reaching for Frankie, following him. It would have been hilarious if the air suddenly hadn't become charged with fury and terror.

Frankie was nearly through the green croquet stakes. LaRiche caught hold of his foot.

I gasped, feeling the zing of the Ghost field activating. Frankie vanished. LaRiche shrieked, staggering back, holding his hand. Probably burned when Jane repulsed his hand from the bubble of Ghost field. Well, that explained her job in all this.

Then a dark rainbow-streaked vortex, just like a gigantic-sized Wishing ball, opened up ahead of me, along the border of Neighborlee.

And Daniel and I were just sitting there, waiting for the goon squads to turn on us. Hadn't Angela told us to get out of there?

The vortex opened up and at the other end I clearly saw the quarries north of Neighborlee. Something shimmered across the rocky surface of a lower level. The ground rippled like it was water. Mrs. Von Helado let out a howl like nothing I had ever heard before. Any monster movie that reproduced that sound would win an Academy Award. Swirls of dark light reached out from the vortex and wrapped around Von Helado and Kerri and LaRiche and their minions, and suddenly they were being yanked into the swirl and through.

And so were Daniel and I.

Too late, I reached with my telekinesis for the back of the stage, the closest solid object, to anchor myself. I felt like I went down a spiral, stretched out, like something in a weird, Escher-based cartoon. My mental grip on the stage held for two heartbeats. Daniel held onto me and my chair. Then my fingers slipped free.

We spun around for what felt like hours, and yet just a few heartbeats. The worst part was that somehow this felt familiar. Maybe I had dreamed something like this?

Or had I gone through another vortex like this, years ago? Like when I was a toddler, and they found me on the side of Old Mill Road? Was this how I had come to Earth? So maybe I really was an alien? Or at least from another dimension, like the members of the Hunt?

Then with a thud and a snap of the axle of my wheelchair, we landed. I went sprawling. Daniel scrambled to get hold of me, to keep me upright, but my forward momentum yanked him down on top of me.

Actually, it was a good thing we went flat, even if he did knock the air out of me. The goon squads landed harder than we did, on the other side of that glowing, throbbing, amoeba-like pulsing just under the uneven surface of the stone of that lower plateau in the quarries. My hand slapped down on the edge of that glow and I gasped, but managed not to yelp. It stung. It burned.

Whatever was happening here, it was not good.

Can we say "understatement of the millennia"?

Daniel rolled off me, which I appreciated more than I could express. Mostly because I still couldn't catch my breath. He got on his knees and hooked his arm through mine and sort of dragged me backward with him, away from that pulsing, glowing edge of whatever was happening to the stone. He got us behind a pile of smaller boulders. We were both gasping, trying not to make much noise. Not that it mattered right then, because LaRiche and Kerri and Von Helado and their goons were all moaning and griping and struggling to breathe. It was kind of comforting to have proof that they hadn't enjoyed that little fun house ride either.

Then Kerri laughed. It was not a nice sound. Kind of like roofing nails on a chalkboard or maybe plate glass. She staggered back a few steps and pointed at the glowing swirl of colors underneath the surface of the rock. Then she jabbered something that sounded like it belonged in Mordor. Mrs. Von Helado glared at her. Then faster than I could follow with my eyes, she swung back her arm and slapped Kerri hard, so she flew out, into the glowing rock.

Flames and spouts of black light burst up where Kerri landed on her back, and she sank into the rock. She shrieked and writhed and leaped up, aiming at Mrs. Von Helado, who battered her away like someone would flick at a fly. Kerri went flying another direction. Her minions scrambled after her. Mrs. Von Helado smirked, then she turned to LaRiche, who had been watching all this and grinning.

Very clearly, while they seemed to be working together, they didn't like each other.

Then I recognized where we were and I groaned, barely managing to muffle the sound. Not that anyone over there was listening. The minions of all three groups were all snarling at each other and making too much noise to have heard if my phone had rung. Which it didn't. Yet. Fortunately.

And the light and colors coming up through the rock pulsed a little faster, a little brighter, with steam and waves of heat rising up. I was sweating. With our luck, a volcano was going to come up through there, and that wasn't going to be good for Neighborlee.

"What?" Daniel whispered, his mouth almost against my ear.

"I know where we are."

"The quarries. We are still in Neighborlee, right?"

"We have to get to higher ground." Not that it would do us much good, but maybe if I could catch my breath, and we were far enough from the core of the blast when it came, I had a chance of flying us out of there.

Daniel looked over to where we had left my broken wheelchair. Just remembering how we had crash landed, my hip throbbed in a delayed reaction. I was going to have one honey of a massive bruise in the morning. If we lived to see morning.

Under cover of LaRiche and Von Helado snarling at each other, Daniel wrapped my arm around his shoulders and backed away, staying bent over. I finally got my feet under myself and managed to take most of my weight. He still held onto me, which was good, because I couldn't promise my legs wouldn't turn into rubber again. I guided him up one of the switchback paths to a higher plateau, and he managed to keep us out of sight of the bickering goon squads below us.

"Well, we were getting readings of energy and activity down there, sliding through the dimensional walls," Daniel muttered, once we were as high as we could get, and stretched out on our stomachs on the gritty, uneven stone of the plateau. "The question is if that's good for us or good for them."

"I've got the feeling this is a mess we made when we were kids, and it's coming back to bite us," I confessed.

"Huh?" He rolled onto his side so he could look at me without craning his neck too much.

"When I was in middle school, the three of us were sure we were aliens, so we tried to phone home. Y'know, like with E.T.?"

"And?"

"You know how Kurt makes gizmos that work even when the laws of physics say they can't? Well, he made an intergalactic phone, sort of, and set it up here on Halloween, right down there where Kerri almost sank through." I pointed. "There was something weird in the tunnels, some energy moving around, and it made Kurt's homemade Geiger counter go nuts. And then the phone went ballistic, screaming and flashing and bouncing up and down like it was going to launch for the moon. Something was making contact, and we were pretty sure we didn't want to take the call."

"So what did you do?" His mouth twitched like he couldn't decide if he wanted to laugh at me.

"We kind of lied to Felicity and got her riled up. This was when her EM bursts were pretty erratic. We got her upset, thinking Sylvia was stealing her bike. All our bikes were parked over there, beyond that scraggly patch of trees. She blew a fuse and got the phone to blow itself to pieces."

"Whatever you contacted ..." Daniel shook his head.

"We probably made a weak spot or a pinhole or something back then. There have been weird events here in the quarries for years. Big Ugly was able to mess with cars, and make people see and hear things. Maybe he's been scraping away at the barrier for years."

"And now he's planning on coming through."

"But they needed Frankie and Pastor Rocky. Please, God, let them need Pastor Rocky really bad, and their plans are totally messed up --"

A howl of agony echoed through the quarries. I looked down to see Sylvia dragging Kerri by her hair, out into the center of the glowing, steaming, pulsing rock. Kerri's minions leaped to protect her, and Sylvia swatted them away with the same ease Mrs. Von Helado had shown.

Definitely a bad sign for our side.

LaRiche stood back, arms crossed over his chest, looking smug. I caught Mrs. Von Helado waving her minions at him. While Sylvia slashed at Kerri's face with her fingernails, the men swarmed LaRiche and dragged him out to join Kerri. They held him down as Mrs. Von Helado sort of slid and slithered her way out to join them. Her fingers glowed this poisonous green shade as she bent and slashed at LaRiche. He shrieked and cursed and howled, and his BoBs finally leaped into the battle.

"No honor among thieves, huh?" Kurt said

He startled me so much, I nearly shredded my throat from the effort not to shriek. The air tingled with the power of the Ghost field as he and Jane materialized and settled down on the rock next to us.

"You're not supposed to be here for this," Jane said.

"Duh." I managed a smile for her, feeling pretty breathless with the relief that slammed through me like a runaway roller coaster.

"Big Ugly?" Daniel said.

"Feels like him," Kurt said with a nod.

"Now what do we do?" I couldn't yank my gaze away from that free-for-all as all three goon squads turned on each other. I had the feeling it had started out as some kind of sacrifice, using blood and probably pain, maybe an energy jolt of a lot of negative emotions, to power whatever they had planned.

"Try to put a lid on the explosion when it comes." Jane sat up. "Uh oh."

She didn't point, but we all looked where she was looking.

Mrs. Von Helado could fly.

Actually, she was rising straight up out of the tangle of black and bloody. Blood smeared her face, but I had the feeling that blood ringing her mouth wasn't hers to begin with. She glowed, kind of pulsing in time with that creepy melting rock light and had her hands folded primly in front of her. Other than the blood smearing her face, nothing was messed or out of place on her. Not a hair. Not a wrinkle in her clothes. Now I could understand the coldness and slightly nauseated revulsion I sensed in Ethan, the few times he talked about the creepy old woman and her minions, who had tried to get him to sabotage Angela and turn her over to them.

"Not nearly enough power, but you will have to do," she said, and reached out one blood-streaked hand toward us.

"No way," Kurt growled, and caught hold of Jane's hand. The Ghost field snapped into place around us.

Mrs. Von Helado let out another of those inhuman howls and launched at herself at us, going all skeletal and fangy. Kind of like how the angel changed to a monster just before everything went drastically south in the ark-opening scene in *Raiders of the Lost Ark*.

Jane took us up, high, and that hag followed us, mouth open and howling and fingers arched into claws.

I looked down, which probably wasn't smart, and saw the battle was slowing down. Was everybody dying, shredded by each other?

Umm ... no. They were *sinking* into the molten rock. On the plus side, zombie Sylvia had her hands around LaRiche's neck. We weren't close enough to see his face.

Then Mrs. Von Helado crashed into the Ghost field, jolting us, and I kind of got distracted by that.

A glow surrounded her fingers, swirling red hot and gold, and her fingers started to penetrate the Ghost field. Daniel cursed and slammed his hands against those claws. She shrieked and spun away.

Daniel curled up, shuddering, clutching his hands. They were smoking and looked burned, and there were bloody, oozing holes in his palms where her talons penetrated. I tried to wipe his hands with the bottom of my shirt. She must have left some kind of venom, because the cloth started smoking.

"That does it," Jane said between clenched teeth. "Going down."

"Go for it," Kurt growled, and his hand went white with the tightness of his grip on hers.

I hate falling. Ever since I broke my back, I have hated the helpless feeling of falling.

The Ghost field dropped like a guided missile.

Our bubble slammed into Mrs. Von Helado. She shrieked, fury and a new note that I desperately hoped was fear, or at least surprise. I was too busy to pay attention, ripping the bottom off Daniel's shirt to try to wipe his hands clean. I ripped the bottom of my shirt off, just in case that smoke was from my shirt melting right off me. My stomach turned inside out in those eternal few seconds as we plummeted, straight down to the center of that glowing, churning, melted rock. Heads and legs and arms writhed, and some minions still fought to get free. We were going to slam down right on top of them. Into the rock. And keep going. There was no way to stop that killer descent before we were buried.

Yeah, but at least we were taking Mrs. Von Helado with us.

Now I had an idea how Samson felt as he took down the temple with all the Philistines sitting on the roof.

We hit.

The Ghost field cracked, like the crazed surface of antique china. A stink of ash and rot and hot rock and acid gushed in on curls of smoke and choked us. Then the field solidified and we could breathe.

And we sank. Down into the rock. I held onto Daniel's hands and he held onto me, despite the shaking and the sweat pouring down his face and his very evident pain. Molten rock surrounded us, swirling around the globe of the Ghost field. Kurt wrapped his arm around Jane and she strained, in short, snapping pants, like a woman in labor.

"Lanie ..." Kurt looked up, and the sensation of falling didn't slow. If anything, we were falling faster. Like we were being sucked downward. The only light was the weird glow coming off him and Jane now. "Give me all you've got."

"How?"

"I don't know! I just have to try something. We're getting pulled down, and believe me, I do not want to see where we land if we get sucked into wherever Big Ugly has been locked up all this time."

"Been there," Jane whispered, her voice a rasp of strain. Her eyes were bloodshot, and her face had thinned in just those few moments of effort. "Don't want to go back." She tried to smile, and it was a skeleton's grimace.

"Okay. Whatever. What do I do?" I closed my eyes because doggone it, I was scared!

"Just ... let go." Kurt reached through the darkness that surrounded me now and caught hold of my hand. "Like when we go flying and I take over, but ... more. I guess."

"You guess?" Daniel started to laugh, but it turned into a racking cough. I squeezed my eyes as tightly shut as I could, because I had the awful feeling if I looked, I would find him coughing up blood.

God, are You there? Help?

The familiar tingling kind of whisper of air across my skin, of Kurt accessing my gift, and hopefully now my strength, helped me relax. For about two seconds. Then the sensation sank into my skin. I felt something pulling on my veins, the marrow of my bones. If this was what it felt like for a smoothie to be sucked up with a straw, I apologized and promised never to have a smoothie again. Or at least never use a straw. I tried to let go, relax, not tense up every time one of those pulses pulled at me.

"It's okay," Daniel whispered. "Think of the tide. Mom told me. Sharing energy. Push whenever they pull."

Huh?

Then I realized he was right, and every time the pulse of Kurt sucking at my energy grew stronger, I pushed, and envisioned sending pulses of strength out, instead of just sitting there and trying to relax. I pushed and tried to focus on the rhythm and the feeling of Daniel's hands gripping mine. I listened to my thudding heart, trying to make it slow and match the rhythm as Kurt sucked up my energy.

Until I realized I couldn't feel Daniel's hands. Had he let go of me? Was he all right?

I tried to open my eyes.

I didn't have any eyes.

I tried to call to him, but I didn't have any air in my lungs to make a sound.

Was I dead?

I nearly laughed, when I realized I hoped I was dead, and we hadn't been trapped in Big Ugly's side of the dimensional doorway just because I didn't have enough energy to supplement Jane and Kurt to get us out of there.

God? Are You there? Please? Let everything be okay? Did we at least save the town?

~~~~~

Well, of course I didn't die, because how else could I be telling this story, making another confession about the weirdness of Neighborlee and how we kept doing our job as the guardians?

But dang ... none of us enjoyed the recovery.

The short version of the story is that, as far as the Fae version of CSI could tell, Von Helado and Kerri and their goon squads had been pouring all the energy they could into piercing the shield around Neighborlee, working up to the moment they planned to break Big Ugly free. There were signs they planned to sacrifice Pastor Rocky and Ambrose Lux, once he had taken over Frankie again, pouring all their power and the influence
~~~~~

of Pastor Rocky's gift into the mix. The clues were pretty clear that LaRiche had been planning all along to betray his boss, and get Sylvia back into her body. Didn't turn out too well for him. Kerri had been sending energy through the tiny holes she and her minions had drilled in the shield during those really weird months of battle, and doppelgangers walking, and remotely controlling the sleepwalkers in the winter. It looked like she planned to become Big Ugly's queen or consort, or at least a major power player in the new kingdom. Mrs. Von Helado wasn't having any of that, as indicated by her move to make Kerri the first sacrifice, even before they shoved Lux and Pastor Rocky through the semi-permeable spot in the dimensional barrier.

Of course, that diagnosis was just a rough guess of what had been planned or intended. Everything was a pretty big mess, and Von Helado and Kerri didn't leave any notebooks behind, detailing their plans. A bunch of specialists and scientists from the Fae Realm came and set up shop to investigate and analyze and do whatever they needed, to ensure the barrier was solid again. As near as we could figure out, this was just like what happened two summers ago at Eden, when the Rivals got sucked down to be a midnight snack for Big Ugly. The three goon squads and their leaders got their comeuppance. Kind of like eternal oneness with Dormammu.

We couldn't figure out how to explain that big, glossy, multi-colored patch of melted rock at the quarries. It was kind of obvious, since those colors had never been there before.

Maybe we just wouldn't try to explain any of it. Let it become another of the many mysterious of the quarries, and the pattern of weirdness that was ordinary life in Neighborlee.

If we were lucky, the indigestion Big Ugly got from downing this new batch of failed co-conspirators would keep him quiet even longer than when he swallowed the Rivals.

As fall settled in and the last reverberations from the amazingly satisfying results of the Magna Magma "Back from the Dead" concert faded away, we let ourselves enjoy the fruits of our labors and suffering. But not too much. Gloating always guaranteed that eventually we'd have to suffer through another attitude adjustment.

Still, how could we help not snickering and feeling a little giddy with relief sometimes?

Of course, we didn't all live happily ever after. But we had a lot to be grateful for and to celebrate, and dang it, we had learned to enjoy the good things and not let tomorrow's problems spoil the glory of NOW.

Neighborlee Children's Home was safe.

Father Marty and Frankie decided to move to Neighborlee and work with Pastor Rocky on setting up a music school, and train teens for summer rock music mission projects.

Stephen Grandstone grabbed his younger brother by the ear -- I saw it, I can vouch for it -- and got out of town as soon as he was released from jail. To all intents and purposes, the Grandstone estate has been abandoned, left for the government to confiscate for back taxes and other fines.

Life without Grandstones in Neighborlee? How would we survive the shock?

Athena and Wallace's wedding came off without a hitch.

Kurt and Jane were married just before Halloween.

Felicity was indeed pregnant. With twins!

Pete proposed to Meggie Richards at the Fall Festival at WBC.

Holly started showing signs of morning sickness about the same time. With the Fae, morning sickness usually comes out as light shows. She shot off fireworks from the ends of her hair, and her ears developed definite points, and turned purple during the worst of the fireworks. Both she and Maurice were delighted.

As for me and Daniel and those weird looks he was giving me? Well … we're taking it slowly. Keeping it quiet. The last thing we want is to be railroaded by our Star Trek club into having a Trek-themed wedding, pulling out all the stops. But dang … the man is a great kisser.

And that is life as normal in Neighborlee, Ohio.

The End

Maybe …

Afterword:

The YA fantasy series, *The Hunt*, overlaps events in Neighborlee in several places. Want to find out how Stanzer and Dawn and the rest of the Hunt get home? Want to see what happens when Big Ugly encounters Gahlmorag and maybe they both kinda-sorta get what they deserve? Think the Classic Star Trek episode, *The Alternative Factor*. From Season 2. You know, the one with a guy named Lazarus whose makeup keeps changing because -- surprise! -- there's two of him ....

That's all I'm gonna tell you. **Gathering**, from Writers Exchange (www.writers-exchange.com) is the final book in *The Hunt* ... maybe ... I keep coming up with more story ideas for my characters, even after I've written what I think is the final "The End."

So stay tuned, okay?

And if you want to visit Neighborlee more, let me know. Throw ideas at me. I keep all the story ideas and subplots I didn't use, just in case I get inspired for something new. Check out my websites, where you can make contact: *www.YeOldeDragonBooks.com* and *www.Mlevigne.com*.

Thanks for reading!

Neighborlee, Ohio

(Title, Original Title, Release Date)

Confessions of a Lost Kid (Growing Up Neighborlee) 05/20
Semi-Pseudo-Superheroes (Dorm Rats) 07/20
Virtually London (London Holiday) 09/20
Living Proof (that no good deed goes unpunished) (Living Proof) 11/20
Night of the Living Proof, 01/21
Quitting the Hero Biz (Hero Blues) 03/21
Bride of the Living Proof, 05/21
Shrunk: The Exile of Maurice (Divine's Emporium) 07/21
Return of the Living Proof, 09/21
Allergic to Mistletoe (Have Yourself a Faerie Little Christmas) 11/21
Dawn of the Living Proof, 01/22
Angela's Knight (Divine Knight) 03/22
The Living Proof Gets the Blues, 05/22

About the Author

On the road to publication, Michelle fell into fandom in college and has 40+ stories in various SF and fantasy universes. She has a bunch of useless degrees in theater, English, film/communication, and writing. Even worse, she has over 100 books and novellas with multiple small presses, in science fiction and fantasy, YA, suspense, women's fiction, and sub-genres of romance.

Her official launch into publishing came with winning first place in the Writers of the Future contest in 1990. She was a finalist in the EPIC Awards competition multiple times, winning with *Lorien* in 2006 and *The Meruk Episodes, I-V,* in 2010, and was a finalist in the Realm Awards competition, in conjunction with the Realm Makers convention.

Her training includes the Institute for Children's Literature; proofreading at an advertising agency; and working at a community newspaper. She is a tea snob and freelance edits for a living (MichelleLevigne@gmail.com for info/rates), but only enough to give her time to write. Her newest crime against the literary world is to be co-managing editor at Mt. Zion Ridge Press and launching the publishing co-op, Ye Olde Dragon Books. Be afraid … be very afraid.

www.Mlevigne.com
www.MichelleLevigne.blogspot.com
www.YeOldeDragonBooks.com
www.MtZionRidgePress.com
@MichelleLevigne

Look for Michelle's Goodreads groups:
Guardians of Neighborlee
Voyages of the AFV Defender

NEWSLETTER:
Want to learn about upcoming books, book launch parties, inside information, and cover reveals?
Go to Michelle's website or blog to sign up.

Also by Michelle L. Levigne

Guardians of the Time Stream: 4-book Steampunk series
The Match Girls: Humorous inspirational romance series starting with **A Match (Not) Made in Heaven**
Sarai's Journey: A 2-book biblical fiction series
Tabor Heights: 20-book inspirational small town romance series.
Quarry Hall: 11-book women's fiction/suspense series
For Sale: Wedding Dress. Never Used: inspirational romance
Crooked Creek: Fun Fables About Critters and Kids: Children's short stories.
Do Yourself a Favor: Tips and Quips on the Writing Life. A book of writing advice.
To Eternity (and beyond): *Writing Spec Fic Good for Your Soul.* A book defending speculative fiction.
Killing His Alter-Ego: contemporary romance/suspense, taking place in fandom.
The Commonwealth Universe: SF series, 25 books and growing
The Hunt: 5-book YA fantasy series
Faxinor: Fantasy series, 4 books and growing
Wildvine: Fantasy series, 14 books when all released
Neighborlee: Humorous fantasy series
Zygradon: 5-book Arthurian fantasy series
AFV Defender: SF adventure series
Young Defenders: Middle Grade SF series, spin-off of *AFV Defender*
Magic to Spare: Fantasy series
Book & Mug Mysteries: cozy mystery series starting in 2022
Quest for the Crescent Moon: fantasy series starting in 2022